The Morning Star

Book one

of

The Star Saga

S.E Dymek

ISBN: 979-8-9893636-1-2

Printed in the United States

First edition October 2023

Second edition March 2025

This book is a work of fiction

First Printing, 2023

Dedication

To Aaralyn, Ivy, and Caiden. My biggest inspirations
for everything I do. To my husband, Aaron, who is
my biggest support.

Acknowledgments

I'd like to thank my parents, close family, and all my inner, dearest friends who listened to me babble about ideas and were willing to read them. I love you all. Thank you to all my readers!

About the Author

S.E Dymek is an upcoming author who has published **The Alpha's War Series:** Including Between the Alpha's War, Breaking the Alpha Council, and The Beta's Betrayal **The Star Saga:** Including The Morning Star, The Evening Star, and The North Star available with Barnes and Nobles, Amazon, Kindle, and other book selling sites. She is also published on several ebook platforms. She has a passion for writing romance novels including paranormal romance novels and fantasy. All of her works include twists and turns, keeping her readers on their toes. She is a mother of three and loving wife. When she is not writing; she is working as a veterinary technician. Born and raised in Rhode Island, she has found her second home in Texas.

Follow her on social media:
Facebook: S.E Dymek
Instagram: sedymek
Tik Tok: @sedymek

Website: www.Sedymek.com

Chapter One
Escape

Darkness overtook them. She couldn't see her hand in front of her face. She could feel her heart as it pounded in her chest, her lungs burned inside of it. A pair of small arms clung around her neck. Hanging on for life. As she forced her legs to keep running.

Run. Run. Run.

The word screamed in her head. She could feel her legs grow weak. No. She couldn't stop. She had to keep going. *Please!* She begged her legs. She couldn't fail. Branches of passing trees scratched and pulled at her skin as if they were reaching out, trying to stop them. She knew it would come and she hated herself. Something caught her foot and they fell forward. Her body crashed to the ground, the little arms that were wrapped around her neck let go and she tumbled away from her.

"Claire!" Morgan yelled in between gasped breaths.

Her body shook as she got up from the ground. Her vision blurred. The trees blocked the small amount of light that came from the pale moon. She could barely see as she frantically searched for Claire.

"Claire!" She yelled again, panicked.

She needed to find her. They couldn't stay here any longer. She heard a small groan come from the side of her and that's when she saw her outline. Morgan rushed to her side and began to check her over.

"Claire, are you hurt? You okay?" Morgan asked as she brushed Claire's blonde hair from her face.

"I'm okay. Are you?" Claire asked as she got to her feet.

"I'm fine. We gotta go now." Morgan said urgently, as she grabbed Claire's hand in hers.

"Can you run?" She asked Claire.

"I think so. Do you think he's-" before Claire could finish her sentence she was pulled backwards away from Morgan.

"You little bitches." He slurred as he threw Claire.

Claire's poor body slung across the dirt floor of the woods. He chuckled as he followed after her. He clenched his fist in his hands as he tried to contain the urge to rip her apart.

Morgan didn't wait. She ran straight at him and threw herself on to his back. She locked her forearms around his throat and squeezed as tight as she could. He wasn't going to touch Claire again. He choked as she applied pressure. His arms flapped wildly as he struggled. His hands went to her forearms, deep scratches appeared as he dug his nails into her skin. She gritted her teeth and tried to squeeze her forearm even tighter. He started to fight less and a spark of hope filled Morgan's gut.

With all his might he slammed backwards into a tree. The bark of the tree ripped into her flesh. She hung on to him with everything she had. He slammed her again and again into the tree. With each blow her skin ripped and scraped. Her grip wavered as her head bounced off the tree. He seized his opportunity and grabbed her arm. He pulled her forward into the ground.

Morgan laid there stunned. Her body felt like it had shattered. She could hear him as tried to catch his breath in between coughs. *Get up, move. Get up!!* She screamed to herself. She rolled to her side trying to get up. She was trying to move faster. She could hear him coming for her. She frantically tried to get to her feet. His footsteps crunched on leaves as they neared her.

"Bitch!" He yelled, as he kicked her in the ribs.

The kick sent the wind out of Morgan. She gasped as she tried to suck air in, as another kick was delivered. Spit flew out of his mouth as he stood over her.

"Morgan to the rescue. Always have to save the day. Fucking bitch!" He screamed, more spit poured out of his mouth.

Sweat beaded across his forehead and dripped down into his eyes. He cranked his leg back and kicked her again. Morgan curled into herself to block the blows. She heard another scream.

"Leave her alone! Stop it!" Claire screamed at him.

"Almost forgot about you. You. You should have died. She should be here and you should be dead." He growled and his words slurred as he spoke.

Raged filled his eyes as he started towards Claire. Morgan stumbled to her feet. Her mind screamed at her that she needed to do something. She couldn't take much more but she couldn't stay down. Claire needed her. He held Claire by her blonde hair.

"Hey!" Morgan yelled at him and planted her feet.

He let out a low guttural sound as he saw her back on her feet. His hand entangled in Claire's blonde hair as he yanked her around to face Morgan.

"Ya just can't stay down!." He screamed as he dropped Claire and kicked her off to the side.

"Always gotta get up! I'll make sure you can't get up! Ever again this time!" He cursed and charged towards her.

As he came for her, panic wiggled in Morgan's belly, she had to think quickly. She waited till he was just close enough and dropped to the ground. With all her might she swung her legs outwards. She hit him hard and fast, it sent him to the ground with a thud. She went to move towards Claire. When suddenly she felt his hand on her ankle. Before she could react she went forward as he yanked her foot out from under her. He pulled himself up to his knees, his grip tight on her ankle as he began to drag her back towards him. Morgan tried to twist away but he was too strong for her. He flipped her over and began to lean over her. She threw her knee up and connected with his stomach. When he lurched forward from the blow; she smashed her elbow into the side of his face. Blood immediately started to pour from his nose. She shoved him off; as he began to gasp and hold his nose.

She stood and watched him as he prayed that he was done, maybe he just let them go. That thought was shattered as he stood up. She glanced back at Claire who watched in horror. Her body screamed in pain, everything hurt. He was never going to let them go. She took a deep breath as she prepared herself. Her eyes looked over to Claire. One of them needed to get out of this.

"Claire run. Just go." Morgan urged her.

"I'm not leaving you." Claire said through tears.

"It's ok. I'll find you. Just go!" Morgan said her eyes focused on him as he stumbled angrily to her.

His pace quickened and Morgan braced herself as he started to charge at her again. Morgan ready herself for what she figured would be her last fight.

"Morgan!" Claire screamed as something was forced into Morgan's hand.

She didn't know what Claire gave her but she gripped it and swung as he charged at her. It connected with his skull and A loud snap sound that echoed through the silent woods. Whatever she held in her hand had broken into pieces against him. He hit the ground lifeless. Morgan stood there, her body shook as she held the blood stained tree limb. She stood there frozen as she watched his body. She waited for him to get back up. Her mind did not believe he would stay down. Claire approached her slowly and tugged on her hand.

"Come on." Claire whispered, her eyes fixated on his body.

Morgan snapped out of it and scooped Claire and took off running. She wasn't sure how long she ran for but it seemed like forever. The sun just started to come up as her feet hit warm sand. She dropped to her knees, the tiny species of sand dug into her skin. Her body was worn out from the running and fighting. It was hard to even focus to see at this point. She ran until she couldn't anymore and prayed it was far enough away. She gently let Claire tumble into the sand next to her then she collapsed.

Claire was seven years old but much older in spirit. She had to be. She was a very tiny thing and looked just like her late mother. Long soft golden blonde hair and eyes as blue as the sky. Claire laid there looking at the sky. She could smell the salt in the air and without looking knew they were on a beach. She sat up and looked at Morgan. She collapsed on the sand exhausted, bruised, bloody, and beaten. Claire's stomach turned in knots. It was all her fault.

Maybe her father was right? Maybe if she would have died instead of her mother, none of this would have happened? Who knows what better life Morgan would have had if she never existed.

Claire's mother died but not during childbirth. She didn't know if that made it worse. Claire's mother died when she was four. They lived in a small cabin in the woods and not too far from the cabin was a large lake. Even though Claire was only four, she could still to this day smell the snow in the air as she walked out the door of the cabin. The lake gave them all the water they needed.

Claire wanted to be a big girl and help her mother. She wandered out towards the lake and the hole in the ice they had made the previous day. The echo of the ice as it cracked rattled inside her mind. Her skin still stung from the cold water as she crashed through the ice. Her own scream as her body sank into the water she could still hear. She can recall how it felt to give into the darkness and slip away. She was almost gone when warm arms reached in and pulled her out with such force she slid across the ice towards the shore. She scooted herself to land, her eyes looked back to see who had saved her.

Her mother laid on her belly as she tried to make her way across the ice. Each movement she made another crack appeared in the ice. The noise was the only sound as everything else had gone silent.

"Momma!" Claire called to her and inched towards the lake.

"Claire, stay!" Her mother yelled frantically.

Her mother tried to hide the fear on her face as the ice cracked quicker. That look and sound is forever etched in Claire's mind.

"I love you." She yelled as one last but loudest crack happened and she sunk into the icy water.

Claire's mom didn't know how to swim and with the water being so cold she didn't stand a chance. Claire sat on the shore and screamed for help until her voice was gone. Claire had tried everything she could, she tossed sticks to the holes, She yelled and begged for her mother to come back. When her father arrived home to find an empty cabin, he rushed to the lake. The look of horror on his face when he realized what had happened. He raced out onto the ice, he broke pieces of it as he tried to find her. He fell into the water himself but the fear and rage inside of him pushed him forward. A loud scream vibrated the air as he found her. He pulled her body up onto the ice. He dragged her to the shore and craddled her lifeless body in his arms. Her mother's long blonde hair dripped water as it dangled on to the ground. Her head tilted back and her blue eyes glossed over. The deep sobs that escaped her father as he shook and begged God for it not to be true.

Claire still remembers the look that he gave her as he walked by as he held her mother's dead body.

"Momma?" She whispered; the look of such hatred he shot her turned her stomach.

He left her there on the shore to freeze. When Morgan had finally came home, she found him drunk by a freshly dug grave. Morgan had grabbed a hold of shaking him till he told her where he left Claire. Morgan raced to the lake to find Claire. She scooped her up in a blanket and cradled her. Morgan and her were not sisters but cousins. Morgan moved in with them after her parents died. Morgan had been there for her from that moment on.

A groan tore Claire from her thoughts.

"Claire!?" Morgan shot up and began looking around.

"I'm here, it's okay" Claire said to her as she went to her side.

Morgan inhaled with relief as she stood and took in her surroundings. They were on a beach. It was far enough away from where they lived but not far enough away for them at this moment.

She knew by the way his body went limp after she struck him with the tree branch that he had to be dead. Even still, she couldn't stop her mind from as it raced with what if 's. She needed a plan and she needed one quickly. They had to get as far away from here as possible. She scanned the beach. Off in the distance, tall mask of a ship reached up into the blue sky. The white sails seemed to wave at her as she squinted her eyes. It looked to be a cargo ship. If they could somehow get on the ship. They could get off wherever it stopped and start over. This was it, simple enough. Get on the ship, hide till it docked and sneak off. Start over. It would work. It had to work.

"Claire-" Morgan said but then Claire let out a loud gasp.

Morgan's stomach drops as she prepares herself to fight again. She turned and saw nothing. Claire's hands were over her mouth as tears slipped from her eyes.

"Morgan your back," Claire said, as she reached up with gentle hands and touched her bloody back.

Morgan gritted her teeth to suppress the pain. She didn't realize how much everything hurt until that moment. The back of her dress was ripped from the tree branches and bark. She knew her skin had to be ripped open but didn't know how bad. The wetness on her back she had chalked up to sweat or mud from the ground. She looked down at Claire and her bright blue eyes filled with tears. This little girl blamed all this evil on herself. This little girl who never had a chance to be a child. She looked at her and her heart broke. She reached down and rubbed her cheek, wiping the tears away.

"Claire, it's okay. I'm fine; it doesn't hurt. I promise it's fine. we need to go." She smiled at Claire.

"Go where?" Claire asked, confused.

"Listen closely. There's a ship down the shore there. We need to sneak on that ship. We'll hide till it docks and then get off when it does. We'll start all over you and me. Okay?" Morgan asked and squeezed Claire's hand.

Claire nodded and they began to make their way down the beach. They were careful to stay out of sight from the ship so no one would see them. They ducked behind a few rocks just by the ship and Morgan began to survey trying to find a way onto the ship.

Morgan spotted large wooden crates next to the ship. They were long enough and wide enough to fit a grown man. She tugged Claire's hand and they made their way to the crates. No one was around as Morgan began to quietly open them. They were empty. what would they be doing with empty crates? She thought as she led Claire over to the crate.

"Hey, we are going to hide in these crates. There's cracks in the wooden boards so we will be able to get air. Don't worry it will just be for a little while. Take a nice nap and when we dock I'll come get you out. I'm going in this one here. I'll be right next to you." She whispered to Claire.

Morgan could see the fear in Claire's eyes. It tugged at her heart but then Claire straightened her head and nodded and began to climb into the crate. Morgan helped lower her in.

"I promise it'll be okay." She said as she kissed Claire on the top of her head.

Moran quickly opened the empty crate next to Claire's and got in. Morgan prayed that they were not going too far; she was worried for Claire. She could see bits of the sky and sunlight in the crate. It gave her reassurance about the air supply. She heard footsteps and talking coming towards them. Morgan prayed Claire would be quiet.

"These two are the last ones." She heard a deep scruffy voice say as her box was kicked.

Her heart jumped at the kick but she remained quiet and still. The next thing the crate was lifted and carried closer to the ship.

"These must be more food rations." She heard another man groan as he stepped off the ramp and on to the ship.

She was carried a few more feet and then hit the ground with a thud. She had to cover her mouth to stop the cry of pain as her back hit the crate. A second thud vibrated the ground next to her box. Claire, she thought as she looked towards the side of her wooden crate. She placed her hand on the wood, and hated that she couldn't comfort Claire. She wished there was another way for them. She smiled at how brave Claire was. She listened closely to see if she could hear anything else was happening. She could make out sounds of orders being given for the ship to get ready to leave shore. And just like that they were on their way to their new life.

Chapter Two
Caught

"Morgan! Morgan!"

The sound of her name made Morgan jolt upright and hit her head on the wooden crate. She must have nodded off. She paused to listen, to make sure she had heard her name and did not dream it up.

"Let go of me! Morgan!" Claire screamed.

Claire! Morgan's stomach burned with dread. She tried to push the crate open, but the lid was so heavy she couldn't even budge it.

"Now, now girlie. Why you screaming for?" She heard a man chuckle.

Morgan began to panic. She needed out now. She brought her knee up and felt the lid budge a little. She placed her forearm on the cover and pressed up.

"Don't touch me!" Claire's voice felt like a punch in the gut to Morgan as she struggled in the wooden box.

The yell gave Morgan a surge of adrenaline and with all her strength she slammed her knees and arms into the lid and it came loose. She pushed the lid off the crate, her legs stumbled on the edge of the box as she nearly fell. Her blood boiled as she stared at the sight in front of her. Three grown men stood in a circle around Claire. They shoved her back and forth. They hadn't heard her. Morgan glanced around an old lantern hung on the ship's wall right by her. It was the perfect weapon, she thought as she grabbed it. Her hands clasped tightly around the heavy metal handle.

She felt the weight in her hand as she began to move towards them.

She crept up behind the man closest to her and with all her might she swung back and brought the lantern hard and fast down on his head. The lantern shattered as glass rained down around the man. His eyes grew wide and confusion swept his face just before he hit the ground with a thud. The two other men froze, their eyes locked with Morgan. They stared at her with blank looks on their faces as they tried to process what happened and where she had come from. The man that held Claire smirked. He passed her to his partner and snickered, his eyes never left Morgan. He squared his shoulders with a grin on his face as he stood off with Morgan.

"Well, well,well; What do we have here? You want to play too Missy?" He said with a laugh and stepped forward loudly to intimidate her.

Morgan smiled a soft innocent smile as he moved towards her. His eyes spread over her body as he sized her up. No concern or worry in his eyes. Morgan knew he underestimated her. He paused as if uncertain how he wanted to proceed. Morgan took her opportunity. She did not wait for him to make the first move. She stepped towards him and smashed her elbow across his face. The step forward added more power to the blow. A crack rang out as she made contact. She stepped back and the man howled. Blood instantly began to pour down his face. As his hands went to his nose to cover it as he collapsed to his knees.

The sound of pain that came from the man didn't phase
Morgan. Morgan turned to face the man who held
Claire.

"Let her go!" She threatened her voice filled with
anger.

The man looked at his friends on the ground and
became angry. He shoved Claire to the side with such
force she fell. He let out a low growl as he ran at
Morgan. Morgan dropped to the ground as he came at
her. She threw her legs out at his feet as he stumbled
forward. The impact knocked his legs out from under
him and he landed forward into the wooden crates. The
crates bursted as his body struck them. Wooden pieces
scattered about the ground. He let out a small groan and
then went silent. Morgan waited as she watched the
three men carefully. Her hands in fist by her side,
clenched so tightly her knuckles turned white. She
watched as the man with the broken nose began to try
to stand. Morgan walked over to him and delivered a
kick to his back which sent him forward. He landed on
his face, blood sprayed out on the ground and he let out
a painful cry. His body shook on the ground and Morgan
knew he was in too much pain to stand again.

Morgan rushed over to Claire and wrapped her
arms around her tightly. Relief hit Morgan for a mere
second as Claire was safe. Then the sound of footsteps
and voices came from all over the ship. It was the sound
of more of the crew who began to gather. The eyes of
the men were filled with anger, confusion, and
excitement as they fell on Morgan and Claire.

Morgan backed away so her back was to a wall of the ship. No one could sneak up behind her. Her eyes dared any man to step forward.

They swarmed them slowly. They came from all directions, from the ship's upper decks and below. They grew closer but didn't rush at her. They acted as if they waited for something. Some even glanced behind them. Morgan followed their eyes. A man stood on the upper deck. He watched the scene below, with no expression on his face. She tried to make out his features. She could see he had deep brown hair that tucked out from under his hat. He was tall and held himself with authority. She wanted to say a smirk tried to dance on his lips. His eyes left heres and he looked out at the men. He nodded and two men stepped forward out of the crowd.

Morgan clenched her fist, her eyes scanned the ship as she tried to find a way out, a plan of somesorts. There were too many men and they were cornered. She had only one option and it had been her only option for so long. Fight. She studied them as one brave man approached her. His eyes glimmered as he acted like a cat who had cornered a mouse.

" Now, now lassy we aren't gonna hurt ya. Just settle down." He said with a smirk.

Morgan narrowed her eyes at him. She was not about to surrender. Something shimmered at his hip and hope flashed inside of her as her eyes saw it. A sword dangled off his hip. She had spent many nights with her father as he taught her how to fence. She was good. He had been so proud of it. If she could just get the sword.

The man didn't seem too sturdy on his feet and the others behind him looked unsure of the situation. She stood there and waited. Finally the man lunged for her. She spun quickly around him. She now stood in the middle of two men. They both grinned from ear to ear as they thought she had made a mistake. He went to reach for her and she moved away from him. His friend who was more cautious reached out his hand but was very unsure. Morgan watched his hand tremble as he held it out to her. He did not know what to do next. He seemed lost.

Morgan smiled sweetly and grabbed the man's arm who had reached out to her. He was shocked that she touched him. He froze at her touch. The man behind Morgan shuffled his feet, he was anxious as Morgan grabbed ahold of his crew mate. He let out a small growl as if it helped him move forward. Morgan with all her strength pulled the man's arm hard forward as she stepped out of the way. The two men smashed into each other, stumbled and fell over. They laid on top of each other in a giant heap. The men, who watched around them began to laugh. The two men tangled with each other began to struggle and try to get free from each other.

Morgan was fast on her feet and seized her opportunity. She fumbled at the guy's waist to get his sword free. She yanked back and pulled it free. In seconds she stood in the center of the ship, her stance blocked anyone from Claire. She wasn't sure what was about to happen but at least now she had a weapon.

She looked around her, there were so many of them and only one of her. She took a deep breath in, it didn't matter she would fight until she couldn't no more. Her stance was firm as she gripped the handle of the sword tightly. The tip of the sword pointed downwards as she waited for someone to make a move.

Two more men stepped forward this time. They seem to be more sure of themselves. One smiled a toothless smile at her.

"Say whatcha you're gonna do with a sword Missy. Put it down and everything will be okay " He grinned.

"I won't be doing that." Morgan said as she tightened her stance and pointed the tip of her sword at him.

He ran his finger over the top of the blade and then pushed it off to the side. He laughed and looked at the other men in disbelief. He then went to grab Morgan. She moved quickly to the side and slashed at his belt. His trousers fell to the ground. His mouth hung open as he hopped slightly as he tried to keep his balance. Morgan chuckled as she slightly kicked him and he fell over. The men that had gathered around them began to laugh more. The second man took his chances when Morgan was distracted; grabbing her by her waist. As she was picked up she caught a glimpse of the man who stood alone on the top deck. He scowled as he watched. He must be the captain she thought.

Before she could give any more thought to it her back connected with the man's chest. It took everything in her not to scream. Her injuries from the night before were still on fire. Morgan threw her legs forward and brought them back as hard as she could. She connected with the man's groin. He instantly dropped her. He fell to the ground as he held his groin. A moan escaped his lips as he curled into himself. Morgan caught her breath as a growl rumbled through the crowd from above. The captain slammed his fist into the railing frustrated with the situation.

"Let's wrap up this fun, boys. She's just a woman." yelled an older man from the crowd.

Morgan squeezed the handle of the sword as she waited. The men in the crowd hesitated. They didn't want to make the captain more angry.

A much larger bulkier man stepped up. He lightly tapped her sword with his. She responded back with a harsh swing that knocked his sword to the side with force. He raised his eyebrows at her and lunged. Morgan moved to the side and struck him as she did. Blood trickled from a slash in his arm. This just angered him. He aggressively swung at her. She had to use both hands to block each blow. She knew she couldn't match him strength wise and she didn't know how long she could keep doing it. She had to think of something. She was lighter and quicker on her feet than the men. She looked around and spotted a stack of large barrels. If she could just get closer. If he fell into them she may be able to capture his sword.

She blocked each blow with her sword. They drew near the stack. It was time. She had to make him angry. She blocked one of his strikes and then slashed his arm again. Another slice right below the one she had made previously on the same arm. He became frustrated and rage began to rush through him as he saw more of his own blood spilled. He took up his sword and raced towards her. This was exactly what she wanted. Just when he was close enough; she spun out of the way and he toppled into the barrels. They fell in on him and he was stuck.

The captain was enraged. She saw him take off his hat and ran his hand through his hair. She smirked a little bit, his frustration told her she could do this. She was about to ready herself for the next fighter when she noticed a movement from the corner of her eyes. She glanced over towards Claire and a man crept towards her. Claire locked eyes with Morgan. Morgan's stomach twisted and she nodded her head to the side, which told Claire to move. The small girl sunk further into the corner she was in.

Morgan bit her lip as she picked up her sword and harpooned it to the wall. The sword hit the wall with such force as it impaled itself deep into the wood. The sword bounced up and down in front of the man's face. He stopped in his tracks, his eyes followed the blade back to Morgan. Morgan quickly began to walk to Claire. She needed to get to her before the man came out of his fear. A loud crash was heard from behind her, her body rocked with the noise as pain washed over her.

Everything began to get fuzzy as she tried to push on to get to Claire. She felt her body waiver. No her mind screamed as her vision began to tunnel. She crashed to her knees, her hand stretched outwards towards Claire.

"Claire." Morgan whispered as her body slumped forward and she hit the deck, the world went black.

"Morgan!" Claire yelled and rushed towards her but rough hands caught her.

The captain shook his head and another long sigh escaped him. He watched the scene below in frustration, sighing frustrated as he watched the scene below. He didn't have time for this. He ran his hand through his hair once more as he watched the fiery red head finally go down. It was definitely a cheap shot but at least that was over with for now

"Get the little one something to eat and have her sit with Jack. Put the redhead in my cabin. Then get back to work and your stations!" He gritted his teeth, his eyes captured by her red hair that sprawled out on his deck floor. He wasn't sure why he ordered to have her in his cabin; the words just came out. He grumbled, angry at the situation. He gave his orders and quickled turned. The anger he felt vibrated through his footsteps as he stomped back to his cabin.

Chapter Three
The Captain

He stood hunched over his desk. His eyes
burned into the map in front of him. They were behind at
least three days. It had taken him that long to notice the
original map was gone. What he had in front of him was
a copy he made from memory. He gripped the sides of
his desk and dug his fingernails into it. He had studied
the other map so much, he knew it by heart. His blood
boiled at the thought of him having it. The word traitor
echoed in his head. He traced the route on the map.
They were there. He knew they had to be. He needed to
catch up or take a shortcut, something. He wanted to
destroy him, burn his whole world down. Just as he had
done to him. He would make the bastard watch as he
did it.

Fire. He could still smell the smoke. He could still
see the flames as they poured out the windows when he
closed his eyes. Still feel the rain on his skin. It amazed
him that a fire could still burn, still destroy everything,
even in the rain. Sweat beaded across his forehead. His
body began to shake a little all of the rage, pain, and
heartache coursed through his veins as if it was
happening again.

A loud bang forced him from his thoughts. He
looked up. His cabin door had been kicked open as one
of the crew members carried the girl. He didn't speak but
just nodded to the bed. The crewmember nodded
slightly and flopped her down on it and left without a

word. He sank down into his desk chair, the weight of everything pushed down on him. He sighs and sinks into his chair.

His eyes looked over at his bed. The unconscious girl laid almost lifeless in the center of his bed. He would have thought she was dead but he watched her chest rise and fall. Another mess, another thing he has to figure out before he can get what he wants. He threw his feet up on the desk and leaned back.

How the hell did she get on the ship? He thought as he shook his head. What the hell was she thinking? He stared at her thoughts raced in his head.

"You know a ship isn't any place for a woman or a child. Never mind a pirate ship." He said to her annoyed.

He heard her move slightly and she let out a painful sound. She couldn't be already coming to he thought. He groaned and got to his feet. He watched her carefully as he walked over to the bed. He braced himself against the bed post as he looked down at her. Her clothing was torn and covered in dirt. She was covered in dirt. She had bruises around her wrist and forearms. Finger marks? He thought, as he stared at the circular blue marks. His eyes traveled down her body. She was covered in tons of scratches on her leg. She looked like she had been through hell. He knew her life was hard, his annoyance with her and the situation softened a bit. Her face still held light in. Even asleep he could see it. He could see little freckles that went across her nose even through the dirt. She had very long

eyelashes that swept over her. cheek and her pouty mouth was the perfect shade of pink.

His eyes lingered a little longer than they should have on her lip. Her hair was the brightest shade of red he'd ever seen; even with all the dirt and mud scattered amongst it. It reminded him of the red sun on hot days as it scorched the earth. Her eyebrows narrowed and Her face began to scrunch. She let out a small groan of pain. Her chest began to rise and fall quicker. She had started to wake up.

Before he could move the girl jolted up her hands immediately went into fist and she looked like a wild animal ready to fight whoever she needed to. Her eyes darted around the room until they landed on him. She squinted her eyes at him and scooted away from him.

"Where is Claire?" She said harshly.

He smiled, she was out numbered and yet she still had this fire. She would take on anything and anyone she had to. He could see that.

"You know I should be asking the questions. You sneak onto my ship and now are demanding answers." He scoffed at her.

His answer wasn't the right one. She was now on her feet, hands clenched in fist by her side. Her eyes threatened him.

"Where is she?" She demanded as her voice got louder.

He took a deep breath in as he tried to calm himself. " She's with Jack -"

"I want to see her! Who's Jack?" She asked, her words cut him off.

"Jack is my cabin boy. I strongly suggest you do not cut me off again." He gritted his teeth as he spoke.

"Bring her to me." She threatened as she stepped towards him.

His patient was gone, the admiration for her tough exterior vanished. He was angry, frustrated and annoyed all over again. He ran his hand through his hair as he narrowed his eyes at her.

"You sneak onto my ship and now you're giving me orders! On my ship! I should just throw you overboard and see how long you can tread water." He bellowed

She didn't say anything. She kept her distance and was staring him down. He stared at this woman in disbelief. Most men wouldn't stare at him like this. No one spoke to him like this. He could feel his blood pressure rise.

"How did you get on my ship lass!?" He yelled as he came around the side of the bed to face her.

She kept her silence and stood her ground. He wanted to shake her. She infuriated him. How dare she not answer him! Then a thought crept into his head. A thought that made his stomach sink. What if Travis had helped her. What if she was here because of him? That would explain how she would know about the ship. That would explain how she could easily sneak on and no one noticed. What exactly was her plan? She now became a threat. He saw red as he thought of Travis.

In one quick motion he closed the gap between them and pinned her against the wall by her arms. He could feel her wince but didn't care.

"Did Travis send you?" He asked as he squeezed her arms tighter.

"I don't know Travis. We just needed a way out." She said her voice cracked slightly from pain.

He narrowed his eyes at her as studied her face. He couldn't tell if he could believe her or not. She remanded still, her heart pounded in her chest as she tried to think of an escape. She took the opportunity to get away from him. He glared at her but he was too focused on his thoughts. She brought her arms up, his arms went with her. His glare turned to a shock look as she spined and knocked his arms away from her. She then dashed to the door. He may have been stunned for a moment but he followed right behind her. His hand stretched to grab her. He grabbed onto the back of her shirt. His hand touched something wet and when he looked down he saw red. Her back was covered in dried and fresh blood. He let go as he looked from her back to his hand.

She went for the door handle ready to escape. He threw his arm up and pressed on the door. The door wouldn't budge. She was trapped again between him and her way out.

"What happened to your back?" He asked the back of her head.

His warm breath hit the back of her neck and instant goosebumps spread through her body. She tugged on the handle again as she ignored the question.

"Your back." He repeated firmly.

She became angry. How dare he ask her. She turned quickly. Ready to fight but as she turned face to face with him she froze. His body was so close to her while she had no way out, her mind went blank. He went to demand an answer but the anger that flickered in her deep green eyes made him stop. His nose was just inches from hers. Her eyes searched his face as she looked for some answer to what she felt.

She then became uncomfortable with how close he was. She pushed herself back further into the door and ignored the pain. His deep chocolate brown eyes searched her face, she could feel her cheeks burn from their gaze. She tore her eyes from his, she couldn't take the pressure they made her feel. Her eyes travel to his full lips. She knew she just turned a deep shade of red. She tried to focus on something else. He was too close; this was too much. She looked at the top of his head. His hair was dark, almost black and slightly curly. The urge to run her fingers through his hair entered her mind. She had never been this close to a man. Embarrassment and panic rushed through her as her stomach flipped inside of her. She tried to push further away from him but was trapped between him and the door. She bit her lower lip nervously.

"What happened to your back?" He asked softly.

"It's nothing." she said looked down ashamed

He reached out and his fingers lightly touched her cheek. Morgan stiffened at his touch. Scared but there was excitement too. His finger tips moved to her chin as he cupped it. He moved her chin upwards which brought her eyes back to his. Morgan stopped breathing. The way his face had gone from anger and hate, to soft and full of care confused her. Her body didn't know whether to lean into his touch or run for her life.

"Can I look at it? " He asked, his words just above a whisper.

She moved her face away from his hand and pressed further into the door. She winced as she did. She pressed further into the door and went as far back into as she could. She could feel blood as it seeped down her back and into her ripped shirt. He stepped away from her and put his hands up like he meant no harm. His chest hurt from how much fear he could see on her face. She looked like a caged animal as she shrunk away from him.

"Jack!" He yelled, which made her

He raised an eyebrow at her and said "Move away from the door "

Morgan took three careful steps away from the door. The only reason she did was because he said the name of the person who had Claire. A few seconds later the door open and a young boy walked in

"Yes Captain?" Jack asked looking at Morgan curiously

"Bring the girl. I need water and clean rags too." He said quickly.

The boy nodded and ducked out the door as quickly as he came in. Morgan stood there and waited. Her hand fell into her own hand and she began to fidget with her fingers. He wanted to make her comfortable, and wanted her to trust him. He didn't understand WHY HE felt that but he followed it. He walked over to his desk and leaned against it. He gave her space. He hoped it would make her less fearful. He folded his arms across his chest and waited.

It took forever but Jack returned with Claire just behind him. Jack carried a bowl of warm water into the cabin, his face wrinkled as he focused on the bowl. Just behind Jack Claire's bright golden hair bounced. She held the rags tightly in her hand. Her big blue eyes spotted Morgan and she squeaked with happiness. She rushed over to her arms open wide. Morgan leaned down and scooped her up into a hug. Claire's arms squeezed her tightly. Morgan gritted her teeth through the pain. Morgan quickly looked Claire over who giggled slightly.

"Stop. I am fine Morgan." She smiled, grabbed Morgan's hand and squeezed it.

Claire then noticed the blood on her own palm. She glanced at Morgan. Her expression went from happy to worried now.

"Morgan your back, it's still bleeding." Claire panicked.

"No honey, it's just my shirt that's all." She smiled at Claire.

"What happened to her back, Claire?" The Captain spoke up, his eyebrow raised in curiosity.

"It's my fault he hurt-" Claire said her voice caught in her throat as she choked up.

Morgan's eyebrows narrowed in anger as she glared at him. If looks could kill he would have been dead. He matched her stare and Morgan glanced away. She spun Claire towards her and squatted down slightly so they were eye level.

"Claire nothing and I mean nothing is your fault! I am fine. I promise." She smiled at Claire as she spoke firmly.

Claire looked at first skeptical, she didn't believe any of that. Everything was her fault.

"Then what is the water and rags for?" Claire asked sharply.

Morgan looked quickly around. She had to think of something. Claire did not need to see her back. She already blamed so much of this on herself. She found her eyes landed on the captain. Her eyes asked for help.

He cleared his throat and stood up. Claire's eyes went to him.

"I need to clean a few things. Since you two are on my ship, you're going to help. Nobody rides for free. Morgan's going to help me and you're going to go help Jack." He ordered his hands still folded across his chest.

Morgan got a little nervous about Claire leaving again. Claire saw the look on Morgan's face and smiled at her.

"Hey everythings been fine. I've been with Jack. He's two years older than me and He's shown me around the ship. I've been helping him. He taught me how to tie a knot. " She said happily.

" All right. I'm going to stay here with the captain and help him…clean. I will come find you when I am all done." Morgan smiled and patted Claire on the head.

The Captain nodded at Jack who made his way to the door. Jack pulled the door open and waited for Claire. She smiled brightly at Morgan before she followed Jack.. Morgan sighed as the door shut. She could feel his eyes on her. She knew they were filled with questions. Questions she never wanted to answer.

"She'll blame herself if she sees my back. She's had a very hard life and I don't need her hurting anymore." She said very simply

"So whose He?" He pressed his previous question.

She just looked at him and shook her head. She would not talk about this. He sighed and threw his hands down. He grabbed the bowl of water. As he snatched it with annoyance the water spilt a little. He grumbled as he grabbed the rags and walked to the bed. He placed the bowl of water on the night stand and turned to look at her. He motioned for her to come sit. She stood there frozen. Her mind screams no way.

He's growing frustrated " Look Lass I can either help you or I can get another man to help you. Or you could get infection and die of some type of fever and I'll throw your body overboard. It's all up to you. However I have a ship to run and places to be. so make a decision and make it now!"

He was right. She hated that he was. Her stomach twisted and turned inside of her. She swallowed hard and walked over to the bed.

Chapter Four
Fire

"Close your eyes." She demanded as she scowled.

"What?" He asked, confused.

"I have to take my shirt off. I don't want you to see." She said as her eyebrows went up as she spoke and her lips pressed together.

He pushed air out of his mouth in a snort and shut his eyes. Morgan felt her eyes twitch at the sound but paid no attention to it. She slowly took off her shirt. The fabric brushed over the open wounds and scrapes. She winced in pain. She pulled the shirt around to her front to cover her breast. She sat on the bed and faced away from him.

"Ok." She whispered her voice soft and vulnerable.

He opened his eyes. He wasn't sure what he expected to see but this wasn't it. Her back was nothing but blood. He could see two large gashes that were the cause of it but it was hard to tell if there was any other damage or wounds. He dunked the cloth in the water, rung it out, and then carefully wiped her back. Morgan bit down on her lip to keep the cry of pain in. He repeated it again. As he tried to clear the blood away. After a third pass he could finally see her back. He was stunned as he looked at it. Her back was riddled with scars. She looked like someone who had been to battle.

Besides the two large gashes, her back was covered in bruises. She looked like she had been severely beaten. He took a deep breath in.

"What happened?" He asked softly, his voice trembled from the anger he tried to keep at bay.

"What's your name?" She asked to change the subject.

"Gavin. What-" He went to ask again but she cut him off.

"Named after your father?" It was a silly question but maybe it would change the subject.

"Lass-

"I told you we needed away out. That's why we got on your ship." She said calmly.

"The girl, is she your daughter?" He asked as he tried to put this puzzle together.

"No, my little cousin." She snapped.

Her body was stiff but not from the pain. The questions he asked hit a nerve. He could see the annoyance in her body language. He felt sorry for her but didn't care that she was annoyed.

" Your back...husband?" He asked, knowing he was pushing his limits.

"Husband? Pssh no husband" She laughed as a small burst of air shot out of her nose.

His lips curled into a small smile as he watched her red hair move with her laugh. He liked the way it sounded, even though it mocked his question.

"So-" He went to ask another question.

"So are you done? " She sighed, he was relentless.

"You know Lass, I would cut a man's tongue out if he interrupted me as much as you do." He smirked but left his tone as a threat.

"It's Morgan." She said sharply, his threat did not phase her and he could tell a playful smile on her face.

He let out an exasperated sigh. The air from it hit her shoulder and sent a small chill through her. She held a breath in to calm her anxiety. She knew this persistent man was not giving up.

"Look, captain. I would rather not and say we did. I don't want to go trudging down my past. As soon as you dock Claire and I will be out of your hair." She said as she started to get up.

"Sit." He grumbled as he placed on her shoulder, he pushed down slightly as he made her sit back down.

"We need to bandage these to apply pressure." He said as he got up and walked over to desk.

He pulled open the wooden drawer and fumbled around inside of it. Morgan could hear the crinkled nose of papers as they were shuffled about. He found what he looked for in the very back and grabbed the bandage material. Morgan glanced over her shoulder and saw the bandage and she began to panic. He would have to wrap it around her front and he would see her. He rolled his eyes at her as he saw the panicked look. He placed the bandage lightly on her wound. She winced as it touched her skin. He then passed the bandage to her.

"Here you do the front," He said shortly.

She felt a rush of relief as she carefully took the bandage from his hand. Her fingertips grazed his warm skin as she took it and she felt another rush of nerves. She pushed it to the back of her mind as she grasped the white fluffy material and lowered the shirt, carefully. She wrapped the bandage around her chest and brought it to the other side, where Gavin grabbed it and brought it across her back. As he took the bandage and handed it back to her, his eyes landed on her side, her soft round breast peaked out and moved each time she did. He clenched his jaw as he saw it.

He felt himself grow tense at the situation. He cleared his throat as he tried to focus on the wounds and not her. It became difficult with each pass of the bandage. Once the wounds were covered Gavin got up, he needed space from her. He walked to a closet and returned with a shirt and pants.

"These may fit. My first mate was a rather small and thin man." He said as he placed the items on the bed and quickly walked to the door.

He glanced back at her and the look of shock on her face. He clenched his jaw once more and waked out.

The sea air hit him as he leaned back against the door. He needed the cold air at this point. He needed more than cold air, he needed a drink. He watched his men move about the ship as they carried out their duties. He spotted Jack and the girl , Claire cleaned some of the railings. What in the world was he going to do with these girls? He let out a groan in frustration.

"Captain?" One of the men asked as he heard the captain.

"Nothing Earl. Go about your duties. " He dismissed him.

Earl was middle aged. Short and stocky. He hadn't been part of the crew long but he was a hard worker and quiet most of the time. He felt the door open behind him and he nearly fell back into Morgan. She placed her hands on his back to steady him. He gained his balance and he looked at her. She had a sweet silly smile on her face that could melt the heart of the coldest man.

"You ok?" She asked, she tried to cover the laugh that lingered behind her voice.

"Fine." He muttered and moved aside and out of the doorway.

She walked out and went to the railing leaning against it to have a look at the ship. Gavin froze. The pants did more than fit. They hugged every curve on her. His eyes traveled up her long legs and locked on her butt. He felt his throat grow dry. The shirt was loose but you could see her outline and with the pants the imagination could dream the rest up. He wanted to know what it would feel like to run his hand down her thigh. What it would feel like to grab her by the hips. How her bottom would fit nicely in the palm of his hands. He swallowed hard. He tried to take his eyes off her and his thoughts from her body.

"So how can I help?" She asked as she turned to face him.

You could get off my ship. He wanted to yell. She was a huge distraction already and she hadn't even been here a day.His eyes began to wander again with his thoughts. Damn it! He yelled at himself. He needed her to go away. He clenched his fist at his side. Morgan's brow frowned as she looked at him, confused with all the emotions on his face.

"Earl." He shouted, Morgan jumped at the yell and her frown turned into a glare/

"Yes captain?" Earl popped up to his aid.

"Take Morgan here and find something for her to do. Let the men know there will be consequences if there's any misconduct with her." He threatened.

"Aye aye." He said then turned towards Morgan.

"Right this way Miss. We'll find something for you to do." He smiled with a small bow of his head.

Morgan looked at Gavin before she went to follow Earl. She had noticed he kept getting uncomfortable and then angry. The man clearly had emotional problems she thought as she followed after Earl.

Gavin ducked back into his room and sighed with relief as he closed the door. This was going to be bad. This woman is on his ship; Nothing good could come of it. He pulled at his pants trying to loosen them from his discomfort.

"Nothing but trouble." He muttered and then walked over to this map.

His map wasn't a full map. He had remembered it enough and filled in the blanks. His first mate, Travis and he had split the map in half to ensure things would be kept fair. Fair. Gavin scoffed at the word. Travis turned out to be a snake and he could not wait to end him.

The treasure was all they talked about as boys. Now he didn't care about the treasure. All he cared about now was finding Travis and making him suffer. He sank in his chair. The headache, the dull pain that was somehow always there gnawed at his skull. It had worsened in the short time the girl had stepped foot on his ship. He rubbed the bridge of his nose, he was exhausted. He leaned back on his chair as he tried to get comfortable and relax. He found the sweet spot on the worn out leather and felt his eyes grow heavy. Within a few minutes he dozed off.

The rain hit the ground and bounced off it. Puddles formed quickly as he walked home. He hugged the groceries close to his chest so they wouldn't get so wet. He couldn't wait to be home. He wanted to watch her spin about the kitchen as she talked mindlessly about the drama in the neighborhood. She loved gossip. He loved to watch her. The smell of smoke invaded his nostrils as he rounded the corner to their street.

His chest tightened. Something was wrong. He knew it in his heart. He raced up the cobble stone path. His feet carried him up the top of the small incline as quickly as he could manage. As he reached the top, that's when he saw it. His small cottage was engulfed in

flames. He dropped everything in his arms. The carton
of eggs splatter on the stone. The shells cracked open
as he felt like his own chest would. He raced towards his
house. His wife Christina was home. Neighbors had
gathered outside of it. Some with buckets of water as
they tried their best to fight the flames.

"Christina!" He shouted, his eyes searched the
crowd for her platinum blonde hair.

"Christina!" He screamed again and his voice
pleaded for an answer.

There was no answer. His heart pounded as he
looked at the house. His stomach sank as the terrifying
relation hit him. She was inside. He bolted towards the
front door and kicked it open. Black smoke poured out
as the door gave in. It blinded him as he pushed inside.
Smoked filled his lungs as he tried to make his way to
their room. His skin felt the heat from the flames as it
burned down everything around him.

"Chirstina!" He yelled with a cough as he fought
against the smoke.

A crack echoed loudly through the house and he
knew the structure that held it all together was about to
collapse. He tried to move quicker but the further he
went into the house the harder it became to breathe.
The flames crept closer and closer to him. He struggled
to pass the flames. The flames singed his flesh as he
tried to get to their room. Another loud creak echo
followed by a crash. A beam from the ceiling fell down in
front of him. The flames from the fire danced across it.
The beam now blocked the way to their bedroom.

Gavin began to cough non stop, he pulled his shirt up over his nose and mouth to block the smoke. He crouched to get closer to the ground as he tried to find some relief.

"Christina!" He managed to yell between coughs.

His chest tightened and he began to feel weak. His vision began to tunnel and he felt himself began to rock.

"Christinia." He whispered as he hit the ground.

A shock of cold rushed over his body. He struggled as he fought himself to gain consciousness. His chest and lungs burned. He felt like he could not take air in. He couldn't breathe. He forced himself up and inhaled, slowly, air flooded into him. He looked around and then everything rushed back.

"Christina!" He said as he jolted up.

He was weak and almost toppled back over. A neighbor steady him.

"Easy Gavin. I got you." He heard him say.

"Christina?" He said still in a haze.

"We couldn't find her. We barely got to you before it all collapsed." His neighbor whispered.

Gavin's eyes fixated on the burnt rubble. Several men stood around and dumped buckets of water on the collapsed structure. The water hissed as it put out the last bit of the fire. He fell to his knees as he felt his world shatter. He looked at the debris in disbelief.

"Christina. " He whispered as his heart broke as he said her name.

He heard small cautious steps come towards him. Another neighbor approached him. His face filled with sorrow for Gavin.

"Gavin, you can stay with us tonight." He said, placing a hand on his shoulder.

Gavin continued to stare at the debris. He didn't respond. He hung his head in defeat. What could have happened? What went wrong? He thought.

"Why." He whispered as if anyone would have an answer for him.

A loud slam woke him from his nightmare. He sat up, his body still shook from the dream. The smell of smoke was still embedded in his nostrils as if he stood outside his home seconds ago. He nearly jumped up out of his chair at hearing his cabin door shut. Sweat beaded against his forehead as he tried to make out who entered.

"Captain?" A man asked, his voice timid.

"Aye what is it?" He said annoyed

"Well captain. Ya see the thing is. Well the men were talking a d-"

"John, get on with it." Gavin growled.

"Well the man was talking and where are these misses gonna sleep." He asked but he took a step back as if afraid of the answer.

"For God sakes John really one girl and this is how you all act." He said as he shook his head.

"Here. They will sleep in here. No one is allowed to touch anyone. If anything happens to them there will be consequences." He spoke with his eyes narrowed to intensify the threat.

The man nodded a few times before he ducked back out the door. He steadied himself against his chair. His mind returned to the dream. He remembered his hands turned bloody as he searched through the debris. He tried to find anything that would tell him if Christina had been in there. He knew in his heart she had been in there. He had waited for hours outside the burnt down home. He hoped that she would come back. When she never came he raced to the few friends she had houses. She was not there. He dragged his feet back to his burnt down home and sat down on the ground. He did not know what to do with himself. He was lost for the first time in his life. He waited for something to happen. He waited for her. A man approached him. He held his hand out to him and handed him a small piece of paper. It was almost like he had never been there at all. Gavin watched him walk away and then opened the folded paper and recognized the scribbles immediately:

Now that you no longer have any ties to this fake life you were leading; I'll see you on the sea. I'll be where my map ends. My condolences

Gavin's blood boiled as he replayed the memory. His hands shook as his breathing became harsh. He would kill him.

Chapter Five
Tour

Morgan walked slowly into the cabin. She held an asleep Claire in her arms. They had laid on the top deck and watched the stars until Claire had dozed off. They had never seen anything like it before. It was just the ship in the wide open darkness. You could not tell where the water ended and the sky began. Thousands upon thousands of stars lit up the sky and their reflections danced in the water top. She closed the cabin door quietly and turned to look about the room. Gavin was still sour when she returned. The look on face said it all. Morgan stayed in the doorway unsure of what to do. She scanned the room quickly. Then she started towards an empty space in the corner. Gavin raised an eyebrow at her, as she went to set Claire on the floor.

"What are you doing? Put her on the bed." He ordered with a shake of his head.

"It's fine we've slept on much worse. " She whispered.

"The bed." He bellowed loud enough to be intimidating but soft enough to not wake the child.

She didn't argue. Claire deserved to sleep in an actual bed for once. She walked over to the bed and laid Claire gently down. She covered her with the blanket and watched her curl in them with a happy sigh. Morgan leaned down and kissed her head.

Gavin watched the scene. Morgan may not be her mother but treated her like she was hers. The softness that she had when she tended to Claire warmed his heart. Morgan shifted awkwardly as she lingered by the bed. He grinned slightly at her. He softened his expression and moved away from his desk.

"Tomorrow if you and the girl could help Jack clean the upper deck. Then our "cook" could use some of your help." He said as he made his way to the door.

Morgan wanted to ask where he was headed too but didn't. She nodded as she watched him. He lingered by the door as if he wanted to say something else but headed out. Morgan looked about the room. She didn't know what to do with herself. She glanced down at Claire and exhaustion crept up on her. It had been a long day, a long week, heck it had been a long several years. Morgan touched the bed lightly with her hand before she gave in. She climbed into the bed and curled up next to Claire. The bed did feel amazing. She sunk into the softness of it consumed her.

She pulled the blanket up to her shoulder and laid on her side so she could watch the door. It was out of habit. Normally she would not even think about sleeping. She would be on the floor in front of the door just in case he decided to try to get in. It was odd but as she laid there, she felt safer than she had in a long time. Which was absolutely crazy due to the fact she was on a ship full of pirates. She still didn't trust anyone. She knew she was on a ship filled with men. Men who had been at sea for a long time without women. Men who lived a life of breaking rules. She focused on the door;

nervousness settled in the pit of her stomach. It would be ok. She told herself. Her thoughts drifted to Gavin. There was something about him that made her feel safe. For some reason she truly believed that would not let the other men harm them.

Gavin grumbled to himself as he walked to the top deck. He continued to grumble all the way to the wheel of the ship. Where he motioned to let him take over. Jason raised an eyebrow at Gavin. Jason was to do the night shift. Gavin steered the ship in the daytime. Jason had taken over early when Gavin had to go deal with the woman issue. Jason grinned as he saw Gavin frustrated. Jason was a tall man with broad shoulders. He had light green eyes and his head was shaved bald. He laughed as Gavin fidgeted for the wheel. He chuckled once more before he scooted over.

"What's the matter with you Gavin?" He smirked as he handed the wheel over.

Gavin glared at him which made Jason laugh harder. His hand went to his stomach as he laughed.

"Don't even start." Gavin said his eyes dared him to continue.

"I've known you too long for that captain. I think your brown eyes are handsome." Jason said and whacked him on the back.

"Well good maybe I should just string you up then. It will be a great lesson for everyone." Gavin said through his teeth.

"Now, now, Capt. I didn't mean to make you upset." Jason chuckled.

"We're three days behind." He said, his eyes narrowed on the horizon.

"And now I have to babysit." He said with a sigh.

"Well then why are they still on the ship?" Jason shrugged.

A look of annoyance washed over Gavin's face. If he could clench his jaw any tighter it would pop off. Jason squeezed his shoulder. Gavin hadn't named any one first mate after Travis. He would never have one again but Jason was second in command.

"Calm down man." Jason chuckled.

"We are three days behind. I now have to watch the men more because of this woman. And all I wanna do is get to Blind Man's Passage so I can kill Travis." He said his knuckles went white on the wheel from how hard he squeezed.

"I know. We will get there and you will have your revenge. Just take it easy or you'll kill yourself before we even get there." Jason said, squeezed his shoulder tighter.

"You go ahead and sleep, I'm going to take the night shift." He nodded to Jason.

Jason didn't say anything back and went on his way. Gavin stared off into the dark horizon as he watched the stars.

Morgan stared at the door, she couldn't sleep no matter how tired she was. She stared at the door and her mind raced. She could not lie there any longer. She slowly got out of bed and looked around the cabin. She wandered over to his desk. The map he intensely studied was rolled out. It was only half a map. He had drawn the missing sections from memory. She looked over both of them. He had notes and dates of where he wanted to be by when. He was three days behind. He wanted to be by what was marked Blind Man's Passage. She settled in his chair and gazed over the map.

     She frowned deeply, there was not a single dock along the route. She narrowed her eyes as she found one just before the passage, she sighed. She wanted off this ship as soon as possible. There had to be something. She traced different paths and routes but still no other docking sites. She stumbled upon something called Sirens Gully. He would catch up if he went through there. She thought as she traced the passage with her finger.

     " If we were here......and the openings here. . . Then it should be less than a day from here." She whispered to herself.

     The sunrise peeked through the cabin windows. She hadn't slept at all. She began to nod out as she looked at the map. Her head touched the dark brown wood desk and she was out. She didn't hear the cabin door open.

Gavin walked in exhausted. He glanced at
Claire, she was still asleep in his bed. He scanned the
room and his eyes landed on Morgan. She was passed
out on his desk. He felt a little unsettled about her being
near his map. She was reluctant to tell him anything.
Her back was proof of a horrible life but that didn't mean
she was not involved with Travis. Could she even read a
map? He thought as he tried to calm the rage in his
belly. His hands were in fist by his side. He debated on
whether to let it go or go shake her awake and demand
answers. He walked over to her not sure what he was
going to do. Just the thought of Travis set a fire inside of
him. He paused at her side. Her red hair sprawled over
the desk, her lashes fanned over her cheeks. Her lips
were perfectly pouty. She was beautiful. Her eyebrows
quickly frowned and she began to tremble.
        "No. Stop. No!" She said as she began to twitch
slightly.
        "No! No...Claire..stop it. Please stop!" She said
her voice was sleepy but it held so much pain.
        He bit his lower lip as he watched her back as it
shook, her body flinched as if some one inflicted pain on
her. He reached out and carefully shook her.
        "Morgan." He said softly.
        She winced and pulled away from him. She
struggled on the desk as she was still in her dream
state.
        "Morgan." He said louder as she shook her a
little bit harder.

She jolted up,her right hand balled into a fist and went to connect with his jaw. Gavin saw it coming and managed to move back slightly. She didn't miss but it lessened the blow. Her other hand came around in a fist to the other side of his jaw. He blocked it and held on to her arm. She struggled against him as she tried to pull away from him. He pulled her against him and wrapped her in a big hug.

"No no stop." She panicked as she began to kick.

"Morgan! Stop." He said as he tried to break through to her.

She slammed her foot down hard and stomped on his foot. He groaned but didn't let go. She then launched forward and went to throw her head back into his face. He saw it and spun her around so they faced each other.

"Morgan!" He said he let go of her with one hand and grabbed her face.

"I'm not him." He said moved her hair out of her face with his other hand.

She froze at the soft touch. She looked confused and scared, her eyes held back tears. Then suddenly she instantly realized who had her and another type of panic spread across her face.

"Him....Captain." She whispered as she tried to take a step away from him.

"Yeah, you're ok. You were dreaming." He said, hsi hand remained on her cheek.

"Sorry." She whispered, embarrassment on her face and fear still lingered in her eyes.

"What was that? You were fighting so hard." He said, his eyes burned into hers.

"Bad dream." She said and turned her face so his hand had to drop.

She stepped away from him and glanced at the bed. Claire could sleep through anything.

"That was more than a dream." He stated, his body wanted to follow after her. He had to stop himself from moving forward.

"Bad dreams, we all have them. I'll get Claire and we'll let you get some sleep." She said as she walked over to Claire.

She shook Claire lightly as she ignored Gavin who still looked at her. Claire smiled as she woke up and saw Morgan. She hugged her tightly.

"Come on, sleepy head. Let's give the captain his bed back. " She said with a smile.

"That was the best sleep ever. Did you sleep well too? Can we get a bed like this whenever we get to where we're going? It's much better than the ground, " Claire said in almost one breath.

"Oh gosh Claire. It's so early for all those questions but yes we will get you a bed. Come on." She said scooting her off the bed and hustling her along.

"Thank you." Claire shouted over Morgan to Gavin and ducked out the door.

Morgan shook her head and went to follow her out.

"Morgan....it was a him, wasn't it." He said, like he had a bitter taste in his mouth.

He watched her swallow hard. Her body tensed as she tried to find an answer.

"Bad dream." She repeated herself and walked out the door.

She stepped out of the cabin and closed the door behind her. She looked down at the ship. It was magnificent. The ship's deck and railings wood was cherry in color. There were little star shaped details etched onto the rails. The stairs that leaded to the main deck had a gold shimmer line across the top of them that sparkled in front of the cherry color. The mass that held the sails was made out of a light color wood that played well with the gold details throughout the ship. She raised her eyes and followed the mass up to the sails. A dark navy blue flag with a bright sun danced in the wind. In the center of the sun was a star. She gazed at and wondered what it meant.

"The ship is called the Morning Star." Jason said behind her.

"It's amazing." She said as she took everything in.

"Come follow me. I'll show you around." Jason chuckled.

"But I'm supposed to help Jack and Claire." She said her eyes looked at them.

Claire had already grabbed a sponge and was laughing with Jack as he scrubbed down one of the rails.

"They'll be fine." Jason smiled and nodded for her to follow him.

She followed him down the stairs and to the main deck. Everyone shuffled about. Men cleaned and others shifted rops. Everyone had their role. She heard men below the deck as they laughed and carried on. She followed Jason and the laughter went quiet. The chores stopped and they all just watched her walk across. She bit her lip nervously and followed Jason up the stairs to the second upper deck. He went to the back rail and waited for her. His eyes looked over the man and they narrowed slightly. The men quickly went back to work.

Morgan watched the small interaction. She glanced at Jason, who nodded his head to her. She wondered what his position on the ship was. He motioned for her to follow him. They were at the stern of the ship. She spotted the helm and walked over curiously. The wheel of the ship was a light colored wood and it too had stars and suns etched into. Someone spent a great deal of time and took a lot of pride in building this ship. The man steering handed the wheel off to Jason. Morgan stood next to him as she overlooked the ship.

"Have you ever been on a ship before?" Jason asked her.

"No." She answered quietly, her eyes now scanned the ship to find Claire.

She saw her and her chest relaxed a little. She watched her and Jack sit on the stairs. She watched them talk. He reached in his pocket and gave her an apple. She smiled brightly and took it.

"Daughter?" Jason asked, as he watched Morgan.

"Cousin." She answered just as quietly.

"So you don't like to talk? First time I've ever met a woman who didn't want to spend the day chewing at my ear." He smiled as he tried to bait her.

She smirked back and shrugged. She didn't have much to say. She hadn't had much of a life. They stood in silence just watching the ship life and the horizon.

"Jason." He said quietly.

"I'm Morgan." She answered him.

The sun was now completely up in the sky. Morgan was leaning against the rail of the stern. Claire and Jack had made their way there.

"Thank you Jack for keeping Claire company." Morgan smiled at him.

"No problem ma'am. It's nice having someone close to my age around. Also I'm sorry about what you and Claire had to go through." He said sincerely.

Morgan froze and glanced at Claire, how much had she told him. She smiled as she tried to remain calm.

"She told me about her father and I just want you to know that I'll make sure she's safe on this ship. No matter what." He vowed to her.

"Thank you Jack." Morgan said as she stepped back and looked to see if anyone heard his statement.

Jason didn't act like he heard anything. She just didn't want anyone to know too much about them.

Chapter Six
Duel

    He had fallen asleep but not for long it was more like a nap. He stood and stretched, a yawn escaped his mouth. He was still tired. He was always tired. He walked over to the map, like he did every time. He dwelled on their destination. He then remembered she had been over here. He looked to see if there was anything different. Some one ....his pencil marks had been smudged on the side that he drew from memory. She had touched it but for what. Why was she even here...did he believe her.

    A sharp metal noise pulled him from his thoughts. He headed to the door and stepped out of his cabin. He followed the noise to see Jack and Jason. They had swords in hand. The metal from the swords as they hit each other echoed around the ship. They were on the main deck. He glanced to the stern. Thomas was steering, he relaxed a little bit. He scanned the rest of the ship. He saw Morgan off to the side, her eyes followed Jason and Jack's every move. Her hands at her side seem to want to move. He raised his eyebrow and watched. She became frustrated as Jack began to lose. Morgan couldn't take it anymore. She began to coach Jack.

    "Up. Down. Left. Block. Block. Lunge." She called to Jack.

He was startled at first but then began to follow her instructions. Jason had an amused look on his face. As Jack became an actual opponent.

That's it, who is this girl! Gavin thought to himself. He turned on his heels and headed down to the main deck.

"Captain on deck!" One of the crew members spotted him and the rest of the ship shifted out of his way.

Jason took the advantage and maneuvered the sword out of Jack's hand. Gavin came stomped over like a mad bull.

"Sleep well Captain?" Jason smiled at him.

"Sword." He said shortly.

"Aye, aye." He said and handed the sword to Gavin.

"Morgan." He summoned her over.

The crew froze and even Jason had a confused look on his face. She narrowed her eyes at him and headed towards him. Claire followed after her but as Morgan got down onto the deck. She nodded for Claire to stop. Claire moved next to Jack and worriedly squeezed his arm. Gavin held the sword out to her.

"I've been watching you. You know how to use a sword?" Gavin asked with a smile.

"A Little." She said her eyes searched his face as she tried to figure out exactly what was going on.

"Good. How about a wager?" He smiled as he forced the sword into her hand.

"Wager? I don't have anything." She said as she took the sword, becoming defensive.

"No need. I win you answer my questions. That's all." Gavin said shortly.

"And if I win?" Morgan asked.

Gavin smirked in disbelief. This girl really thought she could win. He crossed his arms over his chest and looked at her, mischief sparkled in his eyes.

"I'll take you to whatever dock or place you want to go. Safe passage." He said with a small shrug of his shoulders

Her eyes lit up but she looked at him. She didn't believe him. She clenched her jaw, her eyes narrowed with doubt.

"Anywhere? Any route?" She asked curiously.

He paused at her question. It was a strange request...any route. He became even more suspicious of her. He needed to know what she was about.

"Anywhere, any route " He said as he held out his hand.

She grabbed it quickly and shook. He locked eyes with her as they shook hands. She smiled sweetly at him and with a blink of an eye she grabbed the sword from his waist, backed away from him, and took her stance. He couldn't help it, he laughed out loud.

"That's my sword love." He said approaching her.

She tightened her stance and pointed the sword at him. Her eyes dared him to move forward.

"Well then I think I won?" She smiled at him.

"Sword!" He yelled.

Jason unhooked his sword with an unsure smile on his lips as he stepped forward. Jason did not know what Gavin was up to. He handed his sword to Gavin, his eyes full of questions that Gavin chose to ignore. Jason's sword had a beautiful golden handle that shone in the sunlight. It was much thicker than Gavin's and was heavy in Gavin's hand. Gavin's sword was silver which differed from most of the men on the ship. Morgan tightened her hand around the sword. It was definitely heavier than swords she had used before but she would make this work. They stared at each other for a moment waiting to see who would attack first.

Gavin shrugged and went ahead and sent the first strike at her. She blocked it easily and came back at him with a counter strike. Gavin caught the strike and held his sword in place against hers.

"Hmm." He muttered outloud.

Her green eyes sparkled. She smirked and shoved her bladed forwards against his. Just as quickly as she went forward, she pulled back to get out of the lock. She then slashed at his legs to get distance from him. He stumbled backwards away from her. A look of shock came across his face as he gained footing. She flashed him a smile as she waited for him to come at her again.

Gavin attacked again and she blocked. Their swords played off each other with each hit and counter they made. They moved quickly around the deck like this. The crowd that gathered to watch had to keep their distance as the two danced around in a battle of swords. Gavin caught her sword with his again, which stopped them in their place. Morgan pressed into his blade as she tried to make him waiver.

"How do you know how to use a sword?" He said anger in his voice as he kept her blade locked with his.

"You haven't won. No need to answer questions for you." She muttered as she struggled to free her sword from his.

He narrowed his eyes at her. She went to pull back again but this time Gavin snaked his leg around hers and knocked her to the ground. It didn't work out exactly how he had planned. Gavin felt himself go forward and braced himself. Morgan toppled back into the deck. Her back crashed into the wooden floor and a whimper escaped her mouth. She went to reach for her sword but as she had hit the ground both of their swords scattered across the deck. Gavin's sword went left and Morgan's right. He shifted himself so his arms were on either side of her head and his knees straddled the outer parts of her hips. He stared down into her emerald green eyes as they danced with anger.

"Give." He said forcely.

"Never." She growled.

He went to say something else but Morgan was too quick for him. They had landed near the railings of the ship. She weaved her foot from underneath him and used all her strength to kick off of it. She slid out from under him. He was left staring down at the wooden floor of the deck. Before he could register what happened Morgan had snatched her sword and was in front of him. She pointed the tip of her sword at him.

"Give." She said quietly.

A hush fell over the crew members as they watched. He shifted so he sat back on his knees looking at her. He was a little stunned as he tried to process what happened.

"Give." She said more firmly.

"Now love-" Gavin started to say when a motion caught his eye.

"Cap'n." He yelled as the voice slid a sword to Gavin.

Morgan was already on it. As the sword came towards him. She caught it with her foot stepping on it. She then placed the tip of her blade under his chin. She pressed just a little so he knew she had him. The men around them began to grumble. Some became angry. She heard their blades scrape against their holsters as they became unsheathed. She relaxed her stance and waited for another attacker. Gavin looked around and could see this was about to head south. He stood up as he ignored Morgan and her sword. Morgan frowned her brows at him.

"Now lads this was just harmless fun. I appreciate your sentiments. Get back to your stations before I make things not harmless and not so fun." He said sternly.

The men nodded and the crowd dispersed. Morgan followed Gavin with her sword. He hadn't said that he gave yet. She didn't trust him at all.

"Yes. Yes. Love you won." He said as he waved his hand at her blade.

She pointed it down but held on to it. He went by her and leaned against the railing. He watched the waves made by the ship as it sliced through the water. Morgan wasn't a very trusting person so she stayed where she was. She heard him sigh and he relaxed his shoulders.

"Love I said you won. Put the sword down before I think you're threatening me." He said, his voice sounded sweet but dangerous.

She put the sword down and walked over to him. She leaned against the railing as well. She held the sword out to him. He nodded and took it. He placed it back in its sheath and then shut his eyes as if he was just enjoying the weather. She sat there in silence with him and watched the waves. The ocean calmed her, the woosh sound as they broke against the hull. The ocean reminded her of her father. She smiled softly at the thought. She glanced sideways at Gavin and wondered what he could be thinking.

"So Love, do you have any idea where you want to go?" He asked his gaze still fixated on the water and not at her.

She didn't say anything. He sighed and closed his eyes. She frustrated him so much.

"You won, so where do I take you? Or was that all for not. You don't have a place in mind." He grumbled.

"There's a dock on your way to your destination." She started and she saw him get tense.

"However to get to it you need to detour through Sirens Gully." She said, her eyes monitor cautiously because of his sudden mood change.

He gripped the railing tightly, his knuckles went white. Morgan moved carefully to the side of him.

"How do you know my destination?" He growled.

Morgan stepped further away from him, alarms went off in her head as she could feel the anger pour off of him.

"How do you know about the detour through Sirens Gully?" He asked and turned to face her.

His eyes had so much anger in them. As he took a step towards her. She stepped back,her hands went into fist at her side. Fight or flight activated in her as her stomach began to twist. Jason watched them from across the way and saw the quick change in Gavin. Gavin eyed Morgan like she was a prey he was going to rip apart. He had only seen him look that way once before it was when Gavin told him about Travis;'s betrayal and Christina's murder. It was the only thing that caused this much anger in Gavin. It made him lose all sense. Jason made his way quickly towards them.

Morgan shut down. She had seen this look on men before. She knew all too well what would come. She just prepared herself to be numb. She didn't answer because nothing she would say at this point would help. She backed herself into a corner and assessed her surroundings. She tried to find a way out of this. She was up against the ship's living quarters wall, there were not many options.

"Tell me the truth. You're working with Travis." He said as he slammed his fist into the side of the wall near her head.

She didn't say anything. She tried not to make eye contact. That always made it worse. Her hands clenched at her side. She debated on if fighting would make things worse or not. His rough angry hand grabbed hold of her chin and yanked her eyes up to his. The pressure made her jaw hurt but she forced herself to ignore it.

"Did he tell you what he did?" He asked her but didn't want an answer, his voice trembled.

He slammed his fist into the wall again. Her chin began to throb slightly. She debated bashing her head into his face. Break his nose, her mind shouted. Break his nose and run.

"Did he tell you how he killed my wife?" He said with such anger and hurt.

The pain in his voice stopped her. She looked at him, her face softened as the pieces came together. He was so angry and now she understood why he hurt.

"Your wife?" She asked in a quiet voice as she broke her rule to stay silent.

"Yes my wife." He growled and his hand wrapped up into her fiery hair and yanked her head back.

"He burned her alive. So now I'm done playing games. Tell me how you know. Tell me you're working with Travis. Or maybe I'll burn you too." He said every inch of him shook with anger and pain.

She shut down. She grabbed a hold of his hand that pulled her hair and dug her nails hard into it. She knew he had to be bleeding. He loosened his grip but just to reposition. That's when she threw her arm full force up at him while bringing her body down. His hand was knocked free. She was about to trip him, when his hands caught her. He pulled her back up by the shoulders and slammed her into the wall. She winced from the pain from her back as the wood slapped her opened wounds. He pinned her there, His face was inches from hers. She studied him. She now was angry. She would make him hurt. She had to be smart. She had nowhere to go. The ship was his. Even if she got away and broke his nose, she wouldn't get away, away. Trapped again. She flexed her jaw frustrated and tried to calm herself.

"I don't, I can read and I can read maps. My father was a merchant." She said bitterly to him.

His eyes went back and forth over her face as he tried to see if she had lied. He could not tell. His hand left the wall and captured her wrist.

"You can read…you're gonna read." He growled as he squeezed her wrist tightly.

He started to drag her towards his cabin. She had no clue what was about to happen but there was no way she would go with him. She dug her heels into the ground and yanked her hand hardback. His arm pulled back with her and he whipped around to face. He grabbed her wrist with both hands and pulled her towards the cabin. She leaned her whole weight back from him.

"No!" Morgan yelled at him as she fought hard with her.

"Gavin." A strong voice came from behind him.

Gavin ignored it. She was coming with him and she was going to prove that she could actually read maps. She stepped forward to him and caused him to lose balance. She then yanked back hard and this time got her arm away from him. She flopped to the ground. Gavin, still on his feet, came at her again. She tried to scoot away but she didn't get far. Just as he went to grab her, Jason stepped over her and in Gavin's way.

"Gavin, hold up. What are you doing?" He said as he blocked Gavin from Morgan.

"Get out of my way." He growled.

Jason didn't move. He stood his ground and faced off with Gavin. He was calm unlike Gavin who was about to explode.

"Move Jason, that's an order. " He said, as he went to move around him.

"Gavin, I'm not your second in command right now. I'm your friend, look at yourself. Look at her man. You're attacking a woman." Jason said as he tried to connect with Gavin through his blind rage.

Gavin stepped back. He looked at Morgan on the ground. He knew she must be afraid but she masked all emotion. The scene unfolded in front of him as if he looked at it for the first time. His stomach turned twisted. He felt ashamed. He felt awful. He tried to bottle the rage back up. He felt his body wobble from the adrenaline. He overcame the new rush of emotions, tossed his hands up and turned. He stormed towards his quarters.

"Get back to work." He shouted and slammed the door.

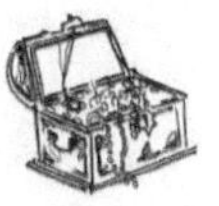

Chapter Seven
Stars

"Are you okay? "Jason asked as he offered his hand to help Morgan stand up.

"I'm fine. Honestly I'm pretty much used to it by now." She didn't mean to let that out but Jason didn't pick up on it.

He thought she was just talking about Gavin.

"He's not like that. The last few months have really changed him. His wife did die in a fire and it was his first mate that started it. Travis, that's why he keeps speaking of Travis." Jason studied her face as he spoke.

She shrugged lightly and waited for him to continue.

"Gavin and Travis grew up together. Did everything together. Became pirates together. They were amazing. Could read each other's minds." Jason started to explain

" Then Christina came along. She was this blonde hair, blue eyes little thing and Gavin melted. No one knew much about her or where she came from but all that didn't matter the moment Gavin laid eyes on her." Jason said with regret.

"I get it his wife died, he hurts. His best friend killed her. Has nothing to do with me." Morgan lashed out, anger shook her voice.

"Hang on Lass. Let me finish." Jason smirked a little.

"Go ahead." Morgan sighed.

"Now back when they were pirating they came in possession of a map. It was some rare treasure. To make sure they continue being fair to each other and they tore it down the middle. Gavin had the end, being the captain he got to keep the part with the treasure. Travis the beginning. They couldn't go after the treasure without the other. Hence the map obsession." Jason winked at her and when Morgan did not act amused he continued.

"So anyways Christina came about and Gavin saw a whole different life. They hadn't even been together more then a month and Gavin retired; brought a small little cottage for them. He took his piece of the map with him. The crew went their separate ways. Some stayed with Travis, others went to find a new captain. It wasn't too long after they started living together that the house fire happened. I found Gavin sitting outside the ashes clinching a note in his hand. It was from Travis admitting he burnt the house down and calling him back to the sea." Jason said, staring at the captain's cabin.

"Since that day the only thing he can think of is killing Travis for taking everything from him." He said softer.

Morgan noted that she felt bad for him but not completely. Every man seems to have some story to justify their actions. She frowned and grabbed her wrist. Gavin's fingerprints bruised her skin. She shook her head.

"Revenge won't do anything. It will just consume him and everything around him. Even when he gets it. Believe me I've watched it happen." Morgan snapped.

She heard a small giggle and knew it was from Claire. She seemed to look herself over, nodded her thanks to Jason and followed the noise.

He slammed the door behind him. He wanted to break something. He wanted to destroy anything. He needed to release all of the wrath that burned inside of him. It began to control him. His eyes landed on his desk. He rushed over to it and gripped it with both hands. The map increased his fury. He swung his arm across the desk. Everything on it crashed to the floor. He needed space, he needed to get away from everyone. He moved away from the desk. He needed to escape. Escape the ship, his mind, the constant reminder that everything was his fault. Travis.

He made his way over to a tall wooden cabinet in the corner of the room. He opened and grabbed a glass bottle. His hand clenched the long neck. He didn't waste any time and pulled the cork from the top of it. He took a long drink. The warm liquor filled his mouth and burned all the way to his belly. He leaned back against the wall and slowly sank down to the floor. He was losing himself. He had to get a grip. It wouldn't be long now and then it would be over. If he wavered or faltered, he could lose everything.

His crew admired him for being leveled. He needed to be that person. He needed to be strong and needed to control himself. He exhaled. He thought about Morgan. She looked frightened of him; her green eyes betrayed her as she had tried to hide it. He gritted his teeth. The image of her trying to get away from him flashed in his mind. He closed his eyes, letting his head slump back into the wall. What was wrong with him?

The sun was setting, Morgan and Claire sat by the railing of the ship and watched the orange and pink lines spread across the sky as the sun ducked behind the ocean. The last little bits of sunlight danced across the tops of waves and gave everything a golden glow. Claire rested her head in Morgan's lap. As Morgan ran her hand through her soft curls. She watches Claire in moments like this; she was almost a kid like she is supposed to be. Morgan could feel her wounds on her back seeping through her bandages. Her whole back was throbbing from earlier. She shut her eyes and pushed back the pain as she listened to Jason and Claire talk.

"So where do you come from? "Claire asked Jason with a raised eyebrow.

"Originally I came from a small island where I grew up with my parents.vThen I became an orphan. I was living on the streets when I met Gavin." He said short and sweet.

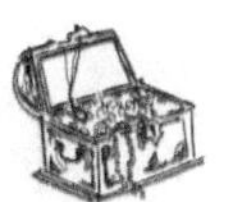

"Morgan was an orphan too and then she came to live with us. Her parents got sick and died. She didn't. She's my cousin. I was lucky she came to live with us. She stopped-" Claire flinched as Morgan had reached over and pinched her.

"So you became a pirate after meeting Gavin?" Morgan asked, trying to turn the conversation.

Jason noticed the exchange between the girls but he left it alone. Morgan clearly didn't want any information out about them.

"Yes....as soon as he got a ship. I became his navigator." He said his eyes on the horizon.

Morgan went back and looked out over the sea. The golden shimmer had faded and the stars started to twinkle.

"How do you know you're going the right way?" Claire asked.

"We use the sun and the sky." Jason answered her.

"But at night there's no sun." She said innocently.

"At night we use the stars." He smiled and pointed up to the sky.

Claire's eyes shifted upwards. Morgan watched a big smile come over her face. She could see all of her thoughts and questions roll across his face as she studied the dark sky.

"But they all look the same, " She stated, still looking upwards.

Morgan looked up at the sky as well, smiled to herself. It warmed her heart that Jason didn't mind the endless chatter. She watched him off and on through the conversation and he had never been annoyed.

"You have to look for the right one." A deep voice said from behind them.

Morgan shifted slightly and sat straighter as she heard his voice. She wasn't sure what to expect and didn't want anything else to continue. Claire didn't notice the change in Morgan's body language and how her guard was now up. Morgan counted his footsteps as he walked across the deck to approach them.

"The right one? They all look the same." Claire said and turned her head one way and then another as she tried to find the "right one."

"Captain." Jason started with a nod as Gavin walked by him.

He nodded back at Jason and squatted down beside Claire. Morgan watches him carefully. She elevated every move he made. Her body on edge, her heart raced in her chest. He didn't seem hostile right now. She watched him smile slightly at Claire as his eye scanned the sky. He pointed upwards as he found the star he looked for.

"Right there. That's the one." He showed Claire.

His eyes slightly glanced at Morgan. She was expressionless, it was close to the blank shut down expression she had earlier.

"That one?" He tore his eyes from Morgan and smiled down at Claire.

"Yes. It's called the north star. If you can find that one you'll always know where you're heading." He glanced back at Morgan who now looked up at the sky.

Claire looked like she was memorizing it. Her brows scrunched together as focused on the star. Morgan cracked a smile looking at her.

"What about fog?" Claire asked.

"Ah lass you're gonna know everything one day." Jason said as he chuckled.

Gavin looked like he was about to answer her when Morgan stood up.

"Claire, that's enough. It's late. Tell Mr. Jason, thank you." Morgan said firmly.

"Ugh fine. Can I ask you more stuff tomorrow?" Claire said as she stood up.

"Of course, Lass." He chuckled.

Claire skipped over to Morgan happily. Morgan ruffled her hair and then looked at Gavin; her face flashed a few different emotions. Concern, fear, nervousness.

"Captain....are we still able to stay in your cabin?" She asked her voice flat but you could tell it took alot for her to ask.

"Of course." He said quietly.

Morgan nodded and made her way to the cabin. Claire chatted away next to her.

Gavin let out a long sigh he held in as he watched them walk away. He ran his hand through his hair, he tended to do this when he was frustrated which was a lot lately.

"Ya know boss you could go talk to her." Jason said quietly.

"I know. I just..." He almost looked defeated.

"Just go talk to her. She's been through alot too Captain. Even a blind man can see that." Jason said as he watched Gavin shift his feet debating with himself.

"You just need to heal, Captain. It's ok. " Jason said quietly.

Gavin stiffened and the nervousness was gone. He needed to get things in order.

"I'll heal when he's dead." Gavin sneered.

Morgan stepped into the cabin. It was dark. She had Claire wait in the doorway so she could find a candle to light. She stumbled as she made her way over to his desk. She had seen a candle on it before. She scraped her foot against something and heard what sounded like paper. She bent down and reached out towards the desk. Her fingers searched the top of it and to her surprise she found nothing. There was nothing on the desk.

"Morgan?" Claire called to her, being a little impatient.

"Hang on." She called to Claire as she reached downwards.

She moved her foot and felt something on the ground. She knew everything was on the floor. She blindly felt around until she felt the candle, she clasped it in her hand and placed it on the desk. grabbing a hold of it. She made her way around the desk. She pulled open the desk drawer. She searched inside the drawer fingertips brushed the small wooden twigs and she knew it was the matches. She grabbed a hold of the matches and then embraced the candle. She quickly lit the candle. She held back a surprise look when she confirmed everything that was one the desk was indeed on the floor. She frowned as she looked at the mess.

"What happened?" Claire asked as she came into the cabin.

Anger....that's what happened Morgan thought. She smiled up at Claire and pointed to the bed.

" I knocked some stuff over trying to find the candle. Now bed." She lied.

"I didn't hear you do that" Claire started.

"Bed." Morgan said and squinted her eyes at Claire.

"Ugh fine." She grumbled and plopped down on the bed.

Morgan began to pick up the mess. She grabbed hold of the map and placed it down first making sure it wasn't damaged. She then picked up the various books and placed them back in their spots. She grabbed his compass, compass rose, and nocturnal from the floor and placed them to the side of the desk. The hour glass that used to sit in the right hand corner was on the floor cracked. Sand spilt out of it. She shook her head in disgust as she bent down and picked up the glass pieces. She spotted a small can in the corner for trash and placed it in there.

She picked up the can and brought it to the desk. She emptied the glass pieces and began to scoop the sand into it. As she did, a bottle rolled out from under the desk. Whiskey. She felt her stomach turn sour as she looked at it. She picked the bottle up and knew it was part of the cause of this mess. She chunked it into the can too.

Claire was tossed and turned while Morgan worked. Morgan looked over at her and found her blue eyes as they stared at her, still full of questions.

"Can you tell me the story?" Claire asked and batted her eyes.

"Ok." Morgan smiled as she dusted the sand from her hands and knees.

She walked over to the bed and sat down.Her back faced the door She brushed a strand of Claire's golden hair out of her eye.

"Once upon a time there were two sisters. One younger sister and an older sister. The younger sister had hair the color of sunshine and eyes bluer and brighter than the sky." Morgan began.

"And the older sister had eyes green like the grass and hair the color of fire!" Claire yelled excitedly.

"Shh. They lived in a small house in the woods; with the golden-haired sister's father. He was a loving father until one day he left and an evil man took his place." Morgan said quietly

"The evil man would punish the girls often but the Fire hair sister would always protect the golden hair sister. She would never ever let anything happen to her. She loved her so much. One day while the evil man was sleeping the fire hair sister came up with a plan. They would leave the house in the woods and find a new home." Morgan said watched Claire's eyes start to close.

"So in the middle of the night the girls ran away. They ran so far away the evil man could never find them. The fire hair sister found them a house to live in. The kitchen in the house always had food. The golden-haired sister could run and play in their yard and be happy. No one would ever hurt them again. They lived happily ever after." Morgan said her voice slowly got quieter as she told the story.

Claire drifted further into sleep with each word Morgan said. She was fast asleep as Morgan finished. Morgan sighed deeply and hung her head.

"I will find happiness for you." Morgan promised as she leaned forward and kissed Claire on the forehead.

Chapter Eight
Scars

"An evil man?" A voice said from the doorway of the cabin.

Morgan took a deep breath and closed her eyes. Gavin....His name rang in her head as she felt her chest tightened.

"Just a story." She said softly.

"I missed the beginning. Want to retell it?" He asked as he leaned on the door frame.

"Not really." Morgan whispered back.

The desk caught his eye and he realized she had cleaned up his mess. Guilt struck his stomach. He glanced back over to her. She hadn't moved or turned around.

"Morgan I. About earlier. I" He started to say.

"It's fine." She said softly her eyes focused on Claire.

She heard him inhale slightly and shift in the doorway. She knew he stepped further into the room.

"I'm not one to say sorry. I never regret anything I do. But I went too far today. It won't happen again." He said softly shifting uncomfortably.

Morgan was about to snap at him about how sorry doesn't ever fix anything but when she looked over at him. She stopped herself. He was covered in remorse. She nodded slightly at him, not sure what to say. She stood and pulled the cover up over Claire more. That's when he noticed her back.

"Come sit." He said as he pointed to the chair.

She raised an eyebrow at him and cautiously crossed the floor to the chair. He began to look through his desk. He pulled out some more bandages and set them down. Morgan was about to argue with him but she knew it would be no use and she didn't feel like fighting. She carefully sat in the chair.

"I'll be right back. Take off your shirt." He said as walked by her to the door.

Morgan watched him walk out. She bit her lip nervously. She knew she had to take her shirt off so he could tend to her wounds but it made her nervous.

"Suck it up." She muttered to herself.

She slowly started to raise the shirt and struggled to get it above her head. The fabric stuck to her wounds. She flinched in pain as she gritted her teeth. She pulled hard as she tried to get it off. She held in a cry of pain as she felt the fabric tear from one of the wounds. She inhaled and slowly exhaled. She knew she had at least one more wound that was stuck to the shirt. She inhaled and held her breath. She tried to prepare herself. Just as she was about to rip the shirt upwards she heard the door open again. She froze.

He cleared his throat to cover a chuckle. She had the shirt half way up, her head covered, and looked like she was stuck. She groaned as she heard him. She quickly pulled the shirt back down.

"Problems?" He asked, raising an eyebrow at her, his lips had a smile lingering on them.

"It's stuck. The wound must have seeped through the bandage and adhered everything to the shirt." She said defeated.

His face turned serious as he saw the red blood that dripped down her back from the first attempt. He walked over to her. She was right. He clenched his jaw as he knew that he was the cause of them bleeding once more. He felt a pain in the pit of his stomach being responsible for it. He set the bowl of water down and rags.

"Hold still." He ordered her as he took his knife from his belt loop.

"Hey, what are you going to do?" She turned quickly.

Her eyes went wide as she looked at the blade and his hand. She took a step back away from him. He caught her hand with his.

"Stop. I'm not going to hurt you." He said softly and pointed back to the chair.

She didn't know why but she believed him. She searched his eyes with hers. She felt safe even after this afternoon. She sighed and sat down with her back to him.

"Hold still." He repeated.

"Could you atleast tell me-

She started to say but then heard the knife slicing through the shirt. She watched her shirt fall down in pieces around her. Gavin had cut away the pieces of bandage and shirt that were not stuck to the wound. Morgan stared down at the floor and then the realization that she was topless hit her. She tried to cover herself. She wrapped her arms around herself and hugged her breast. She was about to protest when she felt water touch her back. She was about to protest when she felt

water touched her back. Gavin held a wet rag to the remaining piece of shirt.

"It should come off easier if it's wet." He stated.

She held her breath. Did he not realize she had nothing to cover herself! Her mind screamed. His eyes wandered over her skin as he waited for the shirt to be damp enough to pull off the wound without hurting her. Even with the wounds and past scars her skin looked soft. Her ears had turned a shade of red from being embarrassed. He found himself wondering what it would be like to bury his face in her neck. To place soft kisses there or tease her bright red ear lobe with his mouth. Although she was covering her breast they were still overflowing her arms. As if begging to escape.

Fuck! He yelled at himself. Focus!

He tested the shirt and it became loose but it was still attached. She winced slightly. He dunked the rag back in the water and reapplied it to the stuck shirt. He needed this to hurry up. His eyes wander to her scars. Most of them were long thin scars. Maybe a whip or switch. His eyes scanned the rest of her back and settled on a large one on her side. It looked brutal. Not thinking his finger traced it. Knife wound? He was growing angry seeing each one. Who and how?

She flinched and moved slightly away from his hand touching the scar. She almost didn't make it with that one. She felt chills run up her spine from his touch.

"An evil man?" He asked with disgust in his voice.

She dropped her head slightly as she debated how much she should say. She wanted him to know she had nothing to do with Travis. She gave in.

"Claire's father. He was a drunk and my uncle. Claire's mother died and he blamed her. I luckily had moved in shortly before it happened and the scars I have were intended for Claire. I just made sure she never got them." She said her voice was very heavy.

His stomach twisted as he glanced over at Claire. He felt the same wrath as before courses through him. How could anyone do this to her or wish to do this to that poor innocent child.

"He deserves to die." Gavin said through his teeth.

The way he said the words Morgan felt that if her uncle stood there Gavin would have killed him. He removed the wet rag and touched the damp fabric and slowly lifted it. It came off with easy. He studied the large gash. He was right, it had broken open again. Jason was right, they had been through enough. He cleaned the wound carefully. The other one looked really good and this one would in time. He grabbed the bandage material and gently placed it over the wound. He passed it up front to Morgan who wrapped it around the front and then handed it back to him. After several passes her wounds were dressed. Gavin looked at her back. He could not stop looking at the large pink scar on her side. He reached out once more and ran his finger over it again. It was healed but looked recent. Morgan's skin immediately responded with goose bumps. She didn't pull away like she did the first time.

"A knife." She whispered.

He shook his head clenching his jaw. He touched another long thin one that seemed to run from her left shoulder down the length of her back.

"Bull whip." She whispered, her voice cracked.

He went to touch another anger rolling off of him, he flued the rage that was buried deep inside of him with each scar.

"Please." She asked him to stop.

He withdrew his hand and stood. He walked over to the closet and fetched one of his shirts. He walked back over to her. She was still hugging herself even though the bandage now covered most of her breast. Her red hair fell down in waves over the front of her. He paused, she was absolutely stunning. She pulled at her bottom lip nervously and watched his eyes study her. The innocent act had Gavin's mind wandering again. What would be like to taste her lips.

She shifted slightly and it seemed to snap him out of it. His eyes went to hers and he held the shirt out to her. She took the shirt from him, careful not to move too much so her breast wouldn't become exposed. He nodded and then turned his back to her so she could put it on. She placed her head in the shirt and began struggling trying to get it over the bandages. Everything hurts still. She made a small noise of pain. The next thing she knew the shirt was gently being pulled down. His fingers grazed her stomach. She instantly got tingles. Her head popped through the shirt as his hands fell to her waist. He left them there. She found herself lost in his deep brown eyes.

"Thank you" She said in a small voice.

He nodded. He knew he should step back and go about his business. He knew he shouldn't linger here much longer, but the way her eyes looked at him. The way her lips seemed to twitch as they were asking for a kiss. He couldn't get his feet to move. He inhaled and calmed himself and went to take a step back. Her hand stopped him. She traced a small scar that went across his jaw. He froze, the act caught him by surprise. Her plump lips curved into a smile and she raised an eyebrow at him.

"Sword." He smirked.

Fuck it he thought. He stepped into her. His hands curled around her waist and pulled her against him. He lowered his head to meet her lips and Just as he made up his mind. She pulled back.

"I haven't lied to you. I may not answer your questions but I have not lied." She blurted out.

His eyes brows came together as he looked at her. Her eyes pleaded with him to believe her.

"We had to get away. Now you know about my uncle, you know why Claire and I snuck on your ship. That knife wound was bad and if I died Claire would be left at his mercy or worse. So we ran. My parents are gone and what I said about my father is true. He was a merchant and taught me how to read maps. That's how I knew your destination and about Sirens Gully." She said in one long breath.

She watched his face and it was blank. No emotion. Not anger, not confusion, nothing. She looked down nervously not wanting to see his face. What if he didn't believe her?

"I believe you." He said quietly and closed the small gap between them again.

"I promise I don't know Travis or have anything to do with him." She said as looked back up at him.

She saw several emotions flash in his eyes. Anger, hurt, betrayal, and guilt. He stepped back suddenly. He nodded slightly telling her it was ok before he headed to the door. He opened it and hesitated like he was going to say something but just walked out. Morgan watched his back as he left. Her stomach ached as he left. Her chest was tight but not from panic or the need to fight. She wondered if she had said or did something wrong.

Gavin walked out into the sea air. He felt like he could breathe again Travis. The simple word made him shake. Christina. He almost kissed her. What was wrong with him? He gripped the railing of the ship.

"Christina." He whispered hurt ran through him.

He looked across the deck. His responsibilities. Get it together he thought as straightened himself out. He made his way across the deck and to the helm.

"You ok Captain?" Jason asked as he moved to the side so Gavin could take over.

"Fine." He answered,his eyes locked on the horizon.

"Did you talk to her?" Jason asked curiously.

"Yes." He answered shortly, his eyes shifted to the cabin.

"And?" Jason asked sarcastically.

"And have a good night." Gavin growled.

"Ok ok." Jason chuckled, walking away leaving Gavin to himself.

"Jason...." Gavin called to his back.

"Aye?" He stopped and looked at him.

"You were right she's been through alot." Gavin said.

"Make sure nothing happens to them while there on this ship." Gavin said to Jason's silence.

"Aye Captain." Jason said walking off.

Gavin glanced back at his cabin. He felt a strong need to protect her. The images of her back flashed through his mind. Then guilt about wanting her. He sighed, as he ran a hand through his hair. He focused on the horizon and pushed all thoughts from his mind.

Chapter Nine
Nightmares

She took a deep breath in...what just happened?
She felt better that she told him most of everything. It really had bothered her that he thought she could be involved with something so..so evil. She smiled softly as she thought about how he reacted when she touched his scar. Her stomach flipped happily and it felt like she had butterflies that fluttered around in there. She sighed softly and then remembered how he left. What changed? She thought and then realized it was after she said Travis's name.

Christina. The guilt. She swallowed hard. She needed to stop whatever had started between them. He wouldn't be over Christina, not that she blamed him. She didn't want to live in another woman's shadow. Besides, she and Claire had plans. It wouldn't work anyways. She moved the chair closer to the bed. She sat down and watched over Claire while she slept.

She looked down at his shirt and couldn't help but bring it to her nose. She inhaled his scent. It was a mixture of sea air and something earthy. She shut her eyes and relaxed in his scent. She pictured herself in his arms. The warmth that radiated from just his finger tips from earlier. She imagined being wrapped in it. She shook her head knowing it could never be. She propped her foot up on the bed and closed her eyes. She forced herself to get some kind of sleep.

She looked around and it was dark. She could smell the old wood. She knew this place. It was their room. They're back. How? Claire? Morgan frantically looked around and found her curled up asleep in the corner. She felt a little relieved seeing her. Then she heard him. Her stomach knotted up. She quickly placed a chair in front of the door. Please not tonight, please not now. Her heart began to race as he got to their door. He grabbed a hold of the handle and began to rattle it. Claire, she had to hide her. The closet; no he would look there. He began to bang on the door.

"I didn't get to say goodnight!" He laughed drunkenly.

Claire's eyes shot open and terror was written all over her face. Something sharp pierced the door. A tip of a knife shown through the door.

"Open the door. It will be the last goodnight I promise!" He screamed.

Each bang the chair gave more and more. It wouldn't hold much longer. She glanced at Claire, tears silently flowed from her eyes. She scooped her up. The window. She thought quickly. It was small but Claire could fit.

"Hey, I need you to listen. I'm gonna hold you up to the window. Climb out and go hide in our spot. After it's all over I'll come find you." Morgan said as she started to push her up towards the window.

"Morgan, I can't leave you. He's gonna hurt you again." She whispered through the tears.

"Hey he doesn't ever really hurt me. He thinks he does. I'm tougher than him. Don't you worry but I need you to go. I need you to be safe." Morgan kissed her forehead and then shoved her up to the window.

Claire grasped the edges and pulled herself out. Claire looked back. She didn't want to leave her. Morgan smiled and motioned for Claire to go. She shook her head and Morgan shooed her. Claire held back tears as she hopped down on to cold dirt. She raced to their safe spot.

The door busted open behind her and she inhaled sharply. She prepared herself for the fight, she felt herself dissociate and become numb so she wouldn't feel any of it.

"Where is she!?" He screamed.

The smell of alcohol hit her. He stood in the doorway and she could smell him. She kept her back to him. She tried to determine how drunk he was and if she could move around him and escape. She turned and faced him. Her fist clenched at her side.

"Where! Is! She!" He screamed again.

His breath hit her and she wanted to vomit. He swayed in place. She could definitely get around him. She just needed him out of the doorway. She backed up and gave the impression she was frightened. He hated when she would try to run. It was better if she just took the beating. Making him chase her made him angrier. He let out a growl and stepped forward. Just a little more she thought.

"If you don't tell me where she is, I'll kill you and then her." He yelled and spit flew out of his mouth as he spoke.

He stumbled towards her and nearly fell over. This would be easy. She was convinced she would get by him and there would be no beating tonight. She counted his steps as he made them. He stopped short in front of her.

"Did you hear me bitch." He said his body as he shook with anger.

"No." She said quietly.

The look of shock on his face made her want to laugh. She never talked to him in moments like this. It was as if his eyes glossed over even more and he lunged at her. His hand stretched out as he tried to capture her. She was able to sidestep him. He stumbled as he missed her and landed on the floor. She quickly made her way to the door. He didn't waste any time. He got up quicker than she expected.

Just as she reached the door, inches from escaping; something hit her hard in the head. Pain washed through her as she hit the ground. The world was fuzzy. She tried to focus her vision and get up. Pieces of wood were scattered around her in splinters. He had hit her with the chair. She could feel wetness in her hair on the back of her head. She stumbled getting up. Her eyes focused on the doorway. Just a little closer. She was almost there. She was pulled back by her hair. She grabbed the door frame and tried to resist. He growled and wrapped his hand around her hair more. He pulled back and then slammed her forward. Her face

smashed into the door frame. Her vision went dark for a second as she tried to hold onto reality. She felt her skin split above her eyebrow. Blood poured into her eye. She could taste iron in her mouth, her teeth had gone through her lip. She grabbed on tighter to the door frame. She started to sink to the ground.

She heard movement behind her. A sear pain punctured her side. She let out a scream. The pain, It crippled her. She collapsed into the door frame. The pain overwhelmed her. She let go over the door frame and her hand went to her side. Dark red blood stained her side. She pressed her hand to it as everything went dark. She gave into the darkness.

"Die bitch." Was the last thing she heard.

Claire woke up as the sun shined through the cabin windows. She stretched and turned to see Morgan asleep in a chair next to the bed. She carefully got out of bed. She was shocked to see Morgan actually asleep. She never got to sleep. Careful not to make any noise she headed to the door of the cabin and opened it. She found Gavin just on the other side. He looked tired.

"Shh Morgan's actually sleeping." She whispered to him.

He didn't say anything but raised an eyebrow

"She never gets to sleep for long." She explained.

He nodded. Claire walked past him, her eyes searched for Jack.

"He's helping the cook with breakfast." Gavin smiled.

"If Morgan wakes up soon, will you tell her so she doesn't worry?" Claire smiled brightly.

Gavin nodded and watched her scamper off. He smiled to himself as he stepped into the cabin. He immediately saw her. She was fast asleep. He walked slowly over to her. She was beautiful. Even with her head slumped back and her mouth hanging open a bit. She was beautiful. He looked at the chair, that couldn't be comfortable. He went over carefully, picked her up and shifted her onto his bed. He settled into the chair next to it. He was exhausted. He propped his feet up and shut his eyes.

He was about to nod off when he heard her. A small whimper. Gavin opened his eyes to see her face in pain. She twitched slightly. Another small cry escaped her as she began to struggle in her sleep. He reached out to comfort her but she began to fight more. Another whimper came from her and a tear ran down her cheek. His heart twisted in pain as he watched. He didn't know why but he climbed in bed with her and pulled her into his arms.

"Shh you're ok. You're safe. I got you." He whispered to her.

She instantly calmed down. He smiled and rested his chin on top of her head. He couldn't help but enjoy having her in his arms. He closed his eyes and decided to stay like this and went to sleep.

Gavin stirred and opened his eyes. He saw Morgan had shifted herself so her arms were now wrapped around him. Her head rested on his chest. He glanced at the window. It was dark out. How long had they slept? He hadn't slept this long or good in months. He glanced down at her. There was something about her that calmed him. He shut his eyes. He wanted to stay like that a little longer. For once the outside world and chaos that he felt was silent.

Morgan squeezed the warmth. It felt so good she wanted to curl into it. It was like warm sunshine. She nuzzled into it again. She felt safe. She had not felt safe in years. She sighed happily. If only she could stay like this. As she started to wake up she realized that the thing she hugged was moving.

It was breathing! She went to shoot up but something heavy held her in place. The smell of sea air and earth hit her nose. She froze. She opened her eyes slowly, not sure what to expect. Her heart raced in her chest. She had her arms wrapped around Gavin's chest. His arms were wrapped tightly around her as he held her back. She shifted so she could see his face. She paused as she looked at him. Happiness was written on it. In the short time she had been on this ship she had not seen him look happy. He was relaxed, a deep dark brown curl dropped down onto his forehead and danced across. She had to stop herself from reaching out and brushing it aside.

Stop. She told herself. She needed to get out of this situation. How the heck did they end up like this. She slowly pulled her arm away. He moved slightly which allowed her to prop herself up on her elbow. She then carefully started to lift his arm off of her. His brows came together and he began to grumble. She shifted her weight away from him, placed his arm down on his chest and slowly started to creep towards the edge of the bed. If he could just stay asleep she could make it out of there and then they could act like this didn't happen.

She sat up on the edge of the bed and let out the breath of relief. Now all she had to do was stand up and walk out. Mission accomplished, she thought as she started to stand.

"You know, for someone who keeps trying to not be caught. You're not doing a very good job of it on this ship." His warm voice teased her.

She stiffened. She knew a big smirk danced on his lips. She could feel her ears turning red.

"I just didn't want to wake you." She said, trying to grab hold of her confidence as she stood.

She glanced back at him sure enough a smirk was on his lips as he laid there with his eyes closed.

"Sure you didn't, Love." He said his smirk turned into a grin.

"You were awake?" She narrowed her eyes at him.

"Whole time." He chuckled.

"No." She said a sharpness to her voice.

"Yup from the moment you nuzzle your face into my chest and sighed happily....good dream?" He teased, as he opened his eyes.

Her face turned several shades of red. She didn't know it was him! She closed her hands by her side trying to find something to say back. She opened her mouth to call him a name but he spoke first.

"I think we've slept all day. Hungry?" He said as he sat up.

She was but she needed to distance herself from him. This was too close for comfort. She wasn't going to let anything get in the way of her plans. And she wouldn't get hurt that way. She could take a hell of a beating but the promise of something that she could never have. She wasn't ready for that type of hurt.

"All day? No, I have to go find Claire and check on her." She said and then walked to the door quickly.

She was gone before he could say anything else. He was left to stare at the closed door as she basically ran out of it.

Chapter Ten
Safe

Morgan rushed out of the cabin as quickly as she could. She locked eyes with the stairs and raced for them. Her heart pounded in her chest. She needed to get as far away as she could from Gavin. Her mind kept picturing him rushing out of the cabin after. Her feet hit the lower deck and she began to move across it. She tried to be discreet so as to not alarm anyone. She had to put as much distance between her and the cabin. Between her and Gavin. She heard voices near the helm and recognized Claire's. She headed up the stairs to the helm. A smile formed on her lips as she saw Claire. Claire laid back on the deck, her hands up in the air as she pointed at stars. Jason spoke as he stirred and Jack lied next to her his eyes on the sky.

"And what's that one?" Claire asked as she pointed at three stars in a line.

Jason glanced up to recognize the constellation.

"That's Orion's belt. Orion was a great hunter hired by a king. His task was to kill off the fierce beast that terrorized the kingdom. Well the goddess Gaia, who was mother of all animals, was not happy about this. She sent a giant scorpion after Orion. Although he fought hard; his sword was no match for the scorpion. In the end the scorpion ended up stabbing Orion to death." Jason explained.

"Woe." Claire whispered her eyes never left the stars.

"Evening." Jason smiled at Morgan.

"Morgan, you're finally up. Do you know how many times I checked on you? I've never seen you sleep like that! Come lay by me! Jason's telling us stories about the stars." Claire said happily, patting the deck next to her.

Morgan chuckled, thankful for Claire's excitement and made her way over to her lay down. She carefully laid her back against the deck floor and her eyes scanned the sky.

"So if you can't find the north star. It's easy to find Ursa Major. See right there that almost square set of stars with a tail." Jack said to Claire.

She nodded her eyes, followed his outstretched finger and traced the square shape with her eyes.

"You see the last star in the square part or bowel?" He asked her.

She nodded again.

"Follow it diagonally to a smaller set of square stars with a tail and the last star in the tail is the north star." Jack said proudly.

"Now I'll never lose it." Claire whispered her eyes fixated on the star as she locked it in her mind.

Morgan chuckled lightly. Jason and Jack began to talk about another constellation as Claire leaned over to her.

"Did you have a good day?" Morgan asked her, she reached out and ran her hand down her hair.

"I did. I stayed with Jack and then Mr. Jason realized you were not out and about yet. He told me to stay by him. He's going to let me stir one day." She smiled brightly.

Morgan glanced over to Jason. She smiled her thanks to him. He nodded back to her. He was a good man. Morgan trusted him.

"So I went and checked on you because you never sleep. So I thought there was something wrong. And I saw you cuddling with the captain." Claire whispered giggling.

Morgan's mouth turned into an O shape and then a frown. Claire giggled more and Morgan reached over and pinched her.The pinch didn't even phase Claire.

"Do you like him?" Claire asked with a goofy face.

"Claire!" Morgan said and pinched her a little harder.

This only made Claire giggle more. Claire's laugh was infectious and soon Morgan was laughing too.

"Ladies care to let Mr. Jack and I know what all the giggles are about." Jason said looking over amused.

Claire opened her mouth and Morgan's hand clamped over it, her eyes wide as she shook her head no.

"Claire's just tired." Morgan chuckled.

"Don't be a traitor" Morgan whispered to Claire.

Claire giggled and held out her pinky finger.
Morgan looped hers around it. They shook lightly and
Morgan let go of her mouth. Jason shook his head at the
scene. Realizing they all went quiet watching them,
Morgan glanced to the stars. She found seven stars in a
u shape.
Keeping her eyes on the stars she asked outlining them
with her finger

"How about these seven right there?" Morgan
called out to Jason.

"Ariadne's Crown." The voice made her heart
stutter. She could feel her skin flush as she recognized
his voice.

This ship was too small. She thought. She tried
to push the butterflies that fluttered in her stomach down
and away but it was no use. She kept her eyes on the
sky as she ignored everything she felt.

"Captain. Rest well?" Jason asked.

"For the first time in a longer time." He answered,
his eyes darted over to Morgan.

"That's good to hear, captain." Jason chuckled.

Morgan felt another warm rush through her body.
A mixture of nerves and excitement. He slept good next
to her. His words for the first time in a long time bounced
around her brain. An image of them entwined with each
other in bed flashed in her mind. She could feel her ears
starting to burn. She remembered how nice it had felt.
Did he mean what he had said...no stop. She told
herself. She cleared her throat and sat up.

"Come on Claire. I need to get you off to bed."
Morgan said as she nudged her lightly before she got to
her feet.

"But I wanna hear about the crown." Claire
pouted.

Morgan placed her hands on her hip and stared
down at Claire. She made her stance to say she was not
about to budge on this.

"Please." Claire said and batted her big blue
eyes.

Morgan shook her head and started to walk. She
walked slowly to make sure Claire would follow.

"Go on Lass. I will tell you in the morning." Jason
chuckled.

Claire huffed and stomped off after Morgan. The
men behind chuckled at the little girl.

"Night Jack." She uttered as she walked by him.

"Night" Jack smiled back.

Gavin watched Morgan leave. He wanted to
follow after her but he told himself no. He shouldn't
make things more complicated. He shouldn't be feeling
anything like this. Whatever this was. He nudged Jason,
his eyes still watching her walk across the deck. Her red
hair swayed with each step.

"You better keep your eyes on the horizon
Captain." Jason whispered to him laughing.

Gavin grumbled and took the wheel.

"Sleep well." He said sarcastically to Jason.

"I hope it's as good as you did." Jason teased as
he began to stroll to his cabin.

"Jason just because it's been a while since I've thrown someone overboard. Doesn't mean I haven't forgotten how." He yelled at his back.

"Aye aye!" Jason chuckled going into the first mate's cabin.

"Do you need company, Captain?" Jack said from the floor of the deck.

"No Jack You can run along and get some rest." Gavin said his eyes set on the horizon.

Jack got up and started to head off. He paused a second lingering.

"Hey Captain?" He asked his voice saying something was up.

"You alright Jack?" Gavin asked, a little concerned.

"Yeah. I just...well you see. I mean how do you tell if a girl likes you? And if you like her back, how do you let her know?" He asked as he shifted his feet uncomfortably.

Gavin chuckled and nodded his head as if he understood that statement more than he wanted to.

"Claire?" Gavin asked and wiggled his eyebrows at the boy.

"No. Well maybe." Jack said with a shrug.

"Ahh. It's hard. They'll like spending time with you. Laugh at your jokes But if you like this girl you should just tell her." Gavin said to him.

"Yeah maybe." Jack said, and started to head off.

"Jackie...remember They're not staying with us." Gavin spoke and as the words left his mouth he felt a pinch in his gut.

Jack nodded slowly and walked away looking sad. Gavin let out a long sigh. Get yourself together Gavin. He thought as he shook out his shoulders trying to chase away the pain in his gut.

Claire hopped on to the bed. A goofy grin on her face. Mischief flashed in her eyes. Morgan smiled and looked at her as she began to tuck her in. Claire let out a small laugh.

"All right missy out with it." Morgan said and tossed the blanket at her.

"Nothing." Claire giggled and her mouth betrayed her.

"Out with it." Morgan demanded and smacked the bed.

Claire started laughing crazily and grabbed the pillow. She laid on her back and tucked her arms around the pillow. She shut her eyes and let out a romantic sigh.

"Look familiar." She squeaked out as she started laughing.

"Claire Lucille, I swear to god I will smother you with that pillow." Morgan said, wacking her thigh with her hand.

"No you won't." She laughed harder as Morgan sat on the bed.

"You bet your butt I will." Morgan threatened and went to grab her feet.

She tackled Claire and began to tickle her viciously. and begins to tickle her. Claire let out a loud sheik and laughed. Claire giggled till tears began to pour from her eyes.

"Ok That's enough" Claire pleaded.

"Fine but only because you need sleep." Morgan laughed and tossed her foot back.

She straightened out the covers and tucked Claire in. She stood up and looked down at her.

"There snug as a bug." Morgan chuckled.

"Hey Morgan?" Claire asked.

"Mhmm?" Morgan responded and sat down in the chair next to the bed.

"How soon till we leave the ship?" Claire asked, her eyes grew heavy.

"Days maybe? I'm not really sure where the next dock is. I guess it depends if we stay the course or not." Morgan shrugged.

"Okay. I was worried we'd be getting off sooner. I kind of like it here. I feel safe I guess." Clara said with a sigh before she shut her eyes.

The statement pulled at Morgan's heart strings. She did nothing but try to keep her safe and ever since Claire's mom passed; Claire never felt safe.

"I promise wherever we end up, you will always be safe. We're never doing anything like that again." Morgan said, She reached out and squeezed her hand.

"I know. I love you" Claire said super sleepy and sounded like she was about to fall asleep.

"I love you too Claire bear." Morgan said softly.

She watched Claire's chest rise and fall and her breathing became slow and rhythm-like. She knew she had fallen asleep. She sighed and leaned back. There's no way she could sleep. She wasn't at all tired. She shifted in the chair restless.

Her eyes wandered over to Gavin's desk. How long would it be till we get to the next dock? She thought as she got up. She hesitated as she walked over to it. The last time she touched his maps, he about lost his mind. She wanted to double-check to see if she was right. Coming through Siren's Gully. would be the only way to the quickest dock.

She went over and studied the map. She wasn't exactly sure where they were. He hadn't made any recent notation. She knew where they had been. She looked at the little pencil mark from the last time he notated about a day and a half ago. She trailed the path across the map. They should be about here. If they continue the way they are going it will probably be another week before they get to a dock. Her eyes linger on the break off that would lead down Sirens Gully. It would save three days' time if they went through there. Instead of going around it. She grumbled to herself how could she bring it up without upsetting him. She grumbled to herself again. She needed some air. The crew will be asleep, she could get a moment to herself. She glanced at Claire. She was fast asleep. Maybe the sea air will get her a little sleep.

Chapter Eleven
Ariadne's Crown

Morgan stepped out onto the upper deck and closed the door behind her. The sea air hit her and she inhaled deeply. It made her feel alive, made her feel free. She craved the adventure. She had felt nothing like it before. She looked around and the sky was clear and you could see stars from miles away. They held their own light show as they twinkled away. The sound of the waves hitting the ship as it glided across the ocean. Everything was so relaxing. She agreed with Claire, this is the first time in a long time she felt safe. The first time in a long time she felt free. She walked down the stairs to the lower deck and across it. Before she knew it she was up the second set of stairs and on the deck where the helm was. Her hand caught the rail. She had subconsciously made her way to Gavin. His eyes were focused on the horizon. He was so serious all the time. The only thing that seemed to be relaxed on him was his dark colored hair as it ruffled in the wind. She smiled softly to herself as she watched him.

"Can't sleep, Love?" Gavin asked as he spotted her.

"No. For once I've slept plenty." She said awkwardly as she made her way up the stairs.

"Me too, Love." He said to himself.

Morgan walked over to the rail to Gavin's right, and leaned on it as she looked down into the water.

"So how long have you been doing this?" She asked, wanting to fill the silence.

"Ten years or so." He said with a shrug.

"How long have you been captain?" She asked, turning to look at him.

A big smirk came across his face before he answered. " Ten years or so."

She scrunched her eyebrows at him. He seemed young to be captain that long.

"So you just started off as captain?" She asked, a sarcastic smile on her lips.

"Well Love, it is my ship. So naturally yes." He said it was almost arrogant.

"So how did you-

"What were you dreaming about?" He asked to cut her off.

He saw her stiffen and her hand went to her side. She swallowed hard trying to force the words out.

"I...I don't remember." She said barely above a whisper.

"It must have been-" He started to say.

"Ariadne's Crown? Tell me the story?" She cut him off not wanting to spend anymore time in memory lane.

He glanced over at her. He was not used to not having things his way or his answers. He was going to argue but when he saw her he gave. She desperately did not want to talk about it and he couldn't make her.

"There once was a Captain who was traveling on a quest. He had vowed nothing and no one would stop him. However fate had other things in mind. This woman had snuck aboard his ship. She was needing help." Gavin started a funny smirk playing on his lip.

" Now wait a minute-" Morgan started to say and turned around more and facing him.

"Wait, wait; Love, you're gonna ruin the magic." He said as he held up a hand at her.

She rolled her eyes at him and stuck her tongue out at him but she waited.

"Unfortunately the Captain found her hiding. She struck a nerve with the Captain. Her attitude was as fiery as the color of her hair. The Captain decided to let her stay on board until the next dock.....Instead of throwing her overboard." His smirk widened.

"The Captain thinks he could." She said as she narrowed her eyes at him, the end of her lip curled up.

"The Captain certainly could if he wanted to but he secretly liked her feistiness." He said with a wink.

"I'm sure he does." She rolled her eyes at him again motioning for him to get on with it.

"Well even though he didn't mind her....annoyingness. All that much. The sea was still too dangerous for a woman. So at the next dock he had to leave her." He continued.

"The night before he was to leave her the Captain asked the gods to pluck a few stars from the sky. The gods granted the generous and handsome Captain's wish."

"The Captain is awfully fond of himself." She muttered.

"No Love, just honest." He said with a fake look of hurt.

"As a snake." She said playfully back.

"Hey, that would hurt his feelings." He said as he placed a hand on his chest.

"I thought pirates didn't have any?" She said as she raised an eyebrow at him.

"Who said he was a pirate? Making assumptions about the poor Captain. Can I finish the story, Love?" He said as he tried hard to keep his face straight.

" By all means." She chuckled.

"So as I was saying. The gods answered the Captain's request and plucked seven stars from the sky and arranged them into a beautiful crown. As they were ready to leave the fiery red headed at the dock. The Captain gifted the crown to her. He left her there but not without letting her know that if she stood out on the dock at night. The stars on her crown would light the way to her. He would find his way back to her, always." He said the smirk no longer on his lips but replaced by a small smile.

Did he just say that he wanted to find her after she leaves? Always? Morgan thought as her heart raced. She had to think of something quick to ignore what he said.

"Sounds like he was a soft pirate" She chuckled.

"Soft! Soft! He was the most ruthless pirate ever! Maybe I just have a soft spot for Redheads." He said as he winked at her.

"Oh whatever. Ok are you going to tell me the real story?" She said and crossed her arms.

"Nah I like this one better." He said and flashed her a grin.

"Fine, keep your story. I'll ask Jason tomorrow and he'll tell me." She said and shifted her view back to the ocean.

"Want to steer?" He asked and motioned to the wheel.

"Really?" She asked but she had already stepped away from the rail and basically ran over to the helm.

She stopped next to him. He stepped out from the wheel. One hand on the wheel and motioned for her to step in between him and the wheel. She carefully stepped in. He grasped her hand and placed it on the wheel. His hand stayed on top of hers. His warm hands on top of hers sent tingles up her arm. She took a deep breath in.

"Put your other hand on top of mine. Now. Be ready, the sea, she has a mind of her own. Try just to keep the wheel straight and steady. The biggest thing is don't ever let go." He explained to her quietly.

She nodded as she tried to ignore how his warm breath brushed her ear, she suppressed the urge to shiver. This might have been a bad idea. She was more focused on the heat of his body resonating from behind her; then she was the ocean. She wanted to lean back into him. Stop! Focused! She yelled at herself. She straightened herself and focused on the sea ahead of her.

"Do you feel how the current wants to pull to the right?" He asked as he loosen his grip so she could feel it.

She nodded. Her grip tightened and she forced the wheel to stay straight.

"There you go." He said he slowly started taking his hands off hers.

She panicked and grabbed on to him. Using one hand to stir.

"No no no. I'm not ready yet. Are you crazy?" She yelled, She grabbed his hand and placed them back on the wheel.

He laughed an actual real laugh, not one of his condescending ones. His chest vibrated against her and although he laughed at her she liked the sound of it.

"It's not funny." She mumbled a smile on her lips.

"Ok ok." He chuckled.

He explained to her about the wind and the directions of the sails. He pointed out that even at night there was someone in the crows nest to watch for possible dangers. To the left of him was a bell to wake the crew if he needed immediate response from them. She listened to him growing more and more comfortable with the closeness of him. Without knowing she leaned back into him. As he continues to talk about the ship. She got lost in the sound of his voice and the warmth of his body; she didn't even realize the sun was coming up.

A throat cleared behind them and Morgan jumped. She let go of the wheel and pulled away from Gavin like she had been caught doing something wrong. The ship jerked to the right and she almost fell over from it. Gavin was quick and grasped the wheel, straightening it.

"What was the one thing I told you?" Gavin grumbled.

She glanced behind him and saw Jason with a silly grin on his face.

"You let go Lass." Jason laughed.

"Morning" He announced as he came over to Gavin and clapped him on the shoulder

"Aye Morning." He grumbled back at Jason.

"I'm going to go check on Claire. Morning Jason." She announced as she walked by them and before they said anything rushed down the stairs.

Gavin watched her leave. He felt something in his chest and gut. There was this pull to her. He didn't want her to go. He liked the way it felt to have her with him. He wanted to follow after her. Damn Jason. He thought. He liked the feel of her body against his. Her scent....her everything. Damn it. He groaned frustrated.

As if Jason knew what Gavin thought he laughed. Jason went to take the wheel and Gavin shook his head. He needed longer. He needed to clear his head of her.

"No, I'm going to wait a little longer. Get the men up and ready if they aren't already." He grumbled.

"Aye Captain." Jason said as he backed away and started to leave.

"What the hell am I doing?" Gavin mumbled to himself running a hand threw his hair.

"She's a good woman Captain." Jason said over his shoulder.

"Go." Gavin growled.

His eyes focused on the horizon. She was making him forget his pain. He needed his pain to fuel his rage. To push him to kill Travis.

She hurried down the stairs. She needed distance between him and her. She rubbed her arm softly, her mind drifting back to how she felt just seconds ago. The warmth and safety of his arms. Her stomach was doing backflips of...happiness? Is that what this is? She asked herself as she reached the cabin. She opened the cabin door and stepped in. A smile formed on her lips as she saw Claire sprawled out on the bed. She walked over to her sitting on the bed.

"Wake up Sleepy head." She said softly and shook Claire lightly.

Claire groaned and stretched a little bit. Her golden hair tangled around her.

"Come on, it's morning, silly." Morgan chuckled and shook her harder.

"Ugh fine." She groaned and sat up.

"You sleep good?" Morgan asked her.

"Yeah I always sleep good here always." Claire smiled brightly.

It tugged at Morgan's heart a little bit. Morgan stood her eyes going to the desk again. She needed to find a way to talk to him about the alternate route.

Claire's feet hit the floor and the sound caught her attention. She took her eyes off the map and looked at Claire. She wore her dress from the first day. Morgan frowned.

"Hey, it's ok. I was thinking the same thing. Jack gave me some clothes that didn't fit him anymore." Claire said and started over to the corner.

She grabbed them and held them up to Morgan.

"They might be a little big but try them on. I'll see if the Captain has anything in his desk that we might be able to sew with, " Morgan nodded.

Morgan rummaged around in his desk not finding anything. She looked over to another closet. She walked over to it and opened it. She began to search on the top shelf. She bumped into something glass. Her stomach knotted before she even looked at it. The long glass neck of the bottle touched her hand and left a bad taste in her mouth. Alcohol. Her mind flashed back to Claire's father. Before the drinking he wasn't a bad man. He had turned evil over night....maybe it had always been there deep down inside of him.

She pushed the bottle out of her sight and her hand found a case. She pulled it down and opened it. Inside of it was bandages, a small knife, some tweezers, a needle, and thread. A makeshift medical kit she smirked. Although whoever made it was a little silly thinking sewing thread could hold skin together and a sewing needle. She turned and held up the thread and needle to Claire. Her eyes focused on Claire and blunt laughter burst from Morgan's lips. Claire stood as she held her arms out, the shirt draped over her and she

as swallowed up by it. It was entirely too long as well as the pants.

"Come here." She laughed and sat down in a chair.

Claire waddled over to her. Morgan grabbed the scissors on the desk behind her and trimmed the shirt up, she did so with the pants legs, and the sleeves. She then began working on sewing. She needed to take the waist in as well. She didn't realize how thin Claire was. She frowned as she worked. All this would change when they got to their new destination. Claire would never go hungry, be afraid or hurt again. She promised her silently as she worked.

Chapter Twelve
Maps

That was another one of his punishments. If he couldn't beat them to death, he would try to starve them to death.

He was gone and Morgan hoped it would be for a long time. She secretly hoped that maybe something would happen along the way and he would never come back. Morgan pried open the loose floor board. She reached in and pulled out a stale loaf of bread. Her stomach winces in pain seeing the food. It had been a few days since they last ate. He had been hanging around the house too much lately. They couldn't sneak in to grab the bread and Morgan had not been able to sneak off with her makeshift fishing pole she made. She had gotten pretty good at catching fish from the lake. Even though Claire hated going there. She didn't blame her but it was one of the ways she could get them food to eat. Even if she had gotten the pole, a fire to cook the fish would have drawn his attention.

She broke the bread and handed it to Claire. She instantly heard her tiny stomach growl. Morgan gave her a small smile. Claire looked at the bread and Morgan nodded to eat. Morgan took a bite of the bread she had. Although it was old and hard, it was the best thing she had eaten. She glanced over at Claire who happily ate. She took one more bite before she wrapped it back up in the cloth and placed it back inside the floor.

120

She carefully placed the floor board over it. Just like that you couldn't tell.

"Morgan, you need to eat more than that." Claire said, holding out the remaining piece of bread.

"No, I am fine. You finish that. I will catch some fish later and we'll eat that too. You eat all of that for now." She ordered and pushed the bread back.

Claire had taken five more bites before their bedroom door swung open. Morgan's stomach dropped. She hadn't even heard him. He leaned against the door frame holding himself up with it. He was blocking the only exit.

"Who said you could eat?" He growled.

Morgan stood and stepped in front of Claire. He smiled stepping into the room. His eyes showed nothing but rage despite the smile. Morgan glanced at Claire and mouthed the word go to her. She shook her head but Morgan ignored it. She took a deep breath in and bolted full speed into him. He was drunk and he wasn't able to hold his balance. He fell to the ground. Claire saw him fall and headed for the door. Morgan had fallen to but was getting on her feet.

"Go! I'm coming! go!" Morgan yelled to her.

Claire nodded and took off. She knew where to meet Morgan. Morgan stumbled to her feet as she headed for the door. Just as she reached the door he caught her ankle and yanked her down. She kicked furiously but he held on tight. Her knees dug into the ground as she tried to get away. The wood beneath her cracked as she tried to get away. The skin on her knees scraped as she struggled, wood splintered into them.

She glanced back and saw him getting to his knees but his hand still held her ankle tightly. If he got up and got over her, the fight would be over. He would have her captured. She aimed for his face and kicked. Her bare foot crashed into his jaw, she watched his head tilt back, a loud groan escaped his mouth. He let go and she didn't wait another second. She bolted to her feet and raced out the bedroom door.

Claires feet dug into the wet ground as she ran. She was close to the lake. She hated coming here but it was the only place he never came to. She stopped just shy of the lake and turned. She knew where to go and where to hide. Hidden in the trees was a small fort Morgan and Claire built out of fallen trees. It camouflaged them. To the world it looked like an old pile of broken trees that had fallen. She ducked under the trees and sat on the ground. Seconds turned into minutes and minutes felt like hours. Something was wrong. Cliare's stomach twisted. Morgan should have been here by now. Claire ducked out of the fort and cautiously started to make her way back to the house. She hung back in the trees as she reached the house. Her eyes scanned the opening to make sure she was safe. Where was she? Claire thought as she continued to study the house. The house was dark and she could see no movements from inside. No noise, nothing. Her heart raced in her chest. There were only a handful of times Morgan didn't come and it was always bad. She stared at the house longer. Then something caught her attention out of the corner of her eye. Something was laying in the mud.....something with red hair.

Claire scanned the yard and she didn't see him. The mud on the ground splattered about as Claire bolted to Morgan. She crashed onto her knees in front of her.

"Morgan." Claire pleaded as she reached out to touch her.

She paused as her eyes saw Morgan's shirt. It was ripped to pieces, blood seeped out of her back and leaked onto the shirt. Claire didn't know how the shirt was still together. She reached down as her hand shook and touched her lightly. Morgan winced and let out a small groan. She had been whipped. The same patterns that shredded her shirt were etched into her skin. The skin had been ripped away from her body leaving bloody neat wounds.

"Morgan. Hey come on we gotta go. I don't know where he went. I'm sorry I shouldn't have left you." Claire's voice cracked as she held back the tears.

She reached down and slipped Morgan's arm over her shoulder and attempted to stand. Morgan let out a small cry. She went to struggle to get away from Claire.

"Hey, it's me. It's me." Claire said as she held tighter to her.

"Claire?" She asked as she opened her eyes.

"Hey we've gotta get out of here." Claire said and helped her to her feet.

The memory faded from Morgan's mind as she placed the last stitch in the bottom of the pant leg. She smiled as she looked up at Claire.

"Tada!" Morgan smiled now that everything fit Claire properly.

"Perfect." Claire laughed and spun around.

"You should really change too." Claire laughed.

"Well this is all I got right now so it will have to do." Morgan said as she wrinkled her nose at Claire.

"You could always borrow one from the Captain." She giggled.

"Are you hungry?" Morgan asked as she ignored her question.

"Yes!" Claire exclaimed as she grabbed her belly.

"Ok let's go." Morgan grinned as she stood up and took her hand in hers.

Morgan watched Claire smile brightly as she walked with her to the door. Morgan was captivated by how happy Claire seemed. It had been so long for her. Remorse ate at her as she pulled the door open. She stepped out her attention still on Claire when she walked straight into something large and hard. His hand instinctively wrapped around her waist to steady her. Her breath caught in her throat and she froze. She had walked straight into Gavin. The feeling of his warmth radiated to her. She wanted to curl up into him. She could feel her ears burn as they started to turn red. So much for space she thought. She went to step back but his hand didn't want to let go.

"Ah sorry." Morgan said awkwardly.

"It's ok. I didn't mind." He said with a smirk on his lips.

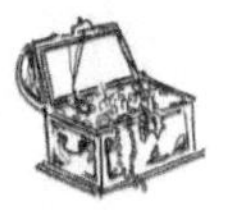

She didn't mean to but she looked up when he spoke. She instantly regretted it. Her eyes lingered on his lips and she felt her heart stumble in her chest. She didn't know if she wanted to smack the smirk off his face or see what he tasted like. She caught a glimpse of something flash threw his eyes....lust. She inhaled and forced herself to take his hand off her waist and placed it back down at his side

"Well we seem to be at an impasse and there's a little girl who's hungry. " Morgan said as she took a big step back. She then motioned for him to go in or out of the doorway.

Gavin didn't realize it but he frowned a little when she took his hand off her waist. He liked the way she felt in his hands. How his hand fit perfectly on her hip. He looked around Morgan and saw Claire. He smiled at her.

"Well I can't stand in the way then." He said as he stepped aside.

Claire popped around Morgan and started walking first. She paused at Gavin with a grin on her face.

"Hey, could Morgan borrow some clothes?" Claire asked with a raised eyebrow.

"Yeah-" Gavin started to say

"Claire." Morgan growled.

"It's fine really." Morgan said as she looked at Gavin.

"Ok great. I'll go get breakfast. Jack's meeting me anyways and you get clothes ok." Claire said as she walked away.

"I, uh Claire!" Morgan yelled at her.

Claire turned around with a bright smile and waved. Morgan looked at her mouth the word no but Claire just giggled and continued on. Gavin laughed as he walked past Morgan into the cabin. He headed over to his closet and pulled out a shirt or two and then looked back at her.

"You'll probably have to try on a few different pants. But whatever is in here you're welcomed to it." He said to her,

She nodded, and yawned a little bit. She walked over to look at the shirts. She saw his attention shift to his desk. He started over there. This might be her chance. She grabbed one of the shirts and cautiously walked over to him. He was marking on the map muttering to himself. She stopped in front of the desk looking down at the map. He raised his head looking at her. A few different emotions passed through his eyes. His guard was up when it came to the map.

"My father would do the same." She smiled softly.

He seemed to soften a little but still watched her closely. He protected the map like it was the most precious thing in the world. The way he hovered over it made her think of an animal that was protecting her food.

"He would come home from his voyage and go right to his study. He would open a map for his next journey and start marking the quickest route. He was known for being one of the fast merchants. If there was a short cut or a way to save time he would find it." She said proudly.

His expression softened as he listened to her. Images of a little Morgan playing at the foot of a tall man who was charting on a map flashed in his head. He took his eyes from the map and looked up at her. He waited for her to continue.

"He began teaching me how to read maps and use the various tools he had. I would help him find short cuts; so he could come home faster. It was a way I could spend time with him. He was never home for long. He was a good man but always gone. Maps remind me of him." She said looking at the map.

"What happened to him?" Gavin asked, his head titled as he asked the question.

Morgan swallowed hard. Losing her parents hurt worse than the beatings her uncle gave her, It was a numb pain that she knew would never go away. She absolutely loved her parents. She had a good life. She was loved. She told herself that it was part of a plan. It was meant to happen so she could save Claire.

"He returned home from one of his trips with a fever. We thought it would pass but it got worse. He broke out in sweats and a horrible rash. Then he couldn't eat. He got so weak his body couldn't go on. We all caught it. I was the only one to live." She said quietly.

"I'm sorry." He said softly.

She smiled her thanks and looked down at the map. She didn't want to live in the sorrow of the memory.

"So what are you muttering about?" She asked.

He frowned slightly looking back at the map and then up at her. He studied her for a second and then exhaled giving in.

"We're behind schedule. Roughly two, three days." He said frustrated running a hand through his hair.

"Well it's your lucky day. I happened to be an expert on all things maps." She said going around the desk to stand next to him.

He watches her carefully as started charting and studying the map. He almost winced the first time her fingers touched the map but he pulled himself back.

"Look here. If we take this way and cut through here. You'll save three days' time." She glanced at him as her finger lingered on Siren's Gully.

He made a face. He had known that's where she would be heading with this. He grumbled to himself looking at it. She was right. It would be the only way to catch up.

"What?" She asked as she turned to face him.

"The men won't like it." He said a growl in his voice

"Why?" She almost laughed.

"I don't know about your father but most sailors are very superstitious. There's a legend saying that no ship has made it through that gully. Some say sirens, others talk about scattered storms." He shrugged.

"Sirens...like evil mermaids." She said a burst of laughter escaped her mouth as her hand quickly went to cover her lips.

"Some legends say they are beautiful women with a tail like mermaids and their songs enchant sailors. They put them in a trance and then lead them to crash into rocky shores or lure them into the waters to drown them. Others say they look more like birds. Still with the same purpose." He smirked.

She laughed more thinking that all the rough men on the ship were afraid of some story. She leaned back into the desk chuckling. Her laughter made him smile, he liked the sound of it. His eyes lingered on her lips. He closed the gap between them pinning her between the desk and him. A playful smile lingering on his lips.

"Or they say they pretend to be red headed maidens. They sneak aboard ships. Looking for help and trick the captains of said ships into falling for them." His voice was deeper as he spoke, his hand going to her hair and twirling a piece around his finger.

She stopped laughing. Her heart which was once light and playful started to race in her chest and she leaned more against the desk, her knees went weak. She felt her breath caught in her throat. She couldn't breath as she realized how close they were. She could hear his breathing slow. She couldn't look up; she knew his eyes were staring at her lips. Instinctively she licked her lips and nervously bit her lower one. His hand went to her cheek. The warmth of it felt good and she leaned into it. His thumb trailed down her cheek and along her jaw until it rested under her chin. He raised her chin up and she kept her eyes down. She knew if her eyes met her she would lose herself.

"Morgan." His voice was heavy as he whispered her name.

Her stomach flipped with excitement as she heard her name come out of his mouth. Her emerald green eyes met his and his mouth claimed hers. His lips placed soft kisses on hers as she slowly started to respond back and followed his movements. His tongue pressed against her lips and demanded her mouth to open. Her body responded by opening her mouth slightly so his tongue could slip in. His tongue brushed against hers and it sent chills down her body. She leaned into him, her hand ran up his shoulder to the back of his head. Her fingers entwined into his dark curls as the kiss deepend. His hand grabbed her waist in response and pulled her even close against him. His other hand ran from the smalls of her back down over her ass.

Alarms went off in her head as she felt his hand start to explore. She pulled back breathless. He was too. He caught his breath and rested his forehead against hers. She tried to find the words to speak. Then the cabin door opened.

"Captain you said you wanted to...to" Jason stopped speaking seeing the two of them.

Morgan went to move away from Gavin but he didn't move. His forehead still pressed against hers, his hand on her waist held her in place.

"Aren't you supposed to be steering?" He growled.

Jason's face held a smirk, as he saw Gavin become irritable, amusement sparkled in Jason's eyes.

"Don't worry I left the helm in capable hands."
Jason said as he tried to hide the humor in his voice.

Morgan jabbed Gavin in the ribs which caused him to shift slightly. It wasn't much but enough for her to squeeze out from him. She started to walk away from him. His hand reached out and caught hers. She looked back at him and frowned slightly

"I need to go check on Claire." She said and pulled her hand back.

Gavin let her hand slip through his and he felt his stomach tighten. He bit back the urge to tell her to stay. He closed his fist and let her go. He watched her walk out of the cabin, each step she had taken pulled at his heart.

Chapter Thirteen
Hurt:

Gavin stood there as he watched the door several seconds after she left. God what was he doing? He thought.

"Captain?" Jason asked amused.

"What?" He growled.

"You asked for me. You said you wanted to go over routes." Jason said with a shrug.

"Fuck. Yes. Damn it." He muttered as he looked down at the map again.

Jason had a silly grin as he walked over to the map. He was happy for Gavin and found his blindness or reluctance to give into his feelings amusing.

"Don't." Gavin warned.

Gavin glared at him and Jason put his hands up in defense. Gavin glanced back at the map. He ran his hand through his hair frustrated. She was right, it would be the only way to catch up. It was going to be such a headache.

"Sirens Gully." Gavin said out loud and locked eyes with Jason as he waited for the back lash.

Jason's eyebrows came together confused. He tried to mull over an appropriate response out of respect for Gavin's title.

"Seriously. You've heard what they say about that passage." Jason said in disbelief.

A smile crept on to Gavins lips as he spoke "Yeah I know evil mermaids."

"No, not even the siren myths. They said the sea isn't right there. The sky's not right there. Gavin you don't want to do this" Jason argued with concern in his voice as he spoke.

" He's fucking getting away Jason! Three fucking days Jason. Don't fucking question me. Tell the men if they don't like it. Tell them to jump fucking over board. I'll man the ship myself if I have to." He yelled, slamming his fist down.

Jason wanted to argue but he knew better. He nodded and didn't say anything else. He left Gavin in his rage. Rage hat would slowly consume his friend and he did not know how to stop it. He prayed maybe the girl would break through it. Jason shook his head as he left quietly. Gavin sat down at his desk as he watched Jason leave. He knew everything he would argue but it didn't matter. He was Captain. What he said went. They will be at Sirens gully by sunset tomorrow. He was not going to let Travis win. He would have his revenge.

Morgan walked out of his cabin as quickly as she could. She could feel her cheeks as they burned with the heat Gavin had awakened in her. What was he thinking? He couldn't have meant it? She thought; her stomach still fluttered around. Her finger tips subconsciously going to her lips. They tingled as they tried to recover too. She shook her head as she pushed the feelings and thoughts to stop. She found her way to Claire, who held up an apple to her as she came to sit by her. Morgan took the apple from her and smiled.

"You didn't change." Claire said to her.

"I know." Morgan answered, taking a bite.

"Why not?" Claire asked.

"I will later." Morgan grumbled as she took another bite of the apple.

There was some commotion on the ship as Jason stepped out of the Captain's cabin.His shoulders were tenson and he shook his head a few times. His frustration and concern was expressed in each heavy step he took. He walked across the deck and approached the helm. Morgan watched him curiously as he took over steering. The expression on his face was unreadable. He began shouting out coordinates and orders. The ship went silent. He repeated what he just shouted and no one moved. What was happening? She thought standing.

"Sirens Gully." One man mumbled.

That's all it took. It was like a slow wave of noise took over the ship. The mumbles turned into yells and then the protesting began. Panic had taken over the ship. Morgan stood up defensively and blocked Claire, in case things went south. The men below were angry and frightened. One man bumped into another. Next thing that happened a brawl broke out on the lower deck.

Morgan scooped up Claire, her blue eyes with fear as she grabbed ahold of Morgan back. She glanced around to look for a safe spot to hide Claire. There was nowhere. She saw Jason and made her way to him. Something said if anything happened he would help her. She ran up the stairs to the helm to Jason.

His eyes narrowed and his jaw clenched. He motioned for the girls to come stand behind him as he began to shout at the men below.The shouting did nothing. More and more men were becoming involved in the brawl.

The Captain's door swung open with a bang. The noise made the men stop in their tracks. Gavin stepped out onto the upper deck. His chocolate hair blew in the breeze. His jaw clenched and his eyes held fire in them. He was wearing his sword and a pistol tucked into his hip. His presence demanded respect and installed fear. Almost all the fighting had stopped. The few who continue must not have heard. Gavin growled, removing the pistol from his hip and firing it into the air. The loud bang echoed around the ship and everything stopped.

"Everyone done?" He shouted, his voice rang out over the silence.

Gavin glared down at them daring anyone to say they were not. A few heads nodded. He tightened his grip on the rail, his knuckles going white as anger poured off of him.

"Sirens Gully." He announced his voice cut through the air like it was a blade.

"Captain, don't you think it's a bit dangerous." One man spoke up, his voice sounded tiny in comparison to Gavins.

"Aye the stories, Captain." Another said.

"Sirens." Another whispered.

"Waters not right there " Their voices mimicked each other, full of fear and caution.

Gavin could feel his jaw about to pop from the amount of tension he squeezed into it. He knew this was going to happen. He was frustrated that he knew and angry that they dared to question him. Gavin cleared his throat and the chatter stopped.

"Are you really being a bunch of cowards!" Gavin bellowed.

"You all are afraid of some stories. Evil mermaids" His lip curled up when he said evil mermaids, it sounded absurd and he had to stop himself from smiling.

Morgan caught it and she relaxed. She couldn't fight back the smile as she watched him.

"We've been through The Dead Man's Passage, Skull Valley, and Silence's Way. Each one of them has tall tails. Each one of them lined your pockets well. I have not once done anyone of you wrong." Gavin spoke to the crowd.

Several shrugged and others' heads nodded in agreement. There was a soft sound of aye's as well. The crowd slowly grew rational.

"You all know why I am doing this. You all know why I've returned to the sea. I do not care for the treasure and as an added bonus you can all split my share of it. But I am going through Sirens Gully like it or not And if you don't like it you're more than welcome to get off my ship." He threatened.

No one said anything. They all continued to stare at Gavin. He nodded to Jason and Jason shouted out the coordinates and orders once more. There was no debating this time. The men went back to work. Gavin's eyes searched across the deck and landed on Morgan's. A smile came to his lips. She was standing there, eyes locked on him but a soft smile danced across her perfect lips. The anger, rage, fighting, and even the firing of a pistol didn't affect her. She stood there with a smile. Most of the men couldn't even look him in the eye but this woman was not only returning his stare but with a smile. He shook his head softly, she's definitely full of surprises. He nodded in her direction and then turned back heading into his cabin. Slamming the door as he did.

Jason smiled softly seeing the exchange. He glanced over to her.

"You know most grown men wouldn't even look at the Captain when he's angry. Here you are smiling. Do you know something I don't?" He asked her.

She smiled bigger and shrugged. " I guess I'm just not afraid of him."

"That is a bit shocking. Each one of those men down there would rather go fight with evil mermaids than challenge the captain." Jason smirked.

Morgan didn't say anything but her smile grew. She shrugged and glanced down at Claire.

"I've seen evil…he isn't it." Morgan said as she locked eyes with Jason. He nodded back because he understood. Claire came around from beside her and leaned into her.

"Pssh I'm not afraid of him ethier." She whispered to Morgan.

Morgan laughed hard and a small cramp started in her side so she leaned slightly over and held her belly. She patted Claire on her head. Jason let out a chuckle as well.

"Come on Claire, let's go find something to make ourselves useful." Morgan said and they headed down the stairs.

They found Jack below the deck cleaning the cannons. He looked at them a little confused.

"We are here to help." Claire announced as she went over to inspect what he was working on.

"Ok ok. You guys can help. But this is a big job. If you do it wrong and we go to fire them… You could blow a hole in the ship and kill a lot of us." Jack explained.

"Ok ok we got it." Claire said as her eyes got wide with shock and then nodded seriously to him.

They began to help Jack carefully. After he showed them, they split up and each worked on different cannons. It seems to take forever. Morgan was double checking Claires and hers. The idea of blowing up the ship was a little scary. After the last cannon. Jack paused looking at all of them.

"Well that went a lot quicker with help." He announced.

"You're welcome. What's next?" Morgan asked.

"Five minute break." Jack laughed.

"Ok." Morgan chuckled.

"So Jack, how did you end up here?" Morgan asked.

"Eh short story is I picked Gavin's pocket. Instead of turning me in or worse. He asked me if I wanted a job." He laughed.

Morgan chuckled. An image of a younger Jack with even more widely hair stealing from Gavin flashed through her head.

"You were a thief!" Claire gasped.

"Um I still kind of am...ya know pirate and all." Jack said with a laugh.

"Why?" Claire asked.

"Um well basically my parents dumped me and I needed to survive. Picking Gavin's pocket was the best thing to happen to me. He gave me a place on his ship, food, clothes and I earned money. He also looked out for me better than any parent I've ever had." He said with a shrug.

Morgan smiled to herself; her soft spot for Gavin growing. The words she said to Jason hours ago held true. There was nothing evil about Gavin.

"Sorry about your parents. I get it though. Morgan looks out for me too." Claire said and then grabbed a hold of Morgan's hand and squeezed

. "Ok what's next?" Morgan asked as she changed topics quickly.

Jack nodded and motioned for them to follow him.

They headed up to the upper deck and began working. By sunset they had secured more ropes and tied more knots then Morgan could even count. They scrub and polish every piece of wood on the ship. Jack even taught them about how the sails were adjusted. Morgan noticed at some point Gavin had taken over steering. Jason had gone off to bed so he could steer at night. Morgan sank to the floor of the upper deck and leaned against the wall of the captain's cabin. Claire plopped down next to her beat.

"I'm hungry and tired." Claire said to Morgan.

"I know darling. We'll go get something." Morgan said going to get up.

Before Morgan could get up Jack was on the top deck. Two plates of food in his hands and a grin on his face. He held them out to each of the girls.

"My hero." Claire announced and took the food.

Jack's face blushed as Claire called him her hero. He smiled a little embarrassed but nodded and then turned to hand Morgan her plate.

"Thank you Jack." Morgan said as her stomach growled.

The food hit the spot perfectly. Morgan set down her plate and then realized Claire was fast asleep against her. A small piece of bread still in her hand as she snored. Morgan lost track of time. The sky had darkened and the stars were out. Morgan turned sideways as she let Claire fall into her arms. She carefully scooped her up and then carried her inside Gavin's cabin. She set her down on the bed and tucked her in. She looked around.

When she stepped inside Gavin's cabin she was exhausted but now that Claire was settled she found a second wind of energy. She couldn't go to sleep now. Sea air should help her, she thought as she ventured outside. The view was captivating every time she looked at it. It may be the same sky and stars and ocean water but it made her feel free. She walked over to the side rail and looked down at the ocean. She glanced at the helm. Gavin crossed her mind. She saw him chatting with Jason as they were switching out control of the ship.

"Ah the captain's play thing." A voice said from behind her.

"Excuse me." Morgan said as she turned to see who was talking to her.

Before she could turn fully around, a hand covered her mouth and pulled her back against him. A hand wrapped around her waist and bear hugged her. She began to struggle against the person as she tried to get free.

"Why should the captain get to have all the fun. " the man muttered into her ear.

Morgan's heart sank as panic flooded her system. She began to try harder to get away. Her arms pulled at him as she tried to break free. The man's hand began to move down over her body, exploring hers. He reached her waist and started to slip his hand under her shirt. The hand that covered her mouth shifted slightly as he touched Morgan's bare stomach. Morgan seized the opportunity. She bit down on his hand as hard as she could. Her teeth crunching through his flesh as blood spilt into her mouth. The man yelled and let her

go. Morgan stumbled forward from his grasp and went to take off her, red hair flew back behind and then she was yanked backwards by her hair. He slammed her into the cabin wall. Something sharp touched her neck and pressed into her throat. She knew immediately what it was. The tip of the knife began to draw blood. She slowed her fighting

"Now bitch. Ethier let me have my fun or I'll slit your throat. Chuck your body overboard and go have my way with that pretty little blonde." He whispered into her ear.

Morgan froze. Claire. She felt like she was going to vomit. The thought of him touching her at all made her insides crawl. She stopped moving all together. The man smiled. He pulled her shirt loose from her pants.

"If we're all gonna die tomorrow in that gully. I am going to have this first." He snickered.

She shut her eyes trying to block everything out. Her untucked shirt was now wrapped in his hand. She wanted to fight, everything in her screamed. She wanted to hurt him but she couldn't. She couldn't let him hurt Claire. She felt him pull on her shirt; in one quick motion all of the buttons were ripped off. He removed the knife from her throat, replacing it with his hand. He then ran the knife up her stomach; cutting away the bandages. The last remaining thing between her and him. She felt her chest exposed. His rough calloused hand captured her breast in his hand and he squeezed hard. He replaced the knife at her throat as if to remind her not to fight.

"Oh that is so nice." He groaned as he fondled her.

Her body began to shake as she closed her eyes not wanting to see him. She felt a tear escape her eye. She heard him groan happily as he roughly played with her breast. She felt him let go and then there was a jingle noise. She opened her eyes and found him fumbling to get the belt of her pants free. Her mind screamed that this can't be happening. She went to fight again and she felt the tip of the knife dig deep into neck. Warm liquid seeped out from the small wound he was making in her neck.

"Move again and I will do exactly what I promised. Or maybe I'll slit your throat in front of her and while you choke on your own blood the last thing you'll see is me with her." He said with a cruel smile on his lips.

Morgan shut her eyes again trying to stop herself from shaking. She told herself to go numb like she would with the beatings. His hand reached out and cupped on her breast again with a chuckle.

"Ahh it's been so long." He said and squeezed it.

His hand traveled down her stomach heading for her belt again. Everything she had faced, now this. Everything she had endured and but never this she felt another tear trying to escape as he pulled the belt loose. Her stomach turned in on itself, this couldn't happen.

"Please." She begged him.

"What's that I couldn't hear -" The man began to choke as the words escaped his mouth.

Warm red liquid hit her as it spewed out of his mouth. The man choking soon turned to gurgles. Morgan opened her eyes and watched the man's face go white. His hand grabbed this throat as blood seeped through his fingers. He began to lose strength and more blood flowed out. Morgan watched the fear in his eyes as he backed away from her. She looked down at herself and she was speckled in red dots. She looked confused as she tried to understand what had happened.

"You fucking low life." She heard Gavin's voice.

Morgan spotted him following the man as he backed away towards the railing. Gavin was calm, his voice barely held anger to it. His normal tense and frustrated back was relaxed. Gavin walked towards him and with the same knife he slit his throat with. The man's eyes pleaded with Gavin to help him. Gavin didn't even acknowledge the look. He pulled his hand back and lunged forward. He stabbed him in the gut. The man choked more as he tried to gasp from the pain. His large bugged eyes staring at Gavin. Gavin snorted at him and slammed his palm into the man's shoulder and shoved him backwards. The man toppled overboard.

Gavin didn't even look back as he plunged in. Within seconds he was at Morgan's side. He cupped her face in his hands. He glanced down as his eyes scanned her, he needed to know if the blood was hers.

"Are you ok?" He said his own voice seemed to want to shake.

Morgan shook her head no. He glanced down at her and saw how exposed she was. He quickly pulled his own shirt up over his head. Taking it off. He placed it over Morgan's head and helped her into it. Morgan's whole body shook and then the tears she had been fighting back began to pour out. She felt weak, she felt lost. She was disgusted. Gavin grabbed her and wrapped his arms around her.

"It's ok I got you. I got you." He said into her hair as he held her tight.

Chapter Fourteen
Trouble

Morgan melted into him as she lost herself. He hugged her tighter trying to squeeze the hurt from her. He suddenly picked her up and cradled her in his arms. He made his way around to the front of the cabin. He needed to get her away from the open, away from the men. He was about to bring her in and she pulled back.

"No Claire! I can't let her see this." She said in between cries.

Seeing her crying; he wanted to drag him back out of the sea and kill him all over again. He nodded slightly and started to make his way towards Jason's cabin. Jack was still up and rushed over to Gavin. She moved wanting him to put her down but he gripped her tighter, pulling her closer to his bare chest.

"I can walk." She whispered trying to wipe the tears quickly away.

He grunted his response as he tightened his grip. She sighed giving into him. She rested her head against his bare chest. She could hear his heart racing. She tried to calm herself by listening to it beating.

"Captain?" Jack asked concerned

"Jackie. Sit outside my cabin. No one is allowed in or out. Watch Claire for me." He ordered as he walked by him.

Jack didn't question the orders, he nodded and raced off. Gavin walked by Jason who paused, concern written on his face. If he wasn't steering he would have been over there. Gavin didn't respond to him. Walking to the door of Jason's cabin he kicked the door open.

"That was unnecessary." Morgan whispered.

He grunted again as he stepped inside. This time kicking the door shut.

"Seriously." She said, rolling her eyes at him.

He walked over to Jason's bed and placed her down. He kneeled in front of her; his eyes wandering over her body as he looked for wounds. Morgan looked confused at him and was about to ask him what he was doing but he placed his hand on her cheek. She naturally leaned into it.

"Are you hurt?" He almost whispered, as if the answer could possibly break him.

"No, I'm ok. Just overwhelmed. I'm used to being attacked but just not like that." She said her voice shook a little as she spoke.

She tried to get her voice straight and she blinked back the tears that threatened to break free. Gavin's eyes narrowed looking at her neck. He went to look at it but Morgan leaned away.

"It's nothing." She said with a small smile.

He ignored her. There was a small slice in her neck. He clenched his jaw. The image of him holding her against the wall with the knife pressed into her throat flashed in his mind. That bastard. He thought.

"See nothing. It's already stopped bleeding." She said with a small smile as she touched her fingertips to the wound and showed him.

He frowned as he looked at her. There was a lot of blood but thankfully it was not hers. He tried to wipe the blood from her cheek.

"Yeah you kind of made a mess." She said with a half laugh as she tried to lighten the mood.

He frowned and got up. He glanced at her before walking to the door. He took a deep breath still looking at her before walking out the door. She instantly felt crushed. Did he blame her? Was this her fault? She stood shaking. She looked down at herself; her arms covered in the man's blood. Tears began to fall down her blood stained cheeks. She tried to wipe the blood on her hands off. It wasn't working. She wiped her eyes trying to get control of herself.

She glanced around Jason's cabin. She had to find something to clean herself up with. She needed to get back to Claire and couldn't go with all this blood. Just as she was about to start searching, the cabin door reopened. Gavin returned carrying a bowl of water, rags, bandage material, and clothing hung over his shoulder. He walked over to Jason's bed putting everything down on his night stand. He raised an eyebrow at her.

"I uh. I thought you weren't coming back. So I was looking to see what I could borrow so Claire didn't see me like this." She said rushed.

"Why would I not come back?" Gavin asked but it was more of a statement, he patted the bed telling her to come.

Morgan walked over slowly. She sat on the bed. She wasn't sure how she felt. Gavin dunked the rag in the water and looked over at her. His jaw was still clenched shut. Morgan's stomach twisted nervously, the thought of him blaming her for this was too much.

"I'm sorry." She said in a small voice, her eyes on the ground.

Those two words stunned him. She was sorry? He sighed, putting the rag down. He narrowed his eyes at her. Trying to understand why she thought any of this was her fault.

"I don't know how to fix any of that but I could be taught whatever job he had on the ship. I don't think I provoked him but if I did-" Morgan began to stutter out.

Gavin's hand was suddenly over her mouth. His eyes searching hers.

"Stop. You're sorry?" He said, letting his hand drop.

"Yeah I-" she started to say again but he put his hand up, shaking his head.

"I'm not. If I could slit his throat all over again I would. Hell if I could do it again he wouldn't be that lucky. That was nice compared to what he should have gotten. I'm the one who's sorry. I know my men are lots of things but I didn't think any of them would dare." He said anger flashed in his eyes.

Morgan stared at him confused. She wasn't sure what to say or how to act. She hated herself for being weak right now. Gavin went back to ringing out the rag and then turned to her.

"Thank you. Captain." She said softly.

He nodded but flinched. He hated the way the word captain came out of her mouth. He pushed the thought back as he began to wipe the blood from her cheek. She pulled away slightly, a smile on her lips.

"I can clean myself up."

"Yeah well you can't see your face. I can't have you walking around looking like this. It's bad enough They're all superstitious right now." He continued.

"Got it. Red head siren and all." She chuckled.

Her laugh was slowly becoming one of his favorite sounds. It instantly made him smile. He dipped the cloth back in the water and then began to wash down her neck. She inhaled slightly as a chill ran down her. Her stomach went from feeling sick to nervous excitement. Gavin smirked a little seeing her body respond. He could see the goosebumps forming on her skin. She cleared her throat.

"It's cold." She said justifying her reaction.

"Mhmm" He said with a smile tugging at his lip.

He scooted back looking at her. He knew she must have blood underneath his shirt she was wearing. He needed to check her back as well.

"What?" She asked, confused.

"Here. You clean up and I'll be back to check your back." He said, handing her the rag.

She nodded as he headed to the door. He saw a quick look of panic run across her face.

"I'll be right back." He promised her.

The panic left her. He lingered in the doorway a second; a playful smirk on his lips. He shuffled his feet for a second before he turned and looked at her, the smirk on his lips deepened.

"I mean I could always stay. I don't mind helping." He said the smirk turned into a devilish grin.

Morgan smirked back and rolled her eyes at him. She grinned and squeezed the wet rag in her hand before he flung it towards him. The wet rag landed on the top of his head with a wap.

"So...this is a yes?" He laughed as he took the rag off his head and moved away from the door.

"No. Get out!" She laughed.

"I don't know. I think you need help." He grinned.

"I've got it." She laughed.

He threw the rag back at her and headed back to the door. He opened it and looked back. She tried to hide her smile as she shooed him. He laughed and walked out. Morgan waited a few seconds before she pulled Gavin's shirt up over her head. Her pervious shirt hung ripped opened underneath. He hadn't wasted a second after realizing she was exposed. She was thankful for how quick he acted. She removed her arms from the ripped shirt. Gavin was right, her whole front was sprayed with blood splatter. She cringed a little as she started to scrub her skin.

Gavin walked out of the cabin thankful for the cold sea air. He had too many emotions going. Jason looked over to the sound of the door closing and saw Gavin.

"Captain." He said to Gavin but it was more of a question.

Gavin sighed, heading over to him. Jason didn't say another word. His eyes studying Gavin waiting for him to speak.

"I killed Rick." Gavin said nonchalantly.

"What? Are you serious? What the hell happened? Damn it! Now's not the time to go around killing crew members. You can't right now." Jason said, upset.

"He tried to rape Morgan." Gavin spat out.

Jason's face drastically changed from anger to worry and he glanced at his cabin.

"Is she ok? Is she hurt?" Jason asked, his voice calmer but now filled with anger too.

"Physically she's ok. She's shook up pretty bad." Gavin said as he ran his hand threw his hair.

"Damn it." Jason muttered again.

"I know." Gavin muttered as well.

He was having the same thoughts. The men will be upset that he killed Rick. What was more upsetting was that this would even happen on his ship.

"Fuck it." Gavin muttered thinking about some of them being upset.

"Aye I agree too but being that we're going through Sirens Gully it might not be the best timing to have this happen." Jason said as he processed.

"You're wrong. I can kill anyone I want. That comes with the title. My ship, my rules. If there's an uproar. They can swim or try to best me." Gavin said angrily.

"Gavin, we're gonna throw the whole crew overboard." Jason said quietly.

"I don't need a crew" He said and slapped Jason on his back.

"Beside you said we. You're already gonna help me. So it won't be the whole crew." Gavin continued with a smirk walking away.

"The two of us running a ships gonna be hard." Jason muttered.

"Hard but not impossible. There will be at least five of us." Gavin laughed.

Jason muttered to himself as Gavin headed back to the cabin. A smile on his face thinking about Jason, Jack, Claire and Morgan being his only crew. He knew there would be an up roar but nothing he wouldn't be able to handle. Worse case he would just make an example out of some. He shrugged at his thoughts as he knocked on the door. He heard a soft "come in." He opened the door and walked in closing it behind him.

Morgan sat on the bed, her back facing the door. Her long red flowing down her exposed back. She had his clean shirt wrapped around her front. He walked over to the bed and sat down behind her. He tried to focus on the wounds but his mind kept going to how soft her skin looked. He reached out, touching her back slightly. His eyes ran down her back. She had two perfect dimples in the smalls of her back. An image flashed of him holding on to her hips; her dimples being the perfect spot for his thumbs as he bent her over. He cleared his throat trying to get his head straight.

"Do they look ok?" Morgan asked, confused.

He brushed her hair over her shoulder. His eyes lingering on her neck. He inhaled slightly imagining being able to place a trail of kisses down it. He wanted to hear her inhale sharply as he did it. His mind wandered to what other noise he could have her make. He wanted to make her melt into him.

"Is it bad?" Morgan asked again, getting worried.

Fuck. Yes, it's bad. He thought to himself but not about the wounds. He needed space from her. He cleared his throat again.

"No, actually they look great. You don't need a bandage on them." He said as he stood.

He needed air now, images of things he wanted to do to her kept popping into his head. He needed out. She didn't need any of that after what just happened to her. He walked quickly to the door. She pulled the shirt over her head and stood.

"Wait." She said to him but looked surprised that it came out.

He stopped and turned to her. His look mirror the same surprised look Morgan had on her face.

"I...I...ugh I hate saying this but I don't want to be alone right now." She said quickly.

He paused in the doorway. His mind screaming at him to go. He looked at her and he couldn't do it. He nodded and came back.

"Ok I'll stay till you fall asleep." He said taking a chair and putting it near the bed.

"Is Jason ok with me staying here?" She asked.

"It's my cabin. He's lucky I let him have one." Gavin grumbled.

Morgan curled up into the bed with a smile playing on her lips as she looked up at him. He raised an eyebrow at her expression asking the silent question.

"You sound like a spoiled brat." She said, yawning.

"No love, just truthful." He smirked.

"Whatever you need to tell yourself." She said closing her eyes

Just as he was getting comfortable he heard her.

"Brat." She whispered and then laughed.

"Go to sleep or I'll show you what a brat I can be." He threatened.

She laughed again letting out a tired sigh. Shortly she was out within seconds. Before she was completely out she felt him tuck her in. He muttered something about something being trouble or the death of him. She was too tired to hang on to the words and sleep came to her fast.

Morgan stretched out in the bed. She didn't have one dream last night. It was refreshing. Just darkness and sleep, her mind completely went off. She turned to her side, opening her eyes. She found a pair of big blue ones staring at her. Morgan let out a squeal. Claire began laughing, holding her side.

"That was awesome." Claire said tears were coming to her eyes. She laughed so hard.

"Jerk." Morgan said and playfully pinched her.

Morgan sat up and realized she was back in Gavin's cabin. She looked around confused. How did she get here? She thought about it as she let her feet hit the ground.

"He carried you in.....he was shirtless." Claire said with a giggle.

"Claire!" Morgan warned her.

"What he was." Claire laughed more.

"What time is it?" Morgan ignored her.

"Somewhere between breakfast and lunch." Claire laughed at herself.

"Oh well I guess we've turned into a comedian overnight." Morgan said as she tried not to laugh.

"Did you eat breakfast or lunch?" Morgan asked her and rolled her eyes.

"Yes and some of Jacks too." She smiled brightly.

"That poor boy." Morgan laughed.

"Come on, let's make ourselves useful." Morgan said, walking to the door.

"Hey Morgan, when we find our new home...can we tell Jack where it is?" Claire asked.

Morgan felt her heart squeeze. She could only nod. They had been there only a short time and the thought of leaving them hurt.

"Good because he's a really good friend and person. I am going to miss him." Claire whispered.

Morgan just simply nodded. She was going to miss them too. She squeezed Claire's shoulder lightly before walking out. Claire follows behind her.

The sound of yelling hit Morgan's ears as she stepped out onto the upper deck; Her hand catching Claire and pushing her back into the cabin.

"Wait here. I don't know what's going on." Morgan said to her as she shut the cabin door quickly.

Morgan slowly walked to the rail of the upper deck and peeked down. A large group of men had gathered. All clearly upset. They were shouting and yelling amongst themselves. Her eyes scanned the crowd searching for him. He was standing tall in front of them all. Jason at his back showing support. Gavin's face was not amused and annoyed didn't even begin to describe it. He looked like he was letting a bunch of children have their tantrums.

"Enough!" Jason's voice rang out over the yelling.

The crowd fell silent. Gavin glared at them all. Anger rolling off of him in waves.

"I'm going to need a new crew." He snarled talking to Jason but loud enough so everyone could hear.

Jason withdrew his sword with a nod. The threat hung in the air. Morgan watched in amazement. The man that cradled her last night, the concern and warmth he expressed was gone. He was deadly. He was hollow. His eyes dared someone to step forward.

"Captain, we mean no disrespect." A small voice started.

What had they seen Gavin do before? Morgan thought. A whole crowd and every man afraid of his wrath. He was outnumbered, logic said they could take him. They all either couldn't count or saw him do unexplainable things. His eyes narrowed on the man speaking. His hand on his sword twitching; like he was fighting his body not to use it. It was like his hand had a mind of its own. The sword, it wanted blood.

"Captain, the boys are just upset. Rick is missing and with us almost to Siren Gully; They're thinking it's a bad omen." The man continued speaking, flinching as he did so.

"Ricks dead." Gavin said shortly. He made a disgusted face saying Rick's name.

"What captain? By who? We need justice." The man pleaded.

"I killed him." Gavin said, a sinister grin appeared across his face.

Grumbles broke out amongst them. Rick clearly had some supporters but not many. It appeared that most of them were more superstitious than loyal to Rick.

"He crossed a line....anyone else wants to cross it." Gavin said.

"You don't break the Captain's orders." Jason's voices echoed.

Silence hung as Gavin waited. His eyes searched the crowd. A voice broke the silence.

"I bet it was because of the girl. Rick said he wanted her. That we should all share her. I think he was right. We should. That way we're all even." A tall thin man began with a grin.

His eyes locked onto Gavin's trying to challenge him. Gavin broke out into a chilling laugh. He nodded to the man. As he laughed more. He held out his arm to the man beckoning him over. He began walking towards him. The men around them cleared away from Gavin as quickly as they could. Morgan stood stunned. Share her? She felt like she was going to vomit. Her stomach knotted up inside of her.

"Peter. Right?" Gavin said, slapping him on the shoulder.

"Aye. Captain." Peter said, confused.

"You know I see your point. We split the treasure. We split rations. Space, time, and duties. You know you're right." Gavin said and squeezed his shoulder tightly and started to walk with him.

Peter had a silly grin on his face. Happy that the captain liked his idea. Almost like he was proud of himself.

"Captain!" Jason said almost like he couldn't believe what he was saying.

"Now now Jason. Mr. Pete here has a point. If we all share her. She won't be a distraction." Gavin said. Peter and him now at the rail, their backs against the sea.

Morgan began to panic. He can't be serious! She looked back at the cabin and she needed a weapon. She could lock Claire and her in the cabin, try to kill anyone who got in.

"Gav-" Jason started to say but Gavin threw up his hand.

"Captain." Gavin said, eyeing Jason dangerously.

"Captain, I have to disagree." Jason said through a clenched jaw.

"Fine, we will use your cabin then." Gavin said to Jason.

Gavin turned to face Peter, laughing a cold sounding laugh as he did. He still had his hand on his shoulder. The rest of the crew was quite not sure what was going on.

"Did you want to go first?" Gavin asked him.

"Captain I would-" Peter started to say.

A loud scream finished Pete's sentence. He looked down at his belly and saw Gavin's dagger plunged deep inside of it. Blood color spit dripped out of his mouth as his hand went to touch the blade. Gavin locked eyes with Pete and twisted the blade. Pete let out another yell and Gavin yanked the blade towards his chest. Peter screamed out in agony, his hands tried to stop Gavin but he was overwhelmed by the pain. Gavin spit in his face as he pulled the blade out. Blood poured out of Peter's gaping wound. He began to cough blood out of his mouth. As his hands covered the hole in his stomach. Trying to keep his insides in. With a forceful shove, Gavin sent him over the rail and into the sea. Morgan watched the graphic scene unfold in front of her. She had slammed her own hand over her mouth to keep from yelling. She didn't want anyone to know she saw what happened.

Gavin turned back around to the crowd who was now completely silent. He held his dagger in his hand and pointed at the crowd. Blood dripped from it.

"Anyone else have any suggestions for me?" Gavin said his eyes were terrifying.

"No! Good! Great! Get back to your post and back to work." Gavin growled.

"Oh and if someone so much as breaths on either one of the ladies on board; I will gut them." Gavin said, staring them down.

The crew quickly dispersed. Some even tripped over their feet as they tried to get to their duties as fast as possible. Gavin's eyes wandered over the crowd on the deck as they left shaking his head. Morgan was frozen on the top deck; still shaken slightly over the site. She dropped her hand away from her mouth and let out the breath she was held in. Gavin's eyes flickered up to her at the sound of her exhale. His eyes were so cold, distant, and deadly. He locked eyes with her for just a second and then looked away he muttered something to himself as he walked away.

"And someone clean up this fucking mess!" He yelled while walking by the blood puddle.

Jason's eyes landed where Gavin had been looking and saw Morgan. He gave her a sympathetic look with a nod. Morgan didn't know if she felt better that Gavin was willing to do anything to make her and Claire safe. Or if she should be afraid with the extent he was willing to go to.

She hung there for a second gathering herself. She watched the man scrub the blood from the deck floor.

Morgan. Get yourself together. She yelled silently at herself. She took a deep breath and shook everything off.

She walked over to the cabin door. Opening the door she slammed into Claire. Claire jumped back.

"Everything ok?" Claire asked, looking behind Morgan.

" Everything is fine. There was a disagreement on board. The captain took care of it but I need you to stay close to me. If I'm not around I want you with Jason or Jack." Morgan said being firm about the last part.

Morgan squeezed Claire real tight and they made their way out of Gavin's cabin. The day was absolutely mind-numbing. Morgan kept busy doing mindless tasks. All the while her eyes kept looking for Gavin. He stayed in his cabin most of the day. When he was out and about inspecting things. He didn't even glance her way. At first she felt bad. She felt like she was the cause of most of his troubles. As the day grew she became more and more annoyed with him. Some type of acknowledgement isn't hard to give. He had even walked by her and didn't even look her way. She stared at him, now the annoyance turned to anger. He was at the helm steering. He had been there for a few hours now. Jason had gone to rest. They were switching off. Claire sat next to Jack laughing as they played a game with some marbles. Morgan grumbled to herself debating on heading up there to confront him. She stood and glanced at Claire.

"Claire, I'm going to go talk to the Captain. Stay with Jack." Morgan said walking by her

Claire nodded and kept playing. Morgan made her way across the lower deck. Her hands clenched as she began to chew on her lower lip. She wanted nothing more than to just call him out on it but she didn't know if she could muster the words. She paused at the stairs that lead up to the helm. She was debating if this was even a good idea.

"You're a good actress." A voice said to her from the right.

"Excuse me?" Morgan asked her eyes finding where the voice came from.

A tall man was leaning against the stairs leading up to the helm. His hair was back in a ponytail. She narrowed her eyes at him, studying him. He had slate gray eyes and his skin was tan from years of being at sea. He looked at her like what he just said was a secret.

"You heard me." He smirked his arms folded across his chest.

"I honestly don't know what you're talking about." Morgan said with anger in her voice.

"It's fine, Doll. We all have a part to play." He said indifferently.

Morgan rolled her eyes and went to start walking up the stairs. He was quick as he reached out and grabbed her. He then pulled her back against him and covered her mouth.

"Shhh we are on the same side." He whispered to her.

"What?" She murmured against his hand.

"Look tonight while he's at the helm. I am getting the map. Once we get through Siren's Gully. They'll be waiting on the other side. I need help getting the map. I think if we both work together and you use your charm. We can do it." He said as he loosened his grip.

Morgan spun in his arms. What the hell is he talking about? Who are they? Gavin obviously had more trouble then he knew. She needed to play along. Let's see how great her acting skills are.

She stepped into him, her eyes narrowed.

"Look I don't know who you are or what you think you're doing but I do not need help. And I don't need someone else fucking this up for me." Morgan said through her teeth and jabbed him in the chest with her finger as she talked.

A grin appeared on his face. She didn't even phase him.

"Chris and we can help each other." He said, still grinning.

"Well out with it." She said as he folded her arms across her chest looking irritated.

"It's been a long time since the Captain's been distracted. Travis was right picking you and the poor abused backstory. And the kid! It's genius. Anyways I have some poison. Simple enough we poison him while you distract him. We get the map. Then they're ambushed right on the other side of the exit to Siren gully. Super simple now you're involved." Chris grinned.

Travis! She choked hearing his name. Morgan changed her surprised look quickly to a smirk. Chris didn't notice.

"When?" Morgan asked him quietly.

"Not tonight he's been steering mostly all day. Jason will steer tonight so we could act tonight. However we do need him to get the ship through Sirens gully. As much as I hate it. He is a good navigator and if anyone is getting us through the gully he will. So we should act just before we are to exit. With him out of the way the ambush should go smoothly. " He whispered to her, his eyes dancing.

"Agreed. Where's the poison?" Morgan asked him, glancing about to ensure no one was listening.

"I'm holding on to that Doll. You just keep working your charm on him. I'll connect with you when it's time." Chris said with a nod going his own way.

Chapter Sixteen
Name

Morgan started to walk up the stairs to the top deck. Her hands shook slightly as she tried to control the beating of her heart, which was racing inside her chest. She reached the top stair and looked towards the helm. Morgan realized that in the brief encounter she had with Chris, Gavin and Jason had switched out. She frowned, walking towards Jason with concern in her eyes.

"Where is he?" Morgan asked Jason.

"Something wrong?" Jason asked, searching her eyes.

Morgan looked around quickly seeing Chris off in the distance and she shook her head no.

"I just need to find the captain." She said her eyes began to wander.

"Lass I think right now it would be best to just give him some space. If there's anything you need I can help you with it." Jason said as he gave her a sympathetic look.

"Oh he'll have all the time he needs once I'm off this bloody ship!" She said remembering how angry she was at Gavin; for avoiding her all day.

She turned away from Jason who wasn't sure what to say or how to act. He was taken back by her anger. He watched her stop at the rail and scanned the deck. She found him talking to one of the crew members. By gestures she could tell her going over

something about the ropes and sails. She hurried down
the stairs towards him. He finished up what he was
doing and started walking away. She knew he saw her.
She gritted her teeth together. He was now purposely
walking away from her.

"Captain!" She shouted out at his back.

She could tell by the way his shoulders moved
that he heard her. He chose to ignore her and kept
going. He was now walking up the stairs to the upper
deck where his cabin was. She picked up her pace.

"Captain!" She yelled to his back once more.

She saw his head tilt confirming that he was in
fact hearing her.

"I need to speak with you!" She shouted.

He didn't slow down. He made it to the top deck
and started making his way to his cabin

Real great! I am trying to save your life! She
yelled at him inside her head. He walked into his cabin
without stopping and slammed the door as Morgan
reached it.   The door slammed shut in her face. She felt
her anger double. The rage that rushed through her
caused her blood to boil. She saw red. Before she could
rethink her actions, she kicked the door open and
stepped inside. She was so angry that her body shook.

She found him facing the door as he leaned
against his desk staring at her. Anger was in his eyes
but she wasn't afraid. She slammed the door behind her.
He stood there as if he was waiting on her.

"I've been trying to talk to you!" She yelled at
him.

He folded his arms across his chest. The same look of annoyance he had given to the crew earlier on his face.

She took two steps away from the door. Her chest rising and falling rapidly with anger. She clenched her fist so tightly by her sides.

"Have you gone deaf now?" She yelled at him again.

A smirk rolled across his lips as he studied her. He noticed she was digging her fingernails into the palms of her own hands as she squeezed them harder shut. He had not seen this version of her yet. No one had dared to yell at him like she was right now. Her eyes burned into him. The way she stood there fearlessly as she tried to control herself. The fire in her made him want her even more.

"Trying to put out fires that someone has made recently." He said his expression was not changing.

A look passed over Morgan's face only for a second. Her stomach twisted in on itself. She didn't mean to be the cause of everything right now. Gavin saw the look of hurt and regretted it. Morgan regained herself quickly and was back to being angry in just two seconds.

"Yeah well I've been trying to do the same. I need to talk to you about it. Maybe if you weren't so arrogant and full of yourself. It would take a second to just listen! Maybe you would see that I'm actually trying to help you not have your whole ship fall apart." She said through clenched teeth.

He was up and off the desk in seconds. He closed the distance between them. He was face to face with her his anger matching hers.

" My whole ship's falling apart!" He growled and backed her up against the door.

"Well maybe it's not the ship! Maybe it's the captain." Morgan said as she tried to match how hateful he was being.

"Or maybe you really are a siren!" He said in a chilling voice.

Before she could stop herself, her open hand was flying towards his face. He was too quick and caught her by the wrist. He held onto her wrist and pinned it above her head against the door. Her eyes scanned his. Almost daring him to do something. His face inches from hers.

"You better watch yourself Love." He threatened

She wasn't backing down. She narrowed her eyes at him.

"Or else what." She answered him, her voice dared him to do something.

The fire in her eyes burned into his. He moved closer trying to intimidate her. She pressed back into the door but her eyes ever faltered. They never let go of his stare. His eyes flickered to her lips that twitched inches from his.

"Fuck it." He said out loud to himself.

Morgan looked confused, her eyes narrowed at him but before she could say anything, his free hand went quickly into her hair pulling her face towards his. His mouth crashed down over hers, claiming it. She tried to fight it but couldn't. Her lips gave into him and her mind turned to nothing. She couldn't think. His tongue eagerly explored her mouth. He sent warm chills through her as her body gave into him willingly. Her tongue brushed back against his.

His hand began to travel from her hair, down her body lingering on her hips as he deepened their kiss. He grabbed a hold of her hip and pulled her against him. A small grunt escaped his lips as her pelvis pressed against his. The noise excited her but tore her from the moment. She moved her mouth from his and placed her free hand on his chest. He let her pull back resting his forehead against hers.

"Gavin I-"

"Say my name again." He said his voice was full of need.

"Gavin." She whispered as she felt her heart skip a beat.

He loved the sound of his name as it came from her mouth. He pictured her laying on his bed saying his name over and over again as he made her moa. He needed and wanted her even more.

His mouth captured hers again and her mind melted. He couldn't get enough of her. The small noises of surprise she made each time he went to kiss her. He wanted to hear more of them. He broke the kiss and began making trails of kisses down her neck. She inhaled sharply and let out a small moan. Her whole body was tingling. His hand began to wander again.

Morgan leaned back into the door. Her whole body flushed as an ache began to form in her core. Her body begged to be touched. She felt him begin to undo the buttons of her shirt as he kissed down her neck. Soon her shirt was completely open and his mouth reached her collar bone. A small noise escaped her mouth as Gavin's hand cupped her breast. His thumb running over the nipple. Jolts of pleasure rippled through her. She was lost in a haze of pleasure.

He placed a trail of kisses down between her breasts. She inhaled and before she could process his mouth captured her nipple. She moaned, her fingers curled into his hair. His other hand grasped her belt. He began to tug and loosen it. Her eyes open quickly. The hand she had woven into his hair she used to tug on it as she tried to get him to stop for a second.

"Gavin." She said breathlessly.

He responded by lightly biting her nipple. She let out a small noise of shock. His hands circled up under her ass. As he let go of her breast he buried his face into her neck applying more kisses there. She moaned into him. In one shift movement he scooped her up suddenly; his mouth back on hers. She wrapped her legs around his waist and her arms around his neck.

He made his way towards his bed. He carefully laid her back on the bed and straddled her. He moved from his mouth and kissed her chin, his mouth worked its way down her throat. He made his way down her center passing between her breast and down over her stomach. Each spot his mouth touched sent cold shivers through her. Her body arched into his mouth as it traveled down, begging for him to continue. He stopped at her belt. His mouth hovering above her pants line as he finished undoing it. She sat up quickly, nearly pushing him away.

"Gavin I....I...I've never-" She started to say but couldn't find the words.

Gavin froze. She's a virgin. The thought didn't cross his mind. It excited him that she had never been touched before but at the same time he didn't want that responsibility. He buried his face into her bare stomach and groaned.

He pulled back sitting on his knees in front of her. He shut his eyes for a second trying to calm himself down. He took several deep breaths in.

Morgan studied him for a second weighing her options quickly. She decided that she wouldn't regret this even if it did happen. She sat up on her knees and gathered strength. He still had his eyes closed. She leaned forward, her fingers curling into his hair and pulled his face towards her. She claimed his mouth this time. He was taken back by the action. As she deepened the kiss he let out a small groan as he took over. He wrapped his arm around her and pulled her into him. He leaned her back into the bed. Straddling her, as

he kissed her. His hand wandered down to her pants. Undoing the button he slipped his hand inside. She froze a little, her breath caught in her throat as she waited for his next move. Her body hyper fixated on each small touch of his hand. The slight stroke of his finger tips sent her body into a frenzy. Gavin paused hesitant at first but seeing her reaction he ventured further.

His hand moved to her center finding her crease. She was already so wet.

His fingers found her bud and he made small circles with his fingers tips. Soft and slow at first but then he quickened his pace. Her body arched into him moving with his hand, her legs went weak and as he begged her to come undone. She pressed her pelvis towards his hand not wanting him to stop. A small moan escaped her mouth against his lips. He bit her lip and pulled it into his mouth.

His fingers traveled from her bud and found her opening. He inserted a finger into her slit slowly. She inhaled sharply as she went still. The feeling was shocking but fulfilling. He began to move his finger in and out allowing her to get used to the feeling. She moaned loudly, arching against his hand. Her body overcomed with the sensation she moved against his hand. When he thought he had given her enough time he added another finger. She let out a soft whimper. Her head tilted away from him. He moved his mouth to her neck kissing and biting the skin softly. His other hand found her breast and grabbed it firmly. His

fingers quickened the pace and her hips were now moving with him. Her whole body was arching. She had never felt like this before but she wanted more.

He studied her face quickly. She was lost in the moment. He smiled to himself quickly getting up. Morgan heard him stand. Confused, she looked for him. He was undoing his pants. He kicked them off to the side. Her eyes widened at the sight of him as he started towards her. She tried to look away from his member. She felt her cheeks burning but before she knew it he was over her. He grasped the sides of her pants and quickly pulled them off of her. He seemed to hesitate trying to judge her response. She saw his hesitation and needed him to know she wanted this. She met him halfway pulling him in for a kiss.

That was all he needed. He smashed his lips into hers as his hand went back to torturing her bud. She moaned against his lips, her hips raising eagerly to meet his hand. He positioned himself near her entrance. He slowly began to push himself inside her. She let out a small noise and he waited, allowing her to get used to him. He stroked her bundle trying to get her mind off the pain. When he felt her relax; He pushed himself full inside her. He still continued to rub her with his finger. Seconds passed and she was back to being in pleasure. Her body ached for him as he filled her. She craved the feeling as a rush of tingles spread through her. He slowly began to move. A groan escaped him at how tight she felt around him. Her body was formed to him. Her hips and body started to move with him as he began to thrust faster.

She clung to him as warmth began to spread over her body. Pressure built up in her core. All of her muscles began to contract. Her toes curled as she felt a release coming. She closed her eyes, throwing her head back into the mattress. Her body arching into him. He felt her organ pulse around him, tightening as he felt her build up. He couldn't take any more. Gavin groaned deeply as he released at the same time as her. Gavin braced himself on his elbows on either side of her. Her eyes still closed a small smile on her lips. He smiled at her expression and leaned up kissing her forehead softly. He rolled to the side of her propping himself up on his elbow looking at her. He ran his finger down the bridge of her nose and over her lips. Her smile grew slightly at the feeling of his touch. He stole another kiss from her lips. Her hand went to the side of his face. He kissed her once more before getting up.

She sat up quickly like the realization of everything and what just happened hit her. She could feel her face was on fire. She began buttoning her shirt quickly. She kept her gaze down as she felt him approaching her. She refused to look at him as she finished the last button. He held her pants out to her, she blindly went to reach for them.

He frowned watching her. Did she regret it? His stomach knotted up on him. God he wasn't good at this stuff. He thought, holding her pants out to her.

"Love." He said softly.

She looked up at him with her big green eyes. A mix of emotions in them. She took her pants from him and began putting them on. She stood up pulling them up.

"Are you ok?" He asked her, he really didn't want to. He didn't want to know if she wasn't.

She nodded, fixing her belt. He gritted his teeth. Stepping towards her.

"It's fine. I'm ok, you can go." She said getting a little flustered.

She didn't know what she expected but she was starting to feel hurt. If he just gets up and leaves she might as well just be a play thing....is that what she is. Shut up, she told herself. His hand caught her face. She refused to look up.

"Morgan." He whispered.

Her eyes shot up to his. He said her name. She was beginning to wonder if he even knew it. Her stomach fluttered with excitement at the thought.

"Are you-" He started to ask her again.

"Say my name again." She said with a smile on her face that border mischievousness as she quoted him from before.

He smirked. His hand went to her waist. His lips lingered just out of reach of hers.

"Morgan." He whispered.

She stepped into him, her pelvis brushing his.

"Don't tempt me, or I'll never let you leave this room." He growled his grip on her hip becoming firmer.

"I don't know if I want you to let me." She whispered as she leaned into him.

He pulled her against him letting her slip back into his lap as his arms went around her. She let out a small noise of want mixed with contentment as she wrapped her arms around his neck. A loud banging on the door made Morgan jump and go to step away from Gavin. He held her there.

"Captain!!" A voice called.

"Can you swim?!" Gavin yelled.

"Gavin." Morgan scolded him.

He smirked his mouth moving towards her as he went in for the kiss. He could just stay here all day with her. Kiss those lips and touch her soft curves.

"Um yes but Captain. Jason is calling for you, we have trouble up ahead." The voice said in a hurry.

He stopped. Jason would only call for him if there was actual trouble. He kissed Morgan's forehead.

"If this is something you guys could handle. I'll kill you both " He grumbled, grabbing Morgan's hand and bringing her with him.

She smiled at the small gesture. He wasn't leaving her.

Chapter Seventeen
Siren's Gully

Morgan dropped Gavin's hand as they stepped out of the cabin. Gavin didn't notice Morgan dropping her hand away, his eyes fixated on the scene before him. Two big cliffs that border a water passage stood in front of them. He looked down the path and the sky was light and seemed to sparkle as if inviting them in. The setting sun gave the entrance a golden hue. Gavin frowned. He left Morgan side and headed as quickly as he could down the stairs and across the low deck. She hesitated, staring at the sky once more before following him. She reached the helm just in time to hear Jason and Gavin talking.

"You said there was an emergency!" Gavin said, narrowing his eyes at Jason.

"Captain, you don't think that the entrance being so happy looking is dangerous?" Jason whispered to him.

"Seriously, when did you become superstitious on me." Gavin said, running a hand through his hair.

"Captain, I have a bad feeling is all." Jason said softly.

Originally Gavin was going to avoid Siren's Gully but as time got away from them he could no longer risk losing Travis. You could see Gavin debating with himself. He let out a grumble before speaking to Jason.

179

"Move! Go take your bad feeling and put it to bed. I'll steer from here on out." He said as he basically shoved Jason from the wheel.

Jason threw his hands up frustrated and walked off to his cabin. Morgan frowned watching the scene unfold. She made a face at Gavin

"Don't" He warned her and looked forward to the horizon.

She rolled her eyes at him and walked away, she heard him mutter a "great". She made her way down the steps, her eyes searching for the little blonde bundle of light. She spotted, her a smile forming on her lips as she made her way towards her. A hand grasped her elbow and pulled her out of sight.

"Did you get the map?" The voice said letting her elbow go.

Morgan had completely forgotten about Chris and what she needed to tell Gavin. Her eyes flickered up to the helm.

"Not yet. He was studying it. I couldn't get close enough to it." She whispered.

"Well we could go with plan b and poison him. Then get the map. " Chris said, shrugging.

"Well, do you have the poison?" Morgan asked frustrated.

"Not on me but I have it." Chris said.

"Well go get it so I can get on with it." She said to him, rolling her eyes.

"You want to do it?" Chris asked, surprised.

"Well I think my charm can get me a lot closer to him then you. It would seem weird you offering him a drink versus me doing it. I'm assuming your poison is powder and has to be drunk." She said annoyed.

"Yes it is. Ok. I'll connect with you later and give it to you. I'm just surprised a woman wants to kill." He shrugged again.

"You have no idea what "women" can do." She said shooing him off with her hand.

He shrugged and headed off. She groaned to herself. She was debating to herself if she should tell Gavin. Should she wait till she had the poison? It would be safer to have the poison so Chris couldn't use it. If she told him beforehand would he believe her without proof? After debating with herself she decided to wait till she had the poison in hand.

"Morgan." Claire said as she spotted her and waved.

Morgan crossed the deck to her. Reaching her she scooped her into a hug.

"What have you been doing, crazy girl?" Morgan asked Claire.

"This and that." She said with a grin.

"Oh really." Morgan laughed.

Morgan stopped laughing as her attention was caught by large stone cliffs the ship was passing. The ship fell silent. Everyone seems to stop and watch the ship pass through the entrance of Siren's Gully. It was like all of the crew was holding their breath waiting for something to happen. Some made the sign of the cross. Others looked like they were praying.

"So it begins. God have mercy on us." Morgan heard a crew member to her right mumble.

"What's going on?" Clairs whispered to her.

"Back to work!" Gavin's voice rang out before Morgan could answer Claire.

The crew jumped back to life and began continuing their duties. Claire grabbed Morgan's hand and began pulling her. Morgan raised an eyebrow at her and began to follow her. Claire leads her to a bucket of water and a mop. Claire grabbed the mop and handed it to Morgan.

"Your turn," She giggled.

"Alright." She laughed while taking the mop.

Gavin watched the crew freeze as they passed the entrance of Siren's Gully. His stomach knotted as well. He grumbled to himself letting his crew's fears reach him. His grip tightened on the wheel as he guided the ship. Once they had safely made it inside the entrance; Gavin looked out over his crew. He narrowed his eyes on them.

"Back to work!" He shouted.

He watched them quickly dismiss their fears and hurry back to their duties. Her red hair caught his eyes. He watched her begin mopping the deck. She wasn't afraid to do anything. He had heard about her cleaning and prepping the cannons. She had helped adjust the sails and tie knotts. If there was something being done around her, she would help. A smile formed on his face thinking about her. She had made a soft spot on most of the crew. Besides the superstition of women being bad

luck at sea, they all liked her. Christina only complained while she was at sea. She hated it and spent most of her time in his cabin bored. She was the reason he left the life. He frowned realizing he was comparing the two. He shook his head trying to clear his thoughts. He put his eyes back on the horizon and began studying the landscape. The passage was narrow and rigid. If you weren't careful you could definitely scrape your ship against the sides. He could tell ahead it would rapidly get wider just as the sun should set. It made him feel a little better since it would be dark.

Nightfall came quicker than he expected. He must have zoned out. He felt a hand grab his shoulder as he blinked back into reality. Jason had come to take over. He glanced down to the deck. It was nearly empty, just whoever was necessary was out.

"You ok Captain?" Jason asked with a yawn.

"Aye." He said moving aside for Jason to take over.

"Lost track of time. We should be out of the passage by tomorrow right at sunset." Gavin continued talking.

"Ok see you in the morning." Jason nodded.

Gavin nodded and headed toward the stairs. Reaching the stairs a strange noise caught his ear. A humming. He glanced back at Jason and his face confirmed that he heard it too. Gavin walked back to Jason. His eyes scan the cliff sides. A wind began to pick up. The ship rocking in the breeze. The wind was becoming stronger by the second. It started pulling the ship towards the cliff sides.

"Sails up!" Gavin yelled out to the few men below on deck.

Jason tightens his grip on the wheel trying to make the ships stay its course. Gavin rushed down the stairs to help the men. They weren't moving faster enough. Two men worked on one set of sails while Gavin started on the other.

"Faster!" He yelled to them as he began pulling on his ropes.

The ship was being pulled closer and closer to the cliff side. The ship leaned into the wind almost tilting. Morgan heard the commotion and rushed out of the cabin. Claire followed behind her. She hit the upper deck stumbling. She quickly saw what was happening.

"Claire, stay!" She yelled to her as she headed to help Gavin.

He was working on the second sail of his post but was struggling with the wind pull. Morgan reached his side. Quickly she began helping him pull. She saw Jack rushing to help with the last remaining sail on the other post. She grasps the rope with Gavin helping him pull the sail up.

"We've got it where it needs to be now but I got to tie it. Can you hold it in place?" He yelled asking her.

She nodded. He slowly let go to see if she could handle the weight of it. She felt the rope cut through the palms on her hands as she held on. She gritted her teeth as her flesh began to rip. She glanced back and he was almost done. She focused her eyes on the side of the cliff that was finally not coming at them. She heard

Gavin exhaled and tapped her on the shoulder. She let go. A small cheer from the men out on the deck was shouted as the ship stopped being dragged.

Morgan glanced down at her bloody palm. She was glad that was over. Gavin raised an eyebrow at her. She closed her hand and shook her head.

"Just let me see." He said as he rolled his eyes.

"It's fine I can tend to it myself." Morgan said to him.

"Damn it. Morgan just let me see it." He said as he became annoyed with her.

"Gavin." Morgan began to say but he didn't listen.

He grabbed ahold of her hand and began looking at it. Morgan tried to get his attention. Her eyes fixated on the sky behind him. It was slowly turning green. The wind was settling down and everything was going still

"Gavin." She said, trying to take back her hand.

"Quit moving." He grumbled.

With her free hand she grabbed his face and yanked it in the direction of the sky. He let go of her hand looking up. This was not good. The world around them was dark but now everything had a green hue to it. It was otherworldly. The silence was eerie. Before they could even move the sea around them began to turn rough. Waves were crashing into the ship rocking it back and forth. Morgan crashed into Gavin as the ship rocked. He steadied her and glanced up to Jason, his expression matched his. This was not good. A loud crack happened and lightning crashed from the sky.

He struck the cliff to the right of the ship and made small boulders tumble into the sea. Waves reached up like arms began to crash onto the deck.

Morgan glanced up at Claire. She let go of Gavin and rushed up the stairs to her. The sky opened up and began to downpour. The ship was under attack and the ocean wanted to claim it. As water began to flood the ship. Morgan reached Claire. Without saying anything she shoved Claire inside Gavin's cabin.

Claire stumbled backwards and a yelp of protest came from her mouth as Morgan slammed the door shut. Morgan staggered to the rail blinded by the rain. Gavin had reached Jason and rang the bell for the crew to get to their post. The waves were so strong he was now helping Jason steer. Lightning struck again, lighting up the lower deck. She saw the crew struggling. She began trying to make her way down the stairs to help. Reaching the bottom, lightning hit the cliff. It was playing target practice with the ship. A small boulder was chiseled for the cliff side and headed for the deck. Seeing a man standing where it was about to hit, Morgan rushed to him and shoved him out of the way. They both fell inches away from the spot. The boulder hit the deck making a large indentation as it slid to the other side towards another group of men.

"Move!! Morgan screamed at them.

They dove out of the way just in time. The boulder slammed into the rail and broke it as the boulder crashed back into the sea. Jack waved his thanks to her as he glanced at the hole in the railing. She nodded to him.

A giant wave came up over the side of the ship. It reached out and grabbed hold of Jack. It pulled him over board. The men around where he was panicked. Gavin was trying to rush down the stairs but the waves crashing kept throwing him back. Morgan quickly reacted. She grabbed a long rope and tied it around her waist. She rushed across the lower deck. Gavin met her at the rail. She didn't say anything but shoved the rope into his arms. Before Gavin could stop her she jumped overboard after Jack.

Gavin's stomach sunk as he saw her dive in. He quickly looped the rope around a nearby post and anchored himself. His eyes on the ocean as he held onto the rope with everything he had.

Morgan hit the water and her skin stung. She tried to see over the crashing waves. The ocean fought hard with her, trying to make her go under. Each wave became taller and taller around her.

"Jack!" She shouted over the waves.

A wave hit her, knocking her under. Below the surface the ocean was calm. She popped up again. Getting her breath.

"Jack!" She yelled again.

"Morgan." She heard a muffled cry.

She spotted him off behind the ship. Waves dunking him repeatedly. It was like they were trying to drown him. One after another crashed over him. Pulling him under each time. Morgan began to swim towards him struggling against the pull of the ocean. It seemed to push her away from him each time she tried to swim towards him. She took a deep breath in and ducked under the water. She began swimming towards him. She could easily navigate the water from under it. She could see his legs now. She broke the surface again, taking another deep breath and going under again. He was just out of reach. She could see his legs growing tired as he struggled to tread the water. She broke the surface again; he was just out of arm's reach. The rope was at its end

"Jack swim to me!" She yelled at him.

"Morgan I can't" He yelled, taking in more water.

"Jack duck under and swim! The waves can't hit you if you do! Jack you have too!!" She yelled trying to move closer to him.

"Jack! Come on!" She yelled at him holding her hand out.

He nodded and took a deep breath and ducked under. Morgan ducked under trying to see where he was. She began to panic not seeing him. Where could he have gone? She came back to the surface trying to see him.

"Jack!" She shouted looking around.

She felt something tugging and pulling her leg. She struggled against it and then was pulled under. Once under she looked down through the salt water. Her eyes stung from the salt water but she needed to see what had touched her leg. She was shocked to see Jack. She quickly reached down and grabbed his arm pulling him with her towards the surface. He could barely hold himself up anymore. Morgan wrapped her arm around him tightly and with the other tugged several times hard on the rope. She felt the rope tighten as they began to be pulled backwards towards the ship.

Gavin held on to the rope with everything he had. His stomach twisted. He needed her to make it. He needed Jack to make it. He should have been the one to jump in. What the hell was she thinking? He held the rope, allowing her to swim out.

"I need eyes on!" He yelled several men stepped up to help.

"I see her! I think she's got this captain!" Walter shouted.

Others came to help him hold the rope. Gavin wasn't moving or letting go.

"She sees him! Give her more rope Captain!" Walter yelled, wiping water out of his face from the crashing waves as they splashed on the ship side.

Gavin cringed. The more rope he gave her the harder it would be to save her.

"Captain, I see him! She can get to him! Give her more rope!" He yelled again.

He gave in and allowed all the rope he could
give her. He looked over to Walter waiting for an update.

"Well!?" Gavin shouted to him.

"I dont know! I don't see them!" Walter shouted
to Gavin as he grabbed a hold of the rail trying to lean
over to see.

His heart sank. "Come on Morgan."

After several long seconds he felt the rope
tugged hard three times.

"Pull!!" He yelled, yanking the rope with all his
strength.

The men with him put all their strength into it as
well. They pulled for what seemed forever. Finally they
saw an arm. Jack reached out and grabbed a hold of the
railing. Gavin rushed to help him up. The men holding
the rope stayed put as they were holding Morgan up.

"I'm so sorry." Jack said to Gavin as Walter came
to help steady him.

"Jackie, thank God you're alive." He said, patting
his head as he passed him off to Walter.

He leaned over, grabbed the rail and held his
hand out to Morgan. She was completely drenched. She
smiled seeing him. His heart unstrangled itself. She
grabbed ahold of his hand and began to pull herself up.

"Are you crazy!" He yelled at her.

"A Little." She laughed reaching the deck.

"I could kill you. You scared me." He whispered
to her, lifting her up.

"I'm a good swimmer." She laughed holding on to
his arms steadying herself.

He grabbed a hold of her for a second not wanting to ever let her go. The men let go of the rope and went back to their stations. The waves were dying down and even the rain was letting up. He kissed the top of her forehead.

"Don't ever do that again, Love." He whispered, stepping away from her.

"Oh yeah because I just wanted to do that." She laughed rolling her eyes.

"Jack." Morgan said, looking for him.

She watched Gavin walk over and grab him. He squeezed him tightly. She heard him call him Jackie and ruffle his hair. Jack was like the son he never had. You could tell by the moment they were sharing. Morgan glanced up to the helm Jason was steering easier. It was still rocky but not like before. Jason nodded his thanks to her. She nodded back.

She went to step away from the rail when a loud crashing noise came from behind her. A wave crashed into the ship. It came up over the rail and engulfed Morgan. It flung her back. She cracked her head hard on the rail as the wave sucked her back into the ocean. The last thing she heard was the snapping of the rope that was holding her.

Chapter Eighteen
Betrayal

Darkness consumed her as she drifted through it. It wasn't darkness like when she was running through the woods trying to escape. It was emptiness, no noise; no sense of overwhelming fear. Just nothing. The nothing of it all was peaceful. She felt like a giant weight was taken off her and she could breathe. She gave into it and enjoyed it.

"Morgan!!" Her name was shouted into the darkness.

She heard it as a distant echo. She opened her eyes staring into the darkness. Did she hear something? Did she forget something? She frowned as she tried to remember.

"Morgan!!"

She jolted. There it was again. Her name. It was distant and faded but she heard it. Who needs her? Who was she forgetting? They needed her.

"Damn it Morgan come on!" He shouted his voice mixed with concern and anger.

"Morgan!! Please!!" A small cry came from a girl's small voice.

"Come back to me." He demanded, his voice broke as he said his plea.

Her frown deepened, the voice was scared and upset. Something was wrong. The first voice she knew. He was always grumpy. She smiled. She enjoyed making him grumble but he was mad. What did she do? The second voice was a girls. Why was she crying? It hurt Morgan's heart. She wasn't supposed to be crying. She needed to stop whatever it was that made her cry. The last was the man again begging her. Why are they sad? She needed to leave.

"I'm coming. Where are you?" She yelled into the darkness.

She was confused. Who are they? The tugging on her heart told her she knew them. She felt pressure in her chest. Like someone was pounding on it.

"Claire! Gavin!" She yelled as her memories all hit her.

She felt a deep pressure in her chest as she began to fight against the darkness. Where was she? She needed to find them.

"Gavin!!" She yelled to the emptiness.

"Claire!"

A strange sensation began to happen, she felt like was being pulled forward by a strong force. She at first fought against but then gave in and let it take her.

She felt her chest crack as she tried to breathe. Her body forced water out of her mouth as she began to violently cough. She tried to sit up to get air.

"Morgan." Gavin whispered in relief.

Her eyes locked with his brown ones, filled with relief. His dark brown hair was soaked as the curls sprawled across his brow and dripped down on his cheeks. He steadied her as another violet coughed forced more water from her lungs. Her chest hurt and felt like it was broken. Sharp pains made it hard to breathe. She winced as she tried to take in her surroundings. The sky was calm. The wind and the storm was over with, it was as if it never happened. She glanced around her eyes and finally focused on Gavin.

"Hi." She forced the words out of her mouth and gave him a small smile.

His hand went to her cheek and he pulled her forehead to his lips. She leaned into the kiss. She could feel the stress leave him as his lips pressed into her forehead. She wanted to wrap her arms around him and just stay like that forever. A small noise broke her concentration. She pulled back and saw Claire. Jack had her wrapped up in her arms, trying to calm and comfort her. Her eyes were red and swollen; tears slipping down her cheeks. Morgan held out her arms to Claire. Morgan's chest throbbed with pain as Claire bolted to her. She ignored it and wrapped her arms tighter around Claire. Claire broke down sobbing as she clung to Morgan.

"You were gone." Claire cried into her shoulder.

Gone? Her mind tried to understand the word. Dead…did she die? Morgan glanced at Gavin quickly and his face confirmed it. She squeezed Claire tighter.

"Hey it's ok. I'm here now." Morgan whispered to Claire; her voice horse from choking and coughing.

Claire continued to cry. Morgan took her off her shoulder and cupped Claire's face in her hands.

"Hey. I'm here. I'm never leaving you. It's ok. Stop crying." Morgan said softly to her and wiped her tears away.

Claire sniffled and nodded as she slowed down and eventually stopped crying. Morgan smiled at her and bopped her on the nose. Claire straightened up and nodded to Morgan as if to say she was better. Before Morgan could process anything else Jack was by her side. He wrapped his arms around her and squeezed her too. She winced again.

"I owe you my life." He hugged her tightly.

"You're welcome." Morgan said and returned the hug.

Jack squeezed her tighter, his body shivered slightly from the emotion that ran through him. He was so scared that they almost lost her. He felt guilt that she almost died because of him. He let out a small sigh.

"Jack its ok. That was not your fault." Morgan whispered to him.

He pulled back and looked at her, the guilt on his face. She shook her head no at him. She bopped him on the nose just like she had done Claire. He cracked a small smile and moved away. Jack wrapped his arm around Claire as they both looked at Morgan.

A cold chill ran through Morgan as she realized how wet she was. The wind made her feel like it was freezing. She was so cold.Morgan went to stand her body ached from fighting the ocean. She felt so bruised and tired. She stood slowly but then felt her legs going weak. She tried to steady herself but as she stood she faltered slightly. Gavin's arm was around her to steady her. Although he was dripping wet. His body rated heat. She leaned into him enjoying being close to him. Without saying anything he pulled her into his arms and scooped her legs off the ground.

"Gavin, I can walk." She whispered to him.

He smirked and didn't move to let her down. He ignored the comment and began to carry her to his cabin. She didn't have the strength to fight him, instead she embraced it and nestled into his chest. He carried her inside the cabin placing her gently down.

"Are you ok?" He whispered his eyes ran over her.

He didn't visibly see anything but then he remembered her head hitting the rail before she plunged into the cold water. His hand began searching her hair for a wound.

"Gavin, I'm fine. My chest hurts really bad but otherwise I'm fine." She said as she grabbed his hands to stop him.

"Yeah that's my fault. I'll need to see if I broke any ribs." He said with a small smile.

"What?" She asked, confused.

"It was something I learned from an old sea captain. One day Travis and I were playing too close to the docks. Travis couldn't swim well and fell in. I was able to get him out but he wasn't breathing. This man came over and moved me out of the way. He began pressing on Travis's chest. After so many times of him pressing on his chest. He would breathe into his mouth and then went back to pressing on his chest. After Travis coughed up a bunch of water and came too. It stuck with me. I had him explain it to me after Travis was ok. Should have left him in the water." Gavin explained his expression turning sour at the mention of Travis's name.

She nodded as she now understood why everything hurt so bad. She shivered again, her body still frozen. Gavin grabbed his coat from his chair and wrapped it around her. He rubbed her arms softly to create warmth. He needed to get her out of the wet clothing, she was not going to stay warm that way.

He headed over to his clothes. He grabbed two shirts and two pants. He walked over to her and held a set out to her. She smiled softly and took them. She then looked at him waiting. She expected him to leave or turn around but instead he pulled his shirt up over his head dropping it to the ground. It landed with a loud noise.

Morgan felt her face flush as her eyes wander from his broad shoulders, down his chest, and over his abs. Her eyes lingered at his waist. The v-shape crease peek out from his pants. His pants soaking wet were glued on to him, hugging every inch of him. He cleared his throat drawing her eyes back to his face. A smirk played across his lips and his eyes danced with mischief. He was fully enjoying catching her check him out.

"Do you need help?" His smirk turned into a grin as he asked, with a step towards her.

"I uh...maybe." She answered with a small laugh.

He stepped towards her; his hands going to the bottom of her wet shirt and carefully pulled it above her head. He let it drop to the floor behind her. She instantly got goosebumps. His hand went to her cheek as his thumb rubbed up and down it. She leaned into him and shut her eyes. She enjoyed the feeling of his hand on her skin. His thumb ran over her lips as his other hand wrapped around her waist and pulled her into him. Her bare breast pressed against his chiseled chest. Shivers went through her body as they touched. His head dipped and met her mouth. His hand moved into her hair and held her close. She met his lips with eagerness as an ache began to form in her core. She placed her hand on his waist and steadied herself as his tongue entered her mouth. She leaned back into his desk. Her hand slowly moved across his pants becoming bolder as she reached his button. She ran her finger over it while debating. She quickly decided as she looped her finger around it, undoing it.

He groaned against her mouth as he felt them come loose. He buried his face into her neck placing kisses there. His hand slipped to her belt undoing it rapidly. The only thing that held her pants up was the belt due to their size. They fell down immediately. A small noise escaped her lips as she felt him press against her. He bit lightly at her neck. Her small noises excited him more.

His hand reached around her back, going to push everything off the desk. His hand swiped at it. Random things fell off... Was something missing? He thought. Morgan grew bold and moved against him. He groaned slightly As he felt herself pressed against his rod. His hands went to her waist about to lift her onto the desk. He glanced at the desk and froze as he looked at it.

"Gavin?" Morgan asked breathy.

He pulled away from her slowly. His heart pounding in his chest.

"My map." He said his voice just barely above a whisper.

Morgan turned around and looked at the desk. The word Chris shouted in her mind. Gavin almost tripped on his pants. They were around his ankles as he tried to rush to the other side of the desk. He kicked them off and continued completely naked. Morgan grabbed the dry shirt and pulled it over her head before following Gavin.

"Gavin." Morgan said, trying to get his attention.

He didn't hear her. His map was gone. He made his way back around to the front of the desk, continuing to panic. His foot kicked Morgan's pants. As he did, a small blue glass vial rolled out from them. It caught his eye. He bent forward picking it up. He squinted at it as he held it up. There was some type of powder inside of it. He went to open it.

"Gavin no!." Morgan yelled, reaching out to stop him.

"What?" He said going to ignore her.

"Stop it's poison!" She yelled, grabbing his wrist.

He paused and his face masked the emotions he was feeling as he looked at her.

"Why do you have poison?" He asked with a hint of anger in his voice.

"Gavin, I've been trying to tell you. It's what I needed to tell you. I've been trying to tell you since the day we um. Well you know." She whispered.

"Morgan. Why do you have poison?" He said his tone sounded deadly as he stepped forward to her.

She stepped back just by habit. Her foot catching her pants. She fell and landed backwards on the floor. Her elbow hit the deck and the floor board gave away. A small compartment was relieved. Someone had pulled up one of the boards up to make it. Gavin glanced at her and knelt by the floor board. Morgan's stomach sank; she knew what was in there. This was clearly a set up. Her mind cursed Chris

"Gavin I know how this looks but let me explain." She blurted out quickly.

He reached in and pulled out the map. He clenched it in his hand. His body shook slightly like he was trying to hold anger in.

"Gavin, it's Chris. He stopped me the other day and told me this plan to poison you and get the map. He's involved with Travis. I kept trying to find a way to tell you but things kept happening" She said, rushing it out as quickly as possible.

"Chris." Gavin said, looking at her.

"Chris was going to poison me and take the map." He repeated what she said.

She nodded. He stood quickly. She couldn't read his face or body language. He quickly put his clothes on. He then headed to the door. He opened it and shouted for Jason.

"Gavin?" Morgan asked.

She saw his shoulder flinch as she said his name.

"Dont." He said not turning around to look at her.

"I would get those pants on if I was you." He said his voice could cut the air around them.

"Gavin I-

"Do you think I am a fool? God I am a fucking fool! Who has the poison Morgan! Who has complete access to this room! Chris?! Chris has been on this ship since before Christina. He's been in here only a handful of times. Chris! You have the poison! You sleep in here!!" He bellowed at her

"Gavin I would never. I swear he's setting me up." She pleaded to him coming towards him.

He held his hand up to her telling her not to come any closer.

"Pants." He said through gritted teeth.

Morgan slipped the pants on quickly just as Jason entered the cabin. He was confused at all the anger he could feel.

"Jason escort Morgan to your cabin. Lock her in. No one is allowed to visit or see her. Except Claire." He orders Jason.

"Gavin no." Morgan said, going to him and grabbing his hand.

He ripped his hand away from her with force.

"A few more hours and you'll be at your dock. Be lucky I don't give you back to the sea." He said his words ripping through her.

She couldn't say anything. She stood there staring at him in disbelief.

"Empty this into the sea; be careful it's poison." He told Jason giving him the poison as he walked by him.

Jason looked at the vial and then to Morgan. Tears swelled in her eyes. He motioned for her to follow him. As they walked out of the cabin Gavin slammed the door behind; breaking Morgan's heart as he did.

Chapter Nineteen
Liar

Morgan stood outside the cabin on the upper deck. This can't be happening, she thought. How could he not believe her? What would she have to gain? She was hurt and angry and then even more angry because she was hurt. She glanced back at the cabin door wanting to go back in. Wanting to talk to him. Wanting to make him understand. She began to turn back to the door but felt Jason's hand on her arm stopping her.

"I'm sorry lass. Orders are orders." Jason said with remorse in his voice.

"Jason I didn't-" Morgan went to explain but Jason pulled his mouth into a thin smile and shook his head.

It didn't matter what she said. She felt herself begin to tremble. She exhaled the breath she was holding in and started to stairs. With Jason close behind her she started down them into the lower deck. She was lost in her own thoughts of what she could do or say to make him believe her. She mindlessly walked across the lower deck feeling like a prisoner as Jason walked behind her.

Halfway across the deck she glanced up and that was when she saw his smug face. Uncontrollable rage boiled through her as she locked eyes with him. Chris inches away from her. His arms folded across his chest and a smile planted on his lips. He looked impressed with himself and then he winked at her

That was all it took. Morgan lost it. Before she could even think she crossed the distance between them. Her hands in fist by her side as she stopped in front of him. If it was possible her eyes would have burned holes right through him.

"Whoa easy doll." Chris said, putting up his hands in front of her; the smug look never leaving his face.

Morgan didn't even give him a second. She stomped her foot down on his. He let out a small yell. A look of shock on his face as he leaned forward. With one quick motion Morgan slammed her elbow into his nose. A loud crack was heard as blood gushed out of him. He grabbed his nose holding it.

"You broke my nose you crazy bitch!" He yelled at her, his hands covered in his own blood.

"You tell him! You did this!" Morgan said, cranked her arm back to throw another punch at him.

She went to throw everything she had in her into the punch to his face but her hand was caught in mid air. She growled, turning around to see who had her.

"Enough!" Gavin's voice echoed through the ship.

All the commotion in the ship stopped. If the crew wasn't already watching from Chris's screams; they were now. Gavin's normal speaking voice demanded attention, never mind when he was yelling. The same voice that even when yelling caused her heart to race and sent shivers running through her. She struggled to pull her arm from his grip. He tighten his grip glaring at her.

"Let go of me." She said turning to face him, her glare matching his own.

He ignored her and began pulling her towards the stairs. She struggled against him. He started walking her up the stairs with him. A thought crossed her mind. She could easily hit him in the back of his legs as he was taking a step. He would fall forward or down and she could escape. She smirked thinking of how he wouldn't even see it coming. He glanced back at her, catching the smirk. He stopped.

"Seriously you're smirking. What? What is it?" He said, turning as he yelled at her frustrated.

"Oh nothing, just thinking that if I wanted to I could take you out on these stairs and get away." She said, taking a step towards him.

The smirk on her lips was deadly and the glare in her eyes confirmed it. He looked at her. Did she always have a plan to attack or run? He was angry. He threw her arm back at her.

"I guess taking me out was the plan all along. Get to Jason's cabin without another incident or I won't regret taking you out. You're only still breathing because you saved Jack." He said only loud enough for her to hear it.

His words stung. How can he really think that? Did everything between them mean nothing? She was fighting back tears of frustration. He shoved past her on the stairs. Her hand caught his wrist.

"Gavin I swear I would never." She said her voice was shaking.

He paused and took a deep breath. She studied his back looking for anything saying he might believe her. His shoulders faltered slightly but then were replaced with tension. He took a step. His wrist slipped out of her grasp and he continued. Morgan stood there feeling broken.

"Chris, clean up your blood." He shouted as he walked across the lower deck.

Jason made his way up the stairs to her. He nudged her softly to get her to start walking and headed towards his cabin. Morgan defeatedly walked behind him. She bleeped everything out. The only noise she could hear was her feet hitting each step. The sound was long and drawn out. As if the step was provoking her. As she reached the top stair little arms hugged her torso. It snapped Morgan out of her trance. She looked down at Claire and smiled.

"Hey Claire Bear." Morgan whispered, scooping her up.

Claire squeezed her back knowing she needed a hug.

"What happened Morgan?" She whispered to her.

"Nothing. I'm going to go take a break in Jason's cabin. In a few hours we will be at the dock and we'll start our new life...problem and worry free." Morgan said to Claire but it was really more to herself.

She needed to remind herself of the game plan. She needed to remember her future was never on this ship. Their future isn't this. Morgan saw Jack hanging by. He looked like he wanted to come over. She nodded

him over and set Claire down.

"Did you want me to come keep you company?" Claire asked Morgan.

Jack came over and he fidgeted nervously. He acted like needed to get something off his chest. He was acting nervous.

"Jack?" Morgan asked him.

Within a split second he squeezed Morgan in a huge hug. He may only be a few years older then Claire but he sure was strong. She hugged him back tightly. She held her breath ignoring the pain in her ribs.

"Jack what's wrong?" She whispered to him worry forming in the pit of her stomach.

"I know you wouldn't. Captain has to know too. I will find a way to show him." He whispered to her.

He was worried about her. She squeezed the boy tighter and smiled. After a few seconds she pulled back. Jason was still waiting but didn't push her.

"Don't go getting yourself into anything Jack. It's fine. Stay away from Chris. He's not a good person." Morgan said to him, studying his face to make sure he understood.

Morgan glanced at Jason and nodded that she was coming. She looked at Claire who seemed torn. Wanting to follow Morgan or hang out with Jack the few more hours that they had.

"Claire bear. It's fine go spend time with Jack. Stay away from that man." She said looking from Claire to Chris who was scrubbing his blood off the deck.

As if he sensed her gaze he looked up at her. Morgan narrowed her eyes at him and he looked back at her just as threatening. Morgan smiled and touched her nose as if to tell him she would break it again if she could. He tensed up and even from across the way the look he gave her was deadly. It was almost as if he promised something bad would happen to her.

She stared back at him, he did not scare her in the slightest. She winked at him with a smile. Telling him to bring it. A look of surprise passed over Chris' face and then anger. He scrubbed the deck floor harder. Morgan tousled Claire's hair and walked to Jason's cabin.

"All right jailer. I'm ready." She smiled lightly at Jason.

Jason frowned slightly and opened his cabin door for her. She walked inside feeling the world close in on her. It's only a few hours, she reminded herself. With nothing to do she made her way to his bed. She could sleep till they docked.

Jack looked at Claire and then around. Without saying anything to her. He grabbed her hand and pulled her. Confused, she followed him. They headed to the back corner of the ship. He looked around again and then back to Claire.

"Jack what's going on?" Claire asked him confused.

"Shhh. So the captain thinks Morgan tried to steal his map-" Jack began explaining.

"What 's crazy! Why would we want his map" Claire said angrily.

"Shhh. He also thinks Morgan tried to poison him-" He started again.

"Is he crazy!-

Jack's hand clamped over Claire's mouth.

"Jeez Claire, will you let me finish and be quiet. I don't want anyone hearing us." He whispered harshly at her.

She nodded as he took her hand off her mouth.

"I believe Morgan. The captain is just too blinded to see that she wouldn't. He's been so paranoid about someone betraying him since Travis. Morgan thinks it was Chris. Now I don't know too much about him. He's always kept to himself. We gotta find something to prove that it was him." Jack whispered to her.

Claire looked like she was debating with herself and then smiled brightly.

"Ok let's do this but we gotta be quick we only got a few hours." Claire said, grabbing his hand.

"Ok but I'm not sure where to start." Jack said thinking.

"Where does he sleep?" Claire asked like it was a no brainer.

"That's a great idea. Most of the men sleep below. It's not much and There's like no beds or anything but everyone claims a spot." He said walking towards the stairs with Claire's hand in his.

He paced the floor in his cabin running his hand through his hair. He was beyond frustrated. He was confused. He was angry. He hated to say it but he was hurt. She betrayed him. He thought she was different. Let himself get weak. He clenched his jaw so tight he felt it pop. He rubbed his cheek as he looked up. His eyes went to the makeshift spot he made in the rafter to hide his map. He was going to set the map back up but he didn't trust it being set up now. He didn't need it anyways. He knew where he was going. His mind kept going back to her. Kept questioning what happened. Kept playing the vial of poison rolling out from under her wet pants. There was no way it could be someone else's. He had literally just pulled her out of the ocean.

Why Chris? He had never seen her talk to him. Chris was a loner always kept to himself. The rage she displayed towards him was so real. Did she know him? Maybe that's why she picked him. He sighed and slammed his fist on his empty desk. He needed a distraction; he could go steer. That always cleared his head. No He would be too close to her. He had locked her up in Jason's cabin that was behind the helm, and now he was stuck in his cabin too. He needed to do something. He needed to keep himself busy somehow. He was the captain of this ship. He wasn't staying in his cabin all day over some woman. He walked to his cabin door and opened it.

He went to the rail overlooking the lower deck; everything was running smoothly. The crew was well in order. Somewhere playing cards and gambling others are finishing up their duties. He couldn't wait to be out of this gully. Couldn't wait to be at that dock. Where he could just send her off and never think about her again.

There's really nothing to do, he sighed running his hand through his hair again. His eyes found Chris and began to wonder. How well did he really know him? He had been on the ship maybe two years now. At least six months of it not being under him as captain.

He made his way down the stairs. His eyes still locked on Chris, he had some questions. Chris tenses seeing Gavin making his way towards him. He shifts uncomfortably. He was studying Gavin and the look of why on his face.

"How's the nose?" Gavin said the question wasn't heartfelt at all.

The innermost part of him found it funny. Maybe even proud that Morgan could hold her own.

"It's doing all right. Is there something I can help you with, captain?" He asked uncomfortably.

"Yeah for some reason Morgan thinks it's you that is behind everything and that I should believe her." He said, masking his expression.

"Captain, I would never poison you." Chris said putting his hand on his chest like it should convince him more.

Gavin nodded slightly and patted him on the shoulder.

"If you find out anything else. You let me know. I need to know if she was the only one plotting with Travis." Gavin said, giving his shoulder a light squeeze.

Chris nodded slowly, his eyes searched Gavin's for some type of answer but there was nothing there. He told himself Gavin believed him.

Jack held Claire's hand as they made their way through the hull of the ship. He was trying to remember where he had seen Chris hanging out. He made his way to the back corner. If he was wanting to be out of the way this is where he would go.

"Jack it's super dark down here" Claire whispered as she bumped into him.

"Well yeah there's not much light. You know, no windows." Jack laughed.

"How much further?" Claire asked as she ignored his laughter.

"I think his spot is over in this back corner." He whispered back.

Claire and Jack made their way over to the corner. A dark blue tattered blanket folded up was in the corner. Two sets of clothing folded up on the side. There was a small wooden crate and a candle sat on top of. Jack dropped Claire's hand and began looking through Chris' belongings. He quickly undid the blanket, nothing. He bunched it back up. Claire checked the pockets on his pants and shirts. Nothing. Jack looked through the empty crate and still nothing. He threw his hand down against His leg.

"There's nothing here" He grumbled.

Claire studied the floor boards. She got down on her knees and ran her hand across them. Everything important they hid in the floors back at her father's house. She traced the grooves with her fingertips and smiled when she found a piece that didn't fit just right. She dug her fingers into it and pried it open. Jack dropped to his knees next to her. A look of shock on his face.

"Back when we lived with my dad. Morgan and I would hide important things on the floor. He would never look there." Claire explained as she reached into the floor.

"Whoa." Jack whispered, looking amazed.

Claire pulled out another vial and a piece of paper. She held them out to Jack, a bright grin on her face.

"This has got to prove that Morgan's right." He said taking them.

The sound of soft footsteps reverberated as they came towards them. Claire quickly covered the hole with the piece of wood and stood up. Jack grabbed her hand and pulled her with him. He was hoping to sneak past the person in the dark. He backed them up against the wall of the ship. Getting himself and Claire as close to it as possible. Hoping to blend in. Claire looked at him, her heart racing. This wasn't going to work. Jack's hand was sweating in hers. The footsteps became louder and Claire's mind was screaming to think of something. Just as the person was reaching them Claire thought of something.

"Found you!! Now it's my turn. Go on, cover your eyes. No cheating." Claire yelled.

Jack literally jumped when Claire shouted. It played right into Claire's lie.

"Hey what are you two doing? You shouldn't be playing down here!" Chris grumbled.

"Hey do you wanna play? You can count first!" Claire said happily, acting innocent.

"No, go on, get out of here. Jack you know better. Besides, you should have some type of chores to be done." Chris grumbled more walking by them.

Claire grabbed Jack's hand again and took off running. She was laughing as they did. She couldn't believe that worked. They raced up the stairs to the lower deck; Sunlight hit Claire's face as she climbed up and out. She waited for Jack laughing.

"You scared me half to death! I can't believe that worked. You are beyond smart." Jack said as he climbed out, and his feet landed on the lower deck.

"You jumped too! It was perfect." Claire laughed, putting a hand on her belly.

"Ok, ok let's see what we got for proof." Jack said calming himself down

He pulled out the vial and handed Claire the paper. The vial was empty but it wasn't at one point. He didn't open it just to be safe. Claire unfolded the paper.

Chris

Mix this into a liquid. A drink. And sever it to Gavin. In 15 minutes he will be dead. Get this done and Travis will surely give you a ship. Get the map after he is dead.

- C

Claire's face lit up; this was the proof they needed. Claire grabbed Jack's hand.

"Come on! We gotta find Mr. Jason! " Claire yelled as she pulled Jack with her.

Chapter Twenty
Illusions

Gavin had left Chris and made his way up to the helm. Jason was deep in thought concentrating on the ocean. Gavin approached him frustrated. Jason raised an eyebrow at him as if to ask what was wrong. Gavin took a deep breath in.

"She was right." Gavin said to Jason in one exhale.

Jason looked at him confused. Gavin took a step closer and lowered his voice.

"Morgan. She's right about Chris. He tried to steal the map and somehow planted poison on Morgan. He's somehow aligned with Travis." Gavin explained, his stomach feeling like it was burning at the mention of Travis's name.

He was doing everything possible to remain in control. Ignoring every impulse he had. All he wanted to do right now was to kill Chris.

"How do you know for sure?" Jason asked.

"I confronted him about Morgan being upset. He immediately said he wasn't the one trying to poison me. That he would never. I never mentioned poison. Only you, Morgan, you, and myself knew about the poison. Possibly Jack if he overheard." Gavin explained gritting his teeth as he did.

"How would he get the poison on Morgan?" Jason asked, as he thought out loud.

Gavins eyebrows narrowed as he thought. When Morgan went overboard, getting them back to the ship, He couldn't carry himself and Morgan on to the ship. He handed an unconscious Morgan to someone. He searched his mind and realized Chris was the one who stepped up to take Morgan from him.

"He had to have planted it on her when he took her from me. When I was carrying her out of the sea." Gavin said processing outloud.

"Why is he still alive?" Jason asked anger filled his face

"If he thinks that we don't know; then I might be able to find something useful against Travis. There's obviously a bigger plan here than just getting me to come back to sea and getting the map." Gavin said, he shifted slightly in his stance to look past Jason.

Jason nodded in agreement.

"Are you going to tell her?" Jason asked with a small smile on his lips.

Gavin bit his tongue. Of course he wanted to. He wanted to rush into the cabin the moment he found out Chris was the one and that she was right. He wanted to apologize and continue where they had left off. Half of his mind was killing Chris and the other was in the cabin with Morgan. He stopped himself as they spoke, from doing both.

"No-" Gavin started to say but Jason cut him off.

"Captain you really should." Jason said ignoring the angry expression Gavin was giving him about being cut off.

"No. It's better this way. We're almost out of the gully. We'll be docking at the dock right outside of it. She'll be leaving. It's better to have her leave angry and upset with me. Instead of....of...of." Gavin explained.

"Instead of? Of what?" Jason asked as he cut Gavin off.

"It's just better this way. Cut me off again and I'm going to cut you for real." Gavin grumbled at him.

Jason went to say something but closed his mouth. He shook his head with a small smile on his lip.

"Mr. Jason!" Claire ran up to him as she dragged Jack behind her.

"What is it Claire?" Jason asked with worry in his voice.

"Here Jack, show him." Claire said, pulling Jack to stand next to her.

Jack was hesitant and looked at Gavin. He didn't want to tell him. He wanted to tell Jason first and then Gavin. Jason looked concerned studying Jack.

"Oh fine gosh I'll do it." Claire said, rolling her eyes.

She reached in Jack's pocket pulling out the vial and note. She walked past Jason and handed it to Gavin.

"My Morgan had nothing to do with it. Here's your proof." Claire said, placing the items in Gavin's hand.

Gavin looked down at the brave little girl and her courage made him smile. He glanced down seeing the vial. It was the same style as the one he had with poison in it. His face turned sour. He stared at the folded up piece of paper. He opened it reading the note. His teeth gritted as he read it. He looked at the signature. C. Not Travis but C. He searched his mind trying to think of a C. He looked down at Claire and patted her head.

"Thank you darling. I'll take care of everything" He said letting her know she could go and that she did good.

She smiled proudly.

"So you're not mad at Morgan anymore?" Claire asked.

"No but we're gonna let her sleep till we reach the dock. Saving Jack took a lot out of her." He smiled and winked at her.

Claire nodded happily and walked back to Jack.

"Jackie no more meddling. Keep Claire close. Go about your business." He said to Jack in a stern voice.

Jack nodded and grabbed Claire's hand leading her off.

"What is it?" Jason asked when Claire and Jack were gone.

He held the vial up to Jason. Jason's eyes narrowed and his face frowned in anger.

"Let me steer." He said to Jason as he walked over to him.

Jason stepped back handing the wheel off to Gavin. As he did Gavin handed the note to Jason. Jason glanced at Gavin as he took it. Gavin didn't say anything but nodded his head telling him to read it. Jason read the note, as he did his hand went to his sword.

"I say we kill him." Jason said the anger in his voice surprised Gavin.

"You're supposed to be the level headed one." Gavin said, trying to make light of the situation.

"Did you read this!" Jason said, crumpling the note in his hand as he shook it at Gavin.

"Aye, why do you think I'm now steering?" He asked; his knuckles going white from how hard he was gripping the wheel.

"Who is C....c...c" Jason said, his eyes wandering over the few crew members on the lower deck.

"I don't know but we need to find out. Go see what you can come up with." He said to Jason.

Jason nodded and handed the note back to Gavin before walking off. Gavin locked his eyes on the sea; it was the only thing keeping him calm. He glanced back at Jason's cabin and he felt his heart tug. He shook his head reminding himself it was for the best. His mind was scattered. Chris, Travis and Morgan. He needed a minute to just zone out. He hoped taking over steering would.

Morgan was exhausted and did doze off.

However, now awake she was pacing back and forth in Jason's cabin. She swore her feet were going to leave grooves in the wood. Her ribs and body ached but she couldn't sit still. She hadn't been awake for long and couldn't take being locked up in the cabin. The only thing her mind kept going back to was that Gavin didn't believe her and that she wished she would have landed the second punch with Chris.

There was yelling and the ship began to rock. She recognized Gavin's voice as he called Jason.

"Claire." Morgan whispered to herself going to the door of the cabin.

She flung open the door and rushed out of the cabin. Her eyes scanned the view trying to figure out what was going on. Jason was at the helm.

"What's going on?" She yelled to him as she headed to him.

He frowned seeing her but didn't mention anything about her being out

"We're about to exit the gully but something is off up ahead. The water is shallow and there are a ton of sharp rocks." Jason explained.

Morgan stood on her tippy toes trying to see what he was talking about. The exit was just like the entrance. A large opening between the two cliffs. The big blue sky and fluffy white clouds stretched out in front of it. Welcoming you to leave. However the ocean was pooling in certain areas, in weird patterns. A small line of current ran down the middle of small pools. As they swirled about. Her eyes caught someone climbing the ropes to the crows nest. She recognized the way he moved. His dark curls blowing in the wind as he climbed. Although the ship swayed he moved effortlessly up the ropes.

"Claire?" Morgan asked Jason as her eyes were still locked on Gavin.

"Captain had her and Jack go in his cabin just in case something strange happens again." Jason explained.

"He's going up to the crows nest to get a better view and give better instructions." Jason told her as he nodded to Gavin.

Morgan looked at the entrance and how fast they were approaching. She glanced at the sails. They needed to slow down. Without saying anything she rushed down the stairs.

"Morgan!" Jason yelled after her confused.

Morgan ignored him as she got to the lower deck. She headed towards the mass. The sails were completely down allowing the ship to go full speed. Morgan began to untie the rope. Another crew member saw what she was doing and headed over to her.

"Hey lass-" He began to ask but Morgan cut him off.

"We need to slow down. Help me untie and pull the sails up." Morgan yelled.

Jason realized what she was doing.

"Alan, Tom, and Paul help her! Pull up the sails." Jason yelled from the helm.

Gavin pulled himself into the Crow's Nest. Getting settled in it. He looked down at the commotion on the lower deck. At first he was angry. What was she doing out? He quickly realized what she was trying to do. She was trying to slow them down. There was a sense of pride seeing her work with the crew. He needed to focus. He studied the horizon and his heart sank. Looking at the cliffs he realized that it was an illusion.

The cliff stretched outwards as the ship would exit. It looked like it was designed to prevent anything from passing through it and no one would realize before it was too late. He looked over the sides of the ship, studying it quickly. The cliff would scrape and possibly puncture the ship as it passed through it. The ship was just a little too wide.

"We need to tilt." He whispered to himself.

"We need to tilt!" He yelled down to the crew.

The crew froze, not sure what to do. Morgan caught his eyes and then glanced forward at the exit. What was he seeing? Tilt how?

"Tilt." She said out loud and looked around.

She looked back up at him and when their eyes met it clicked.

"The cannons." They said at the same time.

"Keep all the sails up." She told the men on the lower deck.

Morgan ran to the opening of the hull. Kneeling down she began climbing down the ladder. Her feet hit the floor as she jumped the last few steps. The men below looked at her confused.

"We need to move all the cannons now! They all need to go to the left. Anything heavy we need on the left." She began yelling at the men down there.

They looked at her dumb founded. She sighed heavily and went to one cannon on the left side and began to unfasten the brackets and ropes keeping it in place.

"Whoa. What are we doing?" One of the men approached her.

"Look if you want to make it out of this gully The ship needs to tilt slightly. We only have a small amount of time before we crash. We need to move now." She said,

You could see the man debate with himself.

"Well you did save Jack. I trust you. You heard her boys! Get these cannons over to the left side." He yelled as he bent down to help Morgan.

The other men down in the hull quickly got to work. Morgan helped push the cannon they untied across to the left. You could hear the ship creek with each cannon being moved. The weight being shifted. She glanced around. She didn't know if it was enough.

"If we have anything else that can be moved to the left and maybe everyone stays on the left side." Morgan said her eyes were still searching the hull for anything heavy.

"And why would we listen to you?" A nasal voice said from a dark corner of the hull.

Morgan turned around to see Chris leaning against the wall. She gritted her teeth, she didn't have time for him.

"By all means don't listen to me. You can hover over the side of the ship without a rope for all I care. I care about surviving and if the rest you want to then I suggest you listen. Stand on the left side." She said, taking her eyes off Chris and looking at all of them.

She then turned sharply without another word and started up the ladder she came down. She pulled herself up onto the lower deck and glanced towards the exit of the gully. They had slowed but the ship was still not tilted. It definitely was leaning but needed more. She looked up at Gavin. She could tell he was thinking. His bad habit of running his hand through his hair when frustrated gave him away.

"Jason, is there anything heavy left to move?" She yelled at him.

Her stomach was flipping from nerves. They couldn't crash, sink, and drown now, not now. Claire and her had lived through way too much to just let this be the end. She watched Jason eyes searching; his calm, cool, and collected self starting to waiver. He shook his head no. Morgan spun to watch the incoming exit. She was gonna puke. She began thinking of the worse and she needed a plan. She could find something floatable to put Claire on. Maybe they could float out and maybe the dock was right there.

"God help us." She whispered.

A loud noise hit the deck behind her. She spun around and was face to face with Gavin.

"Not God Love, just me." He smirked after hearing her.

"Well I'm glad you're going to die with your self confidence still in check." Morgan said, shaking her head at him.

"No one is dying. The captain has a plan." He smiled brightly.

"Well what is it because we're racing towards our doom and we could really use one without the dramatics." She said inches away from shaking him.

"So I need two more people. There's two anchors on this ship. I never saw the use in them but now it's gonna save us. They are amazingly both on the left side. Go to the back of the ship. There's a lever. When I give the signal, drop it." He said pointing toward the back of the ship behind Jason.

"Got it." Morgan said and took off.

"Morgan!" He yelled to her back.

She turned on her heels looking at him.

"Tie yourself to a rail. I'm not going fishing for you again." He smirked at her, throwing a wink her way.

"I thought you didn't care if I went overboard." Morgan shouted at him as she began to walk away from him.

"I care a little." He said to her back as he headed to the front of the ship.

He heard her groan as she finished rushing up the stairs.

"Thomas and Jacob!" He yelled and two men rushed over.

He studied the two of them as if contemplating which one would be better at what task.

"Jacob head to the front of the ship. When I give the order, throw down the anchor. Thomas at the same time I need you to let down the left sails only. Left sails." Gavin instructed.

They both nodded and ran off. Gavin rushed to the center mass and began climbing his way back to the crow nest.

"What in the name of all things holy is going on?" Jason asked Morgan as she started by him.

"We're gonna tilt the ship." She said without even looking at him.

"Bloody hell." Jason said, his eyes shoot up to Gavin as he climbed.

Morgan grabbed a rope near the anchor level and tied it to herself. She then fastened it to the ship's rail. It wasn't a bad idea. She then waited. Her fingers clutching the lever. Her heart was pounding as she listened for Gavin. This has to work. She thought hopefully. Seconds turned into minutes as she waited and then it seemed a lifetime. What was going on? She watched the stone of the cliff passing them. Just as she was about to yell and ask what was happening she heard his voice.

"Drop the anchors!! Drop the sail. Brace yourselves!!" He yelled at the top of his lungs.

Morgan hit her lever. It didn't go. She heard the front anchor plunge into the sea. The sail flapped open. She pulled back the lever and slammed it forward again. Nothing. The rear of the ship began to raise a little instead of tilting.

"Morgan!! Now!!" Gavin yelled again with a slight panic in his voice.

She pulled back and slammed the lever again. Her heart began to sink. It's not working. She glanced over the side of the rail where the anchor was stored. The anchor itself was stuck. The chain was released but the anchor was caught.

" Are you freaking kidding?" She groaned.

She needed something. She frantically looked around. A long pole was in the corner of the ship. She raced to it and ran back to her post. Gavin was shouting her name again. She leaned over the rail shoving the pole against the anchor and using her body weight she pushed down to pry it free from its compartment. She heard the wood breaking from the rail as she pressed down on the pole. A snap was heard as the rail broke. The lever still in the forward position the chain began to move. The pole flung her away as the anchor crashed into the ocean.

As the anchor hit the water the ship tilted left Morgan rolled across the deck heading for the broken rail. She braced herself grabbing a hold of the rope keeping her from going overboard. She stared at the rocks of the cliffs passing by as they started through the exit. She couldn't believe it. It was freaking working. They were going to make it. She felt relief rush through her. A loud snapping sound was heard. Wood was breaking. She heard a yell from the men on the lower deck. Something crashed onto the deck. She closed her eyes and prayed the ship wasn't about to sink.

It was the longest five minutes of her life. She no longer saw the rocky cliffs. There was nothing but a wide open ocean. The blue sky was the most beautiful thing she had seen. She let out the breath she was holding.

"Pull up the anchors!" Gavin yelled.

There was something wrong with Gavin's voice. Morgan told herself it was due to all the hectic things going on and he was fine. Morgan struggled to get to the level. She used all her strength to fight gravity and dragged herself to it. She reached up and grasped the lever. She heard the front anchor wheeling in. She needed hers to go now. She pulled it back and prayed harder. The chain coming back up was the best sound she had heard. She let out a sigh.

As the anchors retreated back the boat untitled almost completely

"Drop the right sails!" Gavin yelled again.

Morgan began untying herself There was something off with his voice! She frowned as concern rushed into her.

"Move the cannons back." He yelled, his voice cracked slightly and there was pounding on the lower deck; letting the men below know to get to work.

The crew began to work and as soon as everything was back to where it was the ship was up right in its normal position. Cheers and clapping echo throughout the ship. They did it. They made it.

Chapter Twenty One
Goodbye

Morgan made her way to the front of the helm.

The men were still cheering and celebrating. She smiled seeing their reaction. She was very relieved to finally be out of the gully. Jason saw her and smiled at her. She walked over and squeezed his shoulder

"I don't know how you all came up or pulled that off but I'm thankful it worked." Jason chuckled.

"Yes Thank god. I heard-" she started to say but then she found her answer.

The crow nest was on the floor of the lower deck. Shattered pieces of wood scattered about. She moved away from Jason, her eyes studying the scene. The mass that held the crows nest was cracked at the top like something just snapped it. It was just the very top so the sails were not damaged. She didn't even realize it but she was moving down the stairs to the lower deck. She was searching for him. Was he in it when it fell? Her feet hit the bottom deck, her eyes scanning the men.

She saw him leaning against the side of the ship. He held himself awkwardly as he was giving orders to the crew. She moved throughout the men making her way to him. Several of the men stopped and thanked her as she made her way she smiled and nodded her eyes fixated on Gavin. Seeing her he went to straighten up but winced slightly, as if he tried to hide something. She stopped in front of him, controlling the urge to touch him. She wanted to find the cause of his pain and fix it.

"What happened? Are you ok?" She asked, taking another step closer, her eyes scanning over him.

"I'm fine. Just a few bruises, nothing major." He smiled at her.

"What happened?" She asked not believing him.

"When the ship tilted the crows nest brushed against the side of the cliff wall. Rough landing." He chuckled.

She frowned. He was hurt. She wasn't sure where and doubted he was going to let her look. She was surprised he was talking to her nicely, never mind not yelling at her about being out and about. She didn't want to push her luck.

"Come on. You need to go lay down for a little bit." She told him.

"Love, I'm fine. I need to make sure everything is going ok." He ignored her suggestion.

"What by hugging the wall?" She said with a smirk.

His eyes narrowed at her but his lips hid away a playful smile. She could see it lingering at the corners of them.

"Fine I'll leave you alone if you can take five steps towards me. Convince me you're fine." Morgan said, as she took five steps away from him.

"I don't need to convince you of anything." He said, his smile faltering.

He was leaning against the wall because the world had been spinning. He hurt but it was his head that was worrying him. He whacked it coming down with the crows nest. He knew he just needed to ride it out. Morgan folded her arms across her chest waiting.

He wasn't doing it. If he did it then he would be wrong and she would try to take care of him. He didn't need anyone to take care of him. He didn't need anyone. If he did need her; he might never let her off this ship. He had to be mean. He had to let her leave.

"You should really be on your way before I decide to have someone put you back in the cabin; where you're supposed to be. " He said, making sure his voice was cold.

"Fine. When you fall on your face I'm not even going to glance your way." Morgan said threw her teeth at him.

Without a second glance she turned on her heels and headed towards Gavin's cabin. She needed to check on Claire. Walking across the lower deck she caught Jason's eye. She nodded towards Gavin. Jason was confused till he looked over at Gavin. He nodded looking back at Morgan saying he understood. Gavin didn't look good.

Morgan made her way to Gavin's cabin fighting the urge to go back and argue with him. She shook it off as she opened the cabin door. Claire and Jack were just standing on the other side of the door. Waiting. Morgan raised an eyebrow at them.

"What the heck happened?" Claire yelled at her.

"We've made it through the gully." Morgan smiled.

"Well duh but everything fell over and we were tossed across the room." Claire said, frowning at her.

"The exit wasn't exactly wide enough to fit through so we had to tilt the ship." Morgan said with a smile.

"Woah." Jack said quietly.

"We should be at the dock in forty-five minutes or so." Morgan said with a small frown.

Claire nodded sadly and looked at Jack. He squeezed her hand lightly.

"You know I'll come visit." Jack told her with a smile.

"Yeah if you remember where we are." Claire said her frown deeping.

"Hey Claire bear. I will make sure Jason and the Captain's have our whereabouts so you can see Jack again." Morgan said her chest felt tight.

"See and I will make sure I memorize the town where we are docking at." Jack said with a smile.

Claire just nodded. Morgan frowned. It was amazing that in these few short days and with all the craziness; that the ship felt like home. The crew felt like family. Morgan glanced around the cabin, she was going to miss it.

Aloud noise tore Morgan from her sentimental thoughts. Jason stumbled through the door holding an off balance Gavin. Gavin's arm draped across his shoulder. Jason's arm steadying his waist.

"Jason, if you don't let me walk, " Gavin grumbled, moving like he was drunk.

Jason sighed and let Gavin go. He stumbled and almost crashed onto the floor.

"Done being stubborn Captain?" Jason said, as he grabbed him.

"Whose steering?" He groaned as Jason helped him walk over to the bed.

"Thomas." Jason said, sitting him down.

Morgan raised an eyebrow at Jason. Jack looked worried at Gavin.

"What's going on?" Claire asked.

Morgan had hit her head enough to know exactly what was going on. She walked over to Gavin studying him.

"How long has it been since he hit his head?" She asked Jason.

"Maybe an hour." Jason said with a shrug.

"You need to rest. It's been enough time where you should be ok. But the world's not gonna stop spinning unless you take it easy. Any vomiting?" Morgan asked, studying his eyes.

"No." Gavin and Jason said at the same time.

Gavin was cradling his head. Morgan sat down next to him and began looking through his hair to see if there were any wounds. She found a good size lump on the back of his head. He winced lightly as she touched it.

"You're going to have one heck of a headache. Jack, can you make the room a little dark? Someones going to need to stay with him. He can fall asleep since it's been an hour but I wouldn't leave him alone." Morgan said, looking at Jack and Jason.

"And how do you know so much about head injuries?" Gavin said from under his hands.

"From experience." Morgan said shortly.

He went to lean back but struggled. Morgan grabbed his shoulders and helped lean himself back. Jack pulled the only shade over the window and the room became dark. She sighed helping him get situated.

"You'll be ok, the spinning will stop soon." She told him.

"I've got him. You can go." She said to Jason who she could tell was debating on what to do.

Gavin shut his eyes trying to ease the spinning. It was worse than he imagined. Not only was his head spinning but with each rock and sway of the ship it made everything worse. He felt a light touch float across his forehead. Morgan found herself brushing a curl of his out of his eyes. Her hand lingering on his cheek. He focused on her touch and it seemed to help ease the spinning. Her thumb began rubbing his cheek, lightly comforting him.

236

"Claire and I are gonna go help Jason" Jack said quietly as he started to follow taking Claire with him.

"Claire stay close to them." Morgan said, glancing her way.

Claire nodded to her as she headed out behind Jason and Jack.

"Feel better." Claire called to him as she left.

The dim light from the outside sun strolled across the bed. It danced across Gavin's face. She smiled softly as the shimmer of light highlighted his lips and strong jawline. Another one of his curls managed to fall down across his forehead. She could not help but caress the side of his face. This man that was strong, ruthless, and tough looked so fragile in this light. She withdrew her hand and sat quietly.

"Dont stop." He grumbled.

She smirked, waiting for the reason why.

"It makes the world not spin so hard." He said softness in his voice.

She smiled, the butterflies in her stomach that had been sleeping woke up. She shifted herself on the bed. Gavin groaned in response to her small movement. She reached over and began to softly rub his cheek. She saw him instantly relax. She traced the outline of his jaw with her finger tips. Like they had a mind of their own, her fingers brushed across his lips. As she touched them she instantly remembered how they felt against hers. A weak smirk formed across his lips.

"You know Love you would be in serious trouble if the world wasn't spinning." He said the threat made her stomach flip with excitement.

"Mhmm." She chuckled.

He went to move slightly like he was going to show her but grunted and laid back down. A laugh escaped her lips.

"My head hurts. I'm glad you're finding this funny." He said in pain.

"I don't. Just shut your eyes and take it easy." She said softly.

She reached forward and lightly ran her fingers through his hair. She felt him relax again. She hummed softly as she played with his curls. She watched his chest rise and fall as he drifted asleep.

She studied his face, she didn't want to forget it. The scar that ran under his jaw. The way his eyes would narrow and his eyebrows dropped down in a scroll whenever she was trying his patiences. The way his lips curled when he spoke to her. She brushed her fingers over them. She sighed, becoming sad. She heard a shout saying they were approaching the dock. She frowned, running her fingers through his hair. She leaned forward and brought her lips to his lips softly. They barely brushed each other. She then placed a kiss on his forehead. He didn't even move from ethier kiss.

"Goodbye Gavin. I hope you find what you're looking for." She whispered to him as a light tap was heard from the cabin door.

Morgan got up slowly and walked to the cabin door, opening it. Thomas stood there with a small smile.

"'I'm here to look after him." He smiled at her.

"He just fell asleep. Keep a watch on his breathing and wake him in about an hour." She whispered to him.

"I will. You be safe, Lass." He said to her as he headed to the bed.

"Thomas, don't let Chris watch him." She said to make her voice very serious.

"You have my word." Thomas said.

She nodded and headed out of the cabin. Walking to the rail; She watched the ship line up with the dock. Two men hopped out. Grabbing the ropes and securing the ship. Another deployed the front anchor. She sighed and scanned the ship one last time. This is it she thought. She found Claire giving Jack a never ending hug. Tears in her eyes as she squeezed him. Morgan made her way to her. She placed a gentle hand on her shoulder.

"Come on Claire bear, why don't we have Jack walk us down the ramp." Morgan said softly to her.

They made their way across the deck to the ramp. Jason was waiting. He scooped Claire up in a hug. Taking her from Jack. He squeezed her tightly and then gently placed her down.

"I'm going to miss your endless chatter little one." He said, setting Claire down.

"You still need to teach me how to steer. So you'll have to come back and see us." Claire said putting on a brave face.

"You have my word." Jason said, ruffling her head.

He glanced at Morgan and held out his hand. She reached for it and as she did he pulled her into a hug.

"We all owe you our lives." He said, squeezing her.

He pulled back resting his hands on her shoulders. The crew behind him began to clap in agreement. A few familiar faces stepped forward and came to her. They reached over Jason and grabbed her shoulder. She blushed and nodded her thanks to them; Jacob, Alan, and Jack.

"He's going to regret letting you off this ship. We all will. Here." Jason told her referring to Gavin and then placed a leather bag in her hand.

"You go get your life started." Jason smiled, pulling away.

She glanced down at the leather bag fill of coins and went to argue but he was ready for her refusal. He shook his head and refused to take it back.

"You go to an inn. See if you can rent a room and they may be able to have a job for you" Jason said giving her advice.

Her eyes began to tear up and she nodded. She felt her chest going tight. She inhaled trying to pull herself together. She reached down grabbing Claire's hand and began to walk down the ramp. It was the longest shortest walk of her life. Hitting the dock she glanced back and waved. The crew and Jason all waved back.

"Good bye." She whispered as her and Claire continued to walk across the deck.

Chapter Twenty Two
The Sunflower Inn

    Morgan didn't look back; the pull to stay was too strong. Claire clung to her hand as she made it into the city. It was a small fishing community she noted as she walked by several stands set up by the dock. The men eyed them curiously. She ignored them as they ventured further. The town opened up into a small market. She thought it was a little strange how it went straight to selling things but if people were new you wanted them to start buying and trading right away; why not Morgan thought.

    "Fresh fruit!" A woman called out to them.

    Claire looked at her letting her know she was hungry. Morgan nodded and headed over to the fruit stand.

    "Go on, which ones do you want?" Morgan said to Claire scooting her up to the stand.

    "We have mangos, papaya, and some coconut. Oh and some melons." The women pointed out the fruit as she said their names.

    "I'll take a mango please." Claire smiled.

    The woman hands it to Claire and takes payment from Morgan.

    "Miss, do you know anywhere that might be looking for help? We're new to the area and I need some work and a place to stay." Morgan said to her.

"Oh The Inn! You can actually get both. They
have rooms and they are looking for some to help. I am
not sure exactly what though. Um, follow this road up
around the bend and you'll see it on the corner there."
The woman smiled at her.

"Thank you so much!" Morgan smiled as she
turned to follow her directions.

"You're welcome." She called Claire and Morgan.

Morgan and Claire made their way down a stone
pass that led away from the dock. Along the way there
were a lot of other venders; Selling various items:
Spices, nuts, fruits, vegetables, and fish. Claire was
fascinated by it all. She kept slowing down to study each
stand. Up around the bend the inn sat. It was a two story
house. It looked like it was made of old pieces of the
ship. Each wood was a plank but a slightly different tone
of wood. They all entwined perfectly. As they
approached it Morgan read the sign. The Sunflower Inn.
A sunflower spun out of wood hung above the doorway.
The door of the inn had a beautiful stained glass
sunflower in it.

Morgan pulled open the wooden door, her eye
catching the help needed sign. She grabbed ahold of
Claire's hand as she walked in. The lower level of the
inn was a bar with several tables set up for eating. The
woman behind the bar smiled brightly at them. She had
long raven black hair and bright blue eyes that matched
how bright her smile was.

"Hello and welcome to The Sunflower Inn. How
can I help you today?" The dark-haired woman smiled.

Morgan approached the bar and smiled at her.

"Hi I actually saw your sign and was interested in work. I also wanted to see if you had any openings for a room, as well." Morgan smiled.

"Can you handle rough men?" The woman asked her, sizing her up.

"Yes ma'am," Morgan said, nodding.

"Hold your own if needed?" The woman asked again, a little unsure.

"Yes ma'am. I can handle my own and anyone else's." Morgan said with a smirk coming to her lips.

"Ok then. You're hired. I need someone to help tend the bar, clean the rooms, and help in the kitchen when needed." The woman explained as Morgan nodded.

"Here take this. It's a key to one of the rooms upstairs. The key will match the door. Your first shift starts as soon as you're ready." The woman said holding a key.

The long silver key matched the sunflower that hung above the doorway but the color of it was blue. Morgan grabbed a hold of it. She glanced at Claire and back at the woman.

"Um ma'am-"

"She can stay in the room or stay with you as long as you're a good worker and she doesn't get in the way." The woman said.

Morgan nodded and turned to leave. She glanced around, not sure which way to go.

"Up the stairs. Um and I'll have some bath water brought up for you. And some women's clothes.....I don't care what your past is as long as it doesn't cause any trouble here." She said with a wink.

Morgan smiled and headed up the wooden staircase. Claire right behind her.

"Does she think we're trouble cause we're wearing boys' clothes?" Claire asked.

"Maybe girls don't normally wear boys' clothes." Morgan explained reaching the door.

"The boys' clothes are much more comfortable than the skirts. And I can do a lot more in them." Claire shrugged.

Morgan saw the first bedroom door had a red sunflower on it. She glanced down at the blue sunflower in her hand and moved to the door that matched. She loved the tiny detail. She looked down at Claire who was still touching her shirt.

"I know." Morgan smiled, opening the door.

It was a small room with a fireplace. Above the fireplace was a painting of a sunflower but like the key it was blue. There was only one bed but it would be fine. For years Claire and her didn't have a bed. Claire saw the bed and smiled brightly. She raced over to it and flopped down on it. The bed squeaked as she laid down. Morgan chuckled watching her. There was a knock at the door.

Morgan hesitated and slowly opened the door. A man with dark almost black hair and jade colored eyes was holding two large buckets of water standing there. He was struggling. Morgan smiled and opened the door wider. She grabbed a hold of one bucket.

"I got this one." She smiled at him.

"Thank you ma-am." He said, returning the smile.

She followed him to the corner where she saw a very small copper tub. He emptied his bucket into and then reached for Morgan's. She handed it to him and he repeated his actions.

"Ok I won't be keeping you. The bath water will only stay warm so long." He said heading to the door.

"Thank you..." Morgan paused, asking for his name.

"Robbie." He said, holding out his hand.

"Morgan and this is Claire." She smiled, shaking his hand.

"Nice to meet you and I'm sure I'll see you around." He said, shaking her hand back.

She smiled, closing the door as he walked out of it. She locked it and then turned to Claire.

"You go first and then I'll go." She said, nudging her to the tub.

Another knock came from the door. Morgan opened it confused. A young girl with straight brown hair and hazel eyes was standing there. In her arms were two sets of clothing.

"Joyce said to bring these up to you." The girl said, holding her arms out.

"Thank you." Morgan smiled taking the clothing

The girl nodded and left as quickly as she came. Morgan shut the door and locked it again. She set the clothing down on the dresser. She looked around, not bad for starting over she thought.

"Morgan?" Gavin asked his head killing him but after sleeping the world had stopped spinning.

"Morgan " He repeated again to her. She was sitting on the edge of the bed leaning against the wall. He squinted his eyes. It was still a little blurry.

"Morgan Thank you." He said to her, sitting up slowly.

She didn't even acknowledge him. She must still be mad about the whole locking her up. He frowned deeply.

"Morgan. I'm sorry. I reacted quickly and it was easy to make you the bad guy. I know you didn't try to poison me or steal the map. Please talk to me." He said ignoring the pain in his head and leaning forward to touch her shoulder.

He grabbed her shoulder lightly and there was something off with her shoulders. It was much broader than he remembered.

"Woah sorry Captain. I nodded off. Are you ok? Do you need anything?" Thomas nearly yelled as Gavin grabbed his shoulder.

"Thomas?" Gavin said confused.

"Aye Captain. Morgan left about an hour ago. We've reached the dock. We are gathering supplies and should be almost ready to head out." Thomas explained.

Gavin frowned. She left. His stomach knotted. He was fighting the urge to go find her. He was fighting himself between knowing letting her go was best and wanting her.

"Captain?" Thomas asked, patting Gavin's hand that was still on his shoulder.

"Good to hear. I'm going to go find Jason. You can return to your duties." Gavin said standing up.

"Aye captain. Glad you're ok." Thomas said getting up.

"Thank you Thomas." He nodded.

"You're welcome." Thomas said as he ducked out.

Gavin steadied himself and then started to walk to the door. His head was killing him. He grabbed a hold of the door and walked out. The sunlight hitting him blinded him for a second. He shut his eyes as his hand went to his forehead to shield himself. It took him a second to adjust. He scanned the ship. Jason was on the lower deck giving the crew orders. They were returning with supplies. He watched them very happily hauled nuts and fruit up on the ship. They had to be careful with the food choices. Things went bad very quickly at sea. He glanced up at the center mass. The crew was already working on making a new crownest. It was a quick one but it would do.

He made his way down the stairs to the lower deck. Jason saw him approaching and smiled at him.

"It's good to see you, Captain." Jason said, clapping him on the shoulder.

"How are things?" Gavin asked.

"Almost set to take off. About 15 minutes we got one more create of supplies. Jacobs's been working with what we had to repair and made a somewhat crows nest." Jason said, looking to the center mass.

"Good." Gavin responded.

"I gave her the pouch of coins like you wanted." Jason said knowing what was on his mind.

"Good." Gavin responded softly, his eyes drifting to the land.

"She'll be ok. She's strong and very capable." Jason said with a small frown.

"I know it's for the best." Gavin said, trying to convince himself.

"Aye Captain." Jason said, squeezing Gavin's shoulder.

"All right boys! Captains back! Move your asses! We leave in 10! If you're not done, leaving regardless. Pick up the pace. We have a date waiting on us." Gavin said, throwing a wink at Jason.

"You heard the captain put your backs in it. Hustle." Jason yelled after Gavin.

Morgan pulled the dark brown skirt up over her hips. The top she had put on was a simple white one. Claire matched her except her skirt was navy blue. Morgan watches her wrestle with it. A smile on her lips. She could hear Claire's thoughts about the skirt being stupid even with her not saying them out loud.

"Claire, did you want to come with me or stay up here?" Morgan asked her.

"I don't want to be alone. I'm coming. Claire said getting up and walking to the door.

"Ok, let's see what we can do." Morgan said, as she held her hand out to Claire.

They made their way to the bottom floor. Joyce was behind the bar. She waved them over. The inn already had a few patrons in it. There was a group of men in the corner. They were opposite another group of men sitting in the corner. The only difference being a platinum blonde woman sat with that group. Morgan's eyes lingered on them as she walked over to Joyce.

"Ok darlings. Little one you're going to sit behind here with me. I'm going to ask you to get me glasses and what not. Morgan, I need you to head over there and get the group's orders. The ones in the right corner were first and then the opposite corner. Here's some paper and a pencil. Let them know Aggie isn't here tonight so no special request for food. We just have the sausage and taters." Joyce said and handed Morgan the paper pad and pencil.

Morgan nodded and walked over to the group of men without the woman.

"Good evening, what can I get you boys tonight?" Morgan asked with a forced bright smile.

"A round of ale." A man with a large beard said.

"Ok a round of ale and if you gentlemen want any food Aggie isn't here tonight; so all we have is sausage and potatoes. Is there anything else I can get you?" Morgan asked.

"Ye new here Lass?" A man with long dirty brown hair asked sizing her up with his eyes. A nasty grin on his face.

Morgan cringed internally. She knew this would happen but not on the first day.

"Aye sir. Today's my first day. I'll go get your ales." Morgan said, turning and heading to the bar quickly.

"You know what they say about redheads." The man snickered to his mates as she walked away.

Morgan rolled her eyes as she approached Joyce.

"I need four ales for that group." Morgan nodded behind her.

"Ok little one you're up. Under the counter beside you get me four tin looking mugs. We don't serve ale in glass glasses. Also judge the men. If they look rowdy they don't get anything but tin. If a fight breaks out ever. I have a shotgun under the bar here. Also a large wooden walking stick in the corner there if you can't make it to the bar." Joyce said to Morgan as she took the tin cups from Claire.

"Another day when Wendy is here I'll go over what's behind the bar and drinks. Go get the other group's order." Joyce said to Morgan.

Morgan smiled. She liked Joyce; she was prepared for most things. She didn't chit chat and was right to the point about everything. Morgan headed over to the other group. The man with the dirty hair is still eyeing her. She approached the second group and they were deep in conversation.

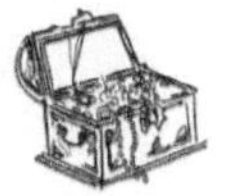

"That little mishap cost us time. Now he's probably ahead of us. We're gonna have to somehow sneak up and ambush him from behind."

"Captain we didn't know. We got a message from Chris that he's docked here now." A small man explained.

Morgan tensed up hearing this. She began to study the men. The one angry and looked like he was in charge had light dirty brown hair and olive green eyes. Are they talking about Gavin? More clenched the notepad in her fist.

"And you're just telling me this now! We need to move then. If we leave now we can still make this all a fucking surprise!" He yelled standing and knocking over his chair.

"Travie. You need to settle down. Gavin is not as smart as you. You have this." The blonde woman with ice blue eyes said as she patted his arm lightly.

"Shut up Christina. If you would have taken care of this back when you were with him we wouldn't have to be doing all this." He said spit flying out of his mouth as he yelled.

Christina stood up and squared off with him. She looked like a spoiled toddler about to throw a tantrum.

"And you just remember that this was my plan. That I put all the work in pretending to love and marry him. Just so that we could benefit from having all of it. So you will not speak like that to me again. The tables can switch real quickly and you've seen me work. So watch your mouth with me." Christina said, jabbing him with her finger as he spoke.

Travis' face twisted into a devilish smile as he grabbed a fist full of Christina's hair. He painfully yanked her head back and forcefully kissed her. Morgan felt like she was gonna vomit. Her stomach felt like it was on fire. Gavin. She had to get to him. She had to tell him. Her mind was panicking. Her face losing all color.

"Can we help you?!" Travis yelled at Morgan realizing she was there.

"Drinks?" Was all she could manage to ask.

"No go." He said waving her off.

She nodded and walked quickly. Approaching the bar Joyce looked at her concern.

"Now darling you're as white as a ghost what happened." Joyce asked her, confused.

"Nothing." She smiled.

"Ok sugar, well take these drinks over to the men in the corner." Joyce said to her sliding the drink tray to her.

Morgan nodded, taking the tray carefully. She felt like she was shaking. She needed to warn Gavin. She had to leave but she was torn. This could be hers and Claire's fresh start. If she didn't leave they could get away with their plan. Gavin didn't even know the woman he had been mourning is alive and behind everything. Claire watched Morgan feeling something was wrong. Morgan walked over to the men and set down the four cups of ale.

"Hey Red there's something wrong with my drink." The man with the dirty hair said.

Morgan was watching the other group of men getting ready to leave. She wasn't paying attention to the man as she went to pick up the drink he was complaining about. A hand grabbed her wrist and pulled her closer.

"Cotton hands to yourself." Joyce yelled as it registered to Morgan that someone had grabbed her.

"Oh come Ms. Joyce I'm just having fun." He smiled not letting go.

"Cotton." Joyce yelled at him again.

Morgan watched Travis and his crew leave. She needed to go. She glances at Cotton whose other hand was starting to travel down her waist. That was enough! Morgan swung the tin ale cup towards his face. As it hit his face his hands dropped from her and went to hold his face. Morgan kicked at his chair leg and he toppled over. Morgan glared at the other men as she stepped away, the tin cup still in her hand as a weapon. They held their hands up in defense.

"I suggest you men enjoy your drinks and be polite." Morgan threatened as she turned and walked back to the bar.

"Joyce I, we gotta go. I'm sorry something came up." Morgan said motioning to Claire to come.

Joyce looked confused and went to say something but Morgan said to Claire

"Claire, we're gonna need our other clothes."

"What...ok." Claire said but before she could say anything else, Claire took off running up the stairs.

"I'm sorry I really am thank you." Morgan said, going to the stairs.

She didn't give Joyce a chance to say anything she was up in the room in an instant. Walking in she almost laughed seeing Claire already changed.

"What are we doing...not that i'm complaining" Claire chuckled.

"We're gonna go save the crew." Morgan smiled.

"Alright!" Claire shouted as Morgan changed.

"Wait what? why? Are they in trouble?" Claire asked.

"Yes long story short those men want to hurt them and we gotta hope The Morning Star is still docked and not gone." Morgan said, looping her buckle and latching it halfway to the door.

"Let's do this!" Claire said excitedly following Morgan.

Morgan pulled open the door and went to walk out. She almost bumped into Robbie.

"Hey sorry Joyce sent me up to see if you're ok?" He said with a kind smile.

"Yeah we are, we just got to leave." Morgan said, taking Claire's hand and stepping around him.

"Hey if it's because of Cotton, Joyce just told him he's not welcome here any more." Robbie said to Morgan's back.

"No, I just found out a friend is in trouble so we gotta go quick. I don't even know if we'll make it in time. I left payment for the room on the fireplace." Morgan said slightly pausing to explain but still heading down the stairs.

"Where do you need to go?" He asked, starting to follow her.

"The dock." She muttered his questions were starting to annoy her.

"Can you ride?" He asked catching up.

She paused and turned around, raising an eyebrow at him.

"Yes, although it's been a while." Morgan said, curious.

"Good. I have a horse you can borrow. Just leave him tied to the entrance of the dock when you get there. Or ride him back if you end up being unsuccessful in saving your friend quickly. Joyce said if you come back the room and job are still yours. She likes you." Robbie smiled.

"Ok I'm out of time. Take me to the horse." Morgan said impatiently.

Robbie nodded and motioned for Morgan and Claire to follow.

Chapter Twenty Three
Taken

Robbie led Claire and Morgan through the small kitchen. They weaved in out of random supplies. Sacks of rice, potatoes, and flour lined the floor as the girls followed Robbie. In the very back of the kitchen was a door that led to the outside. They walked through it. The smell of the sea air fluttered around them and the setting gave the seaside town a warm glow. An old red barn stood out in the backyard of the inn. The red paint was starting to peel away, you could tell it had been there for a long time. Robbie led the girls to it and he Robbie walked through the arch way of the barn.

"I'll get him ready. You two wait here." He said to Morgan and Claire.

Two stalls were set up on either side. An old white horse grazed on his hay on the left and a deep chocolate horse nickered at Robbie on the right.

"Hey guy." He smiled seeing the horse.

The horse nodded his head at him happily as Robbie approached him.

"You want to help some pretty ladies?" Robbie asked him as he scratched the horse's head.

The horse seemed to nod. Robbie grabbed the gear hanging to the right of the stall. He held the bit up to the horse's mouth and fed it to him. The horse took it no problem. He then placed his ears inside the loop and tossed the reins up on his neck. He grabbed the saddle to his left along with his blanket. Robbie placed the saddle blanket on the horse's back and then the saddle. He looped the belt under the horse's belly and tightened it. He then opened the stall. The horse and Robbie headed out of the barn.

Morgan watched the large chocolate horse walk out of the barn. She studied it. It had been a long, long time since she had ridden. The horse's mane and tail was the darkest black she had ever seen. She watched Robbie walk the horse in several circles before stopping and adjusting the belts. After one hard pull Robbie placed his foot in the stir up and bounced lightly The saddle didn't move. He nodded confidently.

"All right ladies. This is Sir Arthur. He is pretty gentle but fast as the wind. He should get you to the dock in no time." He said as he patted the horse.

Robbie cupped his hands and motioned for Morgan to use them to help boost herself onto the saddle. She smiled and walked over to the horse. She stuck her foot in stirrup and used the horn to help pull herself up and onto the saddle. Not using Robbie for help. Robbie laughed.

"Ok then. I see you have this." He chuckled again.

"All right little miss your turn." He said and motioned for Claire to come over.

"Will you help me? I can't do that." She said and pointed at Morgan.

Robbie smiled and picked Claire up by the waist, setting her infront of Morgan.

"Thank you," Claire smiled.

"Your welcome little miss." He responded back to her.

"Thank you." Morgan nodded to him as she adjusted Claire making sure she was in securely.

"Be safe." Robbie told her before he stepped away from the horse.

She nodded to him before tapping the horse to go. The horse set into motion. She tapped the horse with her heels and he began to trott after a few. After a few steps Morgan got used to the rhythm. She remembered quickly how to ride. She squeezed her thighs tight around the horse. She pulled Claire closer to her as she had the horse go full speed ahead. The horse raced back down the curved cobblestone path. All the vendors had packed up their stands for the day. Claire clung to the saddle leaning back into Morgan. Sir Arthur really did fly like the wind.

The air changes as you approach the sea. It feels lighter, open, and free. Morgan knew they were close just by the way the atmosphere shifted. She pressed the horse faster as the dock came into view. She scanned the harbor as she slowed the horse. She felt her stomach knot up not seeing The Morning Star. Pulling back on the reins Sir Arthur came to a halt just as the road turned into the wood of the dock.

She scooted herself back away from Claire as
she swung her leg over the horse and landed neatly on
the ground. She then walked the horse over to the
wooden railing of the dock and tied Sir Arthur there.
Morgan held her arms open for Claire. Claire giggled
before jumping into them. Morgan caught her chucking.

"We have to be quick. I'm praying they're still
here." Morgan said to Claire as she set her on the
ground.

Claire entwined her hand into Morgan's as they
started down the dock. Both of them scan the harbor. It
was a small harbor about five ships could dock at once.
Each empty docking station they spotted made
Morgan's heart sinking further into her stomach.

"Morgan, what are you going to say to him?"
Claire asked her.

"Well I'm going to start by telling him about the
ambush Travis has planned and about-" Morgan said,
fading out as her heart sped up with joy.

"Claire, they're still here! Look there's the Star.
They look like they are about ready to leave. We need to
run." Morgan said, pulling Claire.

Claire laughed, dropping Morgan's hand and
dotting out ahead of her. Morgan smiled seeing Claire
as she began racing to the ship. They turned off the
main dock heading to the ship. Claire would make it to
the shop before Morgan. She was lighter and faster in
short distances than Morgan.

Morgan started off after. Just as she was about to start jogging her foot caught something. She fell forward. Her chest hit the dock with a loud thud. She let out a small groan trying to get her bearings. She slowly stood up. Claire was off by the ship and paused to wait for her. Morgan went to nod to her telling her it's ok; when something weaved into her hair yanking her head hard back. Something cold pressed against her throat. Morgan saw Claire's eyes widen and she went to go to Morgan. Morgan shook her hand by her side at her. She mouths the words go to her.

"You must be Gavin's redhead." A voice snickered into her ear.

"Aye that's the bitch." Another voice Morgan recognized.

Morgans gritted her teeth at the sound of the second man's voice. She could feel the acid in her stomach. Her hand went into a fist at her side. Claire was still hesitating. Go she mouthed again to her. Claire fidgeted and then rushed up the ship's walk away.

"Chris, why don't you tell your friend to let me go; before I break his nose too." Morgan threatened.

Chris stepped forward and with a swift motion smacked Morgan across her face. She felt her lip split and she could taste iron from the small amount of blood that leaked from the cut.

"Shut your mouth bitch." Chris said as he narrowed his eyes at her.

Morgan chuckled at him. He raised his hand at her, threatening. The man behind her shifted as if he was preparing for Chris to hit her again. She took the opportunity. She threw her head back into the man's face. The knife he was holding to her throat left a small cut but the impact of the back of her head into his nose made him drop it. Chris went to grab her to stop her but she ducked slamming her shoulder into his chest. He became off balance and fell. She ducked around him and headed for The Morning Star. Chris reached out and captured her ankle with his hand. Entwining his fingers around her ankle he began trying to pull her down. Morgan kicked at him but he wasn't budging.

"Oh enough of this." She heard a cold feminine voice say.

Something hit her hard over the back of her head. She staggered. Chris pulled on her ankle causing her to fall forward onto her stomach. She struggled as the world became hazy, pixelated, and then black.

"Get her on the ship. We can use her later. If Gavin cares for her he'll cave." Christina snickered.

Claire rushed up the walk way after seeing Morgan urge her to go. She needed to get help. She glanced back to where Morgan was. She froze seeing Chris scoop up an unconscious Morgan and take off with her. Morgan needed help now. Claire rushed past the last of the men boarding the ship.

"Hey!" Several shouted at her as she weaved through them.

She hit the lower deck frantically looking around. She needed Gavin or Jason. She searched and saw the two men at the helm. She took off full speed for the helm. She raced up the stairs speeding past Jack.

"Hi Claire." Jack said casually and then caught himself.

"Claire!" He yelled as he raced after her.

Claire reached the upper deck in no time. She didn't stop as she raced towards Gavin and Jason. Seeing her coming the men looked confused. Claire tried stopping and ended up crashing into Jason.

"Woah there little miss." Jason said, steading her.

Gavin studied her as well and began looking around the ship. His eyes searched the lower deck looking for her. His eyes searched for her bright hair amongst the plain world below. He was a little excited hoping she had come back. Not finding her he glanced back at Claire who was trying to catch her breath.

"Claire, where's Morgan?" Gavin asked concerned.

"They.....took....her." Claire said in three big breaths.

"Who? Who took her?" He panicked.

"Chris." Claire said he was the only one she recognized.

Gavins blood began to boil. He should have killed him when he found out the truth. He walked over to the side of the ship, his eyes searching the harbor. Claire began to tell Jason more. Gavin's heart pounded as he tried to see if he could spot her. He went to head to the lower deck. He would go search on foot.

"Captain there's more." Jason called to him before he could leave.

Gavin paused waiting for more information.

"Morgan....said...Travis....ambush." Claire said, leaning over holding her side.

"Travis....he's here?" Gavin said, his eyes scanning the harbor.

He glanced at Jason before leaving. He nearly jumped down the stairs. Landing on the lower deck he didn't miss a beat. He rushed across it. The men moved frantically out of his way. Making it to the walk way he slammed into Jacob who stumbled off the walk way and into the sea. Gavin didn't even look back. His feet on the dock matched his heart racing in his chest. He needed to find her. His chest felt like it was going to collapse in on itself at the thought of Travis having her. Travis had already taken one person from him. He wasn't letting him take another.

Jason watched Gavin take off like a bat out of hell. He glanced around.

"Jackie!" He yelled trying to find the boy.

He was close by and making his way after Claire already.

"Jackie!!" Jason yelled again.

"Sir." Jack said getting to his side

"Watch-"

" Got it. Go!" Jack said, cutting him off.

Jason nodded, taking off after Gavin. He was going to need help. Travis will definitely have a crew. Reaching the lower deck he headed to the walkway.

"Jacob! Thomas! Alan! With me now!" He yelled over his shoulder making his way to the ship's exit.

The men jumped to attention and without questions. Jacob was soaking wet but it didn't even phase him. They quickly followed Jason off the ship.

Gavin scanned the ships. He wasn't sure what ship Travis had would look like. He must have searched every pier. He got to higher ground trying to make sure he didn't miss any ship. He looked out over the horizon. His stomach clenched as he spotted it. He knew in an instant that it was Travis's ship.

A three mast ship with dark sails. It was the complete opposite of The Morning Star. It was dark. Even the wood the ship was made out of was dark. It's dark sails had a white crescent moon with a small silver star that dangled off the end of the moon. It looked haunting as it sailed towards the open ocean. Ghostly against the sky. Gavin's throat felt like it was closing as he watched it.

Chapter Twenty Four
Captive

Fear rushed through him as Gavin turned on his heel and raced back to The Morning Star. The dock creaked as his foot slammed into the wood. Up ahead he saw Jacob, Jason, Thomas, and Alan as they ran towards him.

"Get to the Star!" Gavin yelled at them.

The men stopped in their tracks and looked at him confused. They glanced at one another trying to understand what Gavin yelled.

"The Star! Get to the ship!" Gavin yelled again, through harsh breath.

Jason heard him this time and the realization hit him. He grabbed Jacob's shoulder and spun him to the ship. He nodded to Gavin as he turned towards the ship.

"To the Star lads!" Jason said to them.

Jason didn't leave them time to understand. None of them moved. He grabbed a hold of Thomas's shoulder and spun him towards the ship as he rushed by. Jason then took off to the ship. Thomas and Alan followed quickly behind. Jacob was still confused as Gavin got to him.

"Jacob come on!" He yelled at Jacob as he passed him.

Jacob lost his balance and stumbled. He caught himself as he dangled over the dock. Trying so hard not to fall in again. He scooted himself back up on the dock just as his feet touched the water. Jacob got himself up on the deck, and took off after them.

Gavin raced up the walkway of The Morning Star. Jason was on board already giving orders to get ready to sail. Gavin's feet hit the floor of The Morning Star.

"We need to leave now!" He bellowed at the crew.

The men quickly began pulling the walk way up. Jacob was still on the dock just in front of The Morning Star as the walkway lifted. Gavin groaned.

"Jacob you better jump or I'm leaving your ass here " Gavin shouted at him.

Jacob nodded, took a few steps back and launched himself at the walkway. The men on the ship holding it groaned as they tried to bear the weight. Jacob began to crawl up it. Gavin shook his head and went to the stairs. He climbed in seconds, the adrenaline rushing through him was making his mind go a mile a minute. All he could think about was how he needed to get to her.

At the top of the stairs he met eyes with Claire. Seeing her his heart sank further. He frowned slightly walking to the back corner of the upper deck. He slammed the lever for the anchor to come up.

Looking out on the horizon his eyes fixated on the dark ship escaping his grasps. Jason met him there, he needed to know exactly what was happening. He knew it was not good..

"What's going on?" Jason asked breathlessly.

Gavin's frown deepened. He grabbed Jason by the shoulder and led him to the side of the ship and pointed to the ghostly ship leaving the harbor.

"Travis has Morgan and he's getting away." Gavin growled.

"Shit." Jason whispered.

"Is she going to be ok? She was sleeping when they took her." Claire's little voice said from behind them.

Gavin felt his mouth go dry. The words she was sleeping made his hand twitch. She better be ok. He thought as he turned around to see Claire standing behind them.

"She will be. Claire, I promise we're going to get her back." Gavin vowed as he reached out and squeezed her tiny hand.

Claire's big blue eyes were filled with tears as she nodded. Gavin squeezed her hand again before going to steer. He checked the ship again, sails were down, anchored up, and walked way was put up.

"I'm coming for you Travis." He swore as he pulled the ship away from the dock.

"Travis." Christina sing songed his name happily as the four of them walked aboard the ship.

"What is it dear?" He answered almost impatiently.

"Look what we have for you." Christina continued in the same sing song voice; overly happily.

"Christina I don't have time for- " Travis started to say annoyed but then saw Chris holding an unconscious woman.

"And you've kidnapped the girl from the Inn, why?" Travis asked, rolling his eyes.

"Because she's not just the girl from the inn. She's Gavin's new girl." Christina smiled wickedly.

An evil grin formed across Travis's face. His eyes danced with sinister excitement. He walked over studying her.

"Oh this is perfect! Are you sure?" Travis said still, his eyes carefully looked over Morgan.

"Yes. Chris confirmed it and we are pretty sure she was on her way to warn Gavin." Christina explained.

A stumbling man came up behind the three. Travis raised an eyebrow at the man. His face smeared with blood and his cheekbones were swollen.

"What the hell happened to you, Clint?" Travis asked him.

He groaned pointing at Morgan. Travis chuckled.

"Oh this is great. How much does he care for her?" Travis said like a child about to win a game.

"He gutted a crew member for touching her and then threatened to kill anyone or all that dared to try to touch her again." Chris said, adjusting Morgan in his arms.

"Yes! Yes! I will so enjoy slitting her throat in front of him and when she is done bleeding out. I'll kill him as mercy." Travis laughed.

"This is going to be epic. First he'll find out that his fake beloved wife was behind everything. And then we will kill the next woman he ever loved right in front of his eyes. " Travis laughed more as he all but danced around.

Travis grabbed Christina by the hair and pulled her in for a forceful kiss. She eagerly met him half way. Chris rolled his eyes and shifted his weight as he held Morgan. He was waiting to be told where to put her. Christina pulled back from Travis and looked at Chris.

"Put her in the cabin. Bind her hands and feet. I am not dealing with any more nonsense." Christina said as she waved Chris off.

Chris nodded and happily headed to the upper deck. He walked over to the first mate's cabin and kicked the door open. He clumsily made his way in, Morgan flopped about in his arms. His eyes spotted the bed and made his way over to it. He dropped her so hard on the bed, she bounced slightly. He walked to the cabin door and looked out.

"You!" He yelled at the closest crew member.

"Me? Aye?" The man replied.

"Get me a rope or ropes quickly." Chris growled before heading back into the cabin.

He paced slightly as he waited. He kept glancing over to Morgan. Different thoughts running through his head. In the pit of his stomach he felt bad for Gavin. He was a good man and captain. Chris reminded himself that he needed to do what was best for himself. After this he would have Gavin's ship and be on his way to his own greatness. Travis had promised him a ship if he helped in Gavin's undoing. He glanced at Morgan making sure she was still out. The girl annoyed him. He admired her strength and ability to fight but that just added to his reason for finding her annoying. He snorted at himself. Admired her. He thought as he found himself walking toward her. She was definitely beautiful. His eyes ran down the length of her body.

Christina was beautiful in a typical way. Men found her stunning with her ice blue eyes, pale, soft; never worked a day in her life skin and platinum hair. She was dainty and that added to her poor me and innocent act she pretended to be. She had the personality of a cat. Sweet loving until she got what she wanted. She would turn around in a heartbeat and dig her claws into you. She had no problem biting the hand that feeds her. She also loved toying with people until she killed them. Gavin was blind to her charm and this cat and mouse game was the biggest thrill for Christina. She came to Travis whispering thoughts of riches and glory into his ears. She was the mastermind behind all of this.

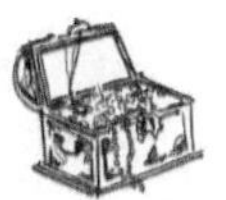

Morgan was beautiful but also warm. Her emerald green eyes sparkled when happy or excited. She had a smile that was infectious. And her sun kissed skin begged any man to touch it. She was strong, confident but he bet she could be sweet. Real sweet. He shook his head. He could see why Gavin fell so easily. He reached out letting her fiery red lock curl around his finger.

"It will be such a waste when they kill you." Chris said very nonchalantly.

The noise of the man walking in pulled him from his thoughts. He fumbled the two ropes hee carried. As he got half way to Chris he held them outwards. Chris walked over to him without a word, snatched them from his hands and shooed him away. The man simply nodded and headed out as quickly as he came in. Chris walked over to Morgan and sat down on the bed next to her. He looked her up and down before deciding it would be better to tie her hands behind her back. He grabbed a hold of her hips and with one swift motion flopped her on to her stomach. He paused to look at her. More thoughts entered his head about how she would feel bent over beneath him. He clenched his jaw and grabbed her arm and began wrapping one of the ropes around her wrist. When he was done with that one he moved on to her other arm; fastening them together behind her back. He did the same to her ankles. Once done he stood up and studied his work. Double checking the ropes to make sure she would not be able to get out of it.

"She does have a nice ass, doesn't she. I mean just look at the way the mens pants just cling to her every curve." Christina said as she leaned against the doorway.

Chris didn't acknowledge her comment. As he stepped away from Morgan. Christina walked over and placed her arm on Chris' shoulder.

"Wouldn't you want to know what she felt like?" Christina whispered in his ear, her finger trailed down the side of his neck.

Chris stiffened uncomfortably as he tried to shrug her off. His thoughts had already wandered there and he fought against them.

"I won't tell you. I could even make sure you weren't disturbed." Christina said in the same whispered tone.

"Get off of me Christina." He growled at her.

"Easy boy." She chuckled as she stepped away from him.

"That won't be happening. I might have low standards but they're not that low." Chris said in a low threatening voice.

"Oh well, too bad. It would have been worth adding to Gavin's misery. Letting him know another man had what was his. Maybe I can convince someone else." She laughed as she headed to the door she came in.

"That won't be happening. Killing her infront of him will be enough. Why don't you go practice your acting skills for when we face off with Gavin." Chris said through gritted teeth.

If she had a tail it would be twitching. Chris smirked imagining her as a pissed off cat. Chris could see the smoke coming out of her ear holes. In her mind no one told her what to do. She took a few steps towards him. The gray skirt she was wearing swooshed around her. She reached into her partly pulled back hair and pulled out a red rose hair pin. The rose hair pin turned into a small blade as she pulled it from her hair and pointed it at Chris. Chris eyed her waiting for her to make a move.

"You forget your place." Christina said, stepping towards him.

"What's going on here darling?" Travis said, as he waltzed into the room.

"Chris was thinking he could tell me what to do." Christina said tighten her grip on the blade.

"Not telling her what to do. Just what wasn't going to happen." Chris said with a shrug.

"Look I don't have time for your back and forth. Gavin saw us leaving and now we don't have the surprise of an ambush." Travis said as he glared at them.

Chris didn't say anything else, his eyes stared down Christina. He was not going to let her get a cheap blow in. Christina all but hissed and placed her blade down on the nightstand next to the bed. She took a deep breath in as she calmed herself. Travis began pacing, muttering to himself.

"Why don't we just wait for them then." Chris said with a shrug.

"What?" Travis asked as he stopped pacing and looked at him confused.

"Well they are now chasing us. They know our plan to an extent. Why not let them catch up and just square off. We have Morgan as leverage and he still doesn't know that Christina is alive. It might be enough of a shock to have the upper hand without the surprise aspect." Chris explained.

Travis hand went to his chin as he pondered what Chris said. He glanced at Christina, a smile forming on his lips.

"Well darling let's get this show on the road." Travis said to Christina an equally awful smile formed across her face.

"Chris, watch the girl. I am going to let the crew know to get a little further out in open water and to ready the cannons." Travis said excitedly.

"Come darling, let's make you look like you've been a captive." Travis laughed, grabbed Christina by the hand and led her out of the cabin.

Chris sighed heavily at them as they left. Maybe he could just kill those fools and take this ship. He groaned sitting down facing Morgan.

"Babysitting duty and holding people's hands are what I'm best at lately." He grumbled folding his arms across his chest.

"This "show" better be quick. I have other places to be. Maybe they'll all kill each other." He mumbled as he kicked his feet up.

Chapter Twenty Five
Show time

The Morning Star left the harbor and was now in the open ocean. The ship moved as fast as it physically could. Gavin's eyes were locked on Travis's ship. He studied it. There was something off. He narrowed his eyes as they continued towards it.

"Captain?" Jason asked.

"Travis is waiting for us." Gavin said a hint of surprise in his voice.

"Waiting." Jason mimics Gavin's tones.

"For as long as I've known him he has never been a straightforward person." Gavin muttered to himself.

"Aye. He's very manipulative. Gavin keep your guard up. I doubt this will be just an exchange." Jason frowned.

"Let the men know something is up. To be ready for a fight." Gavin said quietly.

The world was foggy. She could hear talking. She went to move but couldn't. Her head hurt so bad. The pain throbbed deep into her temples.

Where was she? She struggled to move and felt something rough against her skin. She knew instantly it was ropes. She was bound by her wrist and ankles. She started to remember what happened before the world went dark. She stayed still trying to gather as much information as possible. She did not need anyone to know she had come too.

"We need to capture the Morning Star without causing a whole lot of damage to the ship." A voice said.

"His guard will definitely be up but if we act like we want an even exchange the map for the girl. Then maybe we can lure him on to our ship." The voice continued.

"He wants blood Travis. More specifically your blood. And he's one hell of a swordsman." Chris said, his voice flat.

"I know that! We will take the map first, act like we are going to give him the girl. Then we will have Christina escape and run into his arms." Travis smiled.

"Him seeing poor little me all disheveled but alive will overwhelm him." Christina chuckled.

"Aye and then we won't even have to match swords with swords. As they make their big reunion Christina can take him out in her loving arms." Travis laughed.

"And the Star?" Chris asked.

"Yes, yes boy. I don't have use for two ships. The Star can be yours once he's dead." Travis said as he shook his head at him.

"Come my dear. It won't be too much longer now." Travis said as he took Christina's hand.

Chris sighed as he watched them leave the room. He didn't trust Travis but he didn't have too many options now. He glanced over at Morgan. He walked over to the bed and plopped down next to her. Purposely making her roll.

"I know you're awake." He said to her,

"You're all cowards." Morgan said angrily into the bed.

She tried to adjust herself but without the use of her hands or feet struggling was all that happened. Chris laughed at her and then looped his arm through hers and swiftly sat her up. The world began to spin and she began to fall forward. He let her go forward just to be an ass. He stuck his leg out so she wouldn't smash her face. She landed on her knees.

"You bastard." She muttered to him having no choice but to lean into him to keep from landing on her face.

"I actually knew my father but not for very long. Hmm maybe you're onto something. I had no manly role model growing up." He said shifting away from her.

Without his support Morgan landed on the ground on her side. She groaned as she hit the ground. Whatever Christina hit her with really messed with her head.

"You know, doll. This could have all gone differently. You should have stayed at the inn. Now you get to die alongside him." Chris said as he shoved her lightly with his foot.

"He's going to kill you." Morgan said as she gritted her teeth.

"Oh I doubt that. First seeing you and then his long lost beloved wife. His whole world is going to shatter even more. He won't be able to tell up from down. He won't be killing anyone." He chuckled, placing his foot on her hip and rocked her back and forth.

"Head hurt doll? Being pistol whipped will do that uh. Much worse than a broken nose." Chris laughed.

"Not Gavin. Travis." Morgan said as she shut her eyes trying to make her stomach stop from being nauseous.

Chris stopped. He looked down at her. He didn't think about that. Would he? No, why would he. There was no need to kill him. Like he said he has no use for two ships. Chris thought to himself.

"You believe him? Look at what he's doing to Gavin. He's known Gavin since they were boys. Gavin saved his life. You're nothing to him." Morgan said, sensing his thoughts.

"Yeah but he doesn't need two ships." Chris said, trying to sound confident.

Morgan began to laugh even though it hurt. Chris stood suddenly and kicked her in the chest. The tip of his boot caught her lip as he did. It made the cut on her lip crack wider. She instinctively curled her lip inwards and tasted blood.

"Need and want are two different things" She coughed.

Chris growled slightly as he stomped away. He left Morgan on the floor. She heard the cabin door open and slam shut. Realizing she was alone she began to try to snake across the floor. She had to get free. Had to stop this. She wouldn't let them hurt Gavin. She saw a desk in the corner of the room, there had to be something sharp on it that she could use to cut the ropes. She began to wiggle her feet back and forth trying to slither. Her feet caught the night stand next to the bed. It stopped her movements and she struggled to get her feet out from under it. She scooted herself forward and wiggled her feet. She nearly took the nightstand with him and as she did she heard a cling. Something hit the floor. She curled into her stomach trying to see what it was.

Seeing the red rose blade on the floor her heart fluttered. She flipped herself over and began to back up to the blade. She could feel the cold steel just out of her grasp. She scooted back more, hitting her head slightly on the bed as she did. The pain was enough to make her go out again. She fought through it as a wave of nausea passed through her. She would not let herself fail.

"Come on." She whispered as her fingers played against the blade.

She let out a long aggravated breath. Just a little closer she thought. Finally she was able to loop her pinky finger around the handle and pull it into the palm of her hand. Using her feet she pushed off the bed. Giving herself some distance between herself and the bed. She curled her feet up towards her butt and bent her back towards her feet. She was in a ridiculous looking u-shape but it worked. She began to lightly saw at the ropes that held her feet together. She could feel the ropes loosen as they began to fray. Her body ached and she could no longer hold the position. She began to work on her hands. She could go back to her feet in a second. She was able to go much faster than her feet. She could feel the rope becoming looser.

"I'm getting her!" Chris shouted just outside the cabin door.

Morgan froze. She quickly slipped the blade up her sleeve and held it in place by closing her fist slightly around the end. Chris marched into the room as loudly as he left.

"Come on Doll. It's a good day to die." He snickered to her as he lifted her up off the ground by her elbow.

She swayed and almost fell again. "Yeah you remember that." She growled at him.

He tightens his grip on her as he silently threaten her. He attempted to pull her forward but she almost fell again.

"Ugh I'm going to have to carry you." He groaned.

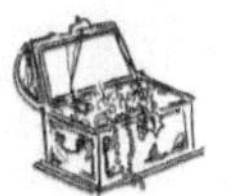

He leaned down and tossed her over his shoulder. She let out a groan As she slumped over his shoulder.

"Ugh believe me doll I don't want to be carrying you ethier." He grumbled as he kicked open the cabin door.

"Then untie me." She growled against his shoulder.

Chris laughed. "I'm not dumb."

Morgan let out a long sigh as she flopped around over his shoulder like a sack of potatoes. She tried to see what was going on. There was lots of noise. Her red hair flung over her face and blocked most of her view. All she could make out was men rushed about the ship. She bounced down the stairs on Chris's shoulder to the lower deck. She lifted her head as he slowed down. The Morning Star was pulled up alongside Travis's ship. Travis stood in the center of the lower deck, sword on his hip, and arms folded across his chest. He looked so proud of himself. A smug smile was planted on his face as he watched The Morning Star. Chris walked over and stood just behind Travis. He slung Morgan off his shoulder and placed on the ground. She began to rock slightly.

"Oh for fuck sake." Chris grumbled and steadied her by the shoulders.

"Untie my feet. I'll be able to stand right." She said as she rolled her eyes.

Chris debated but didn't want to chance her escaping. Morgan focused her eyes and began to scan The Morning Star. She spotted him. Her breath caught in her throat and her chest ached. He was just across the way pacing the lower deck. He looked like an animal ready to attack; dangerous and deadly. He stopped suddenly as if he felt her presence. Their eyes met and the world seemed to slow and stop. Pain and anger flashed across his eyes. He moved to the side railing, he needed to get her! Morgan smiled at him to let him know she was ok. She left his gaze and scanned the ship once more, her eyes panic going back to him. As if he knew who she was looking for he nodded to his cabin. Claire was safe. She felt relief wash over her.

Suddenly she was yanked forward by her hair. Travis's fist in her hair she had no choice but to collapse into Travis's chest as he held her by the hair. His hand began to stroke her cheek as he locked eyes with Gavin. He was baiting him, his smug smile turned into a grin as he pressed Morgan further into his chest. Gavin fell for it and felt himself losing it inside. His grip tightened on the ship's rail. His knuckles turned white, his jaw was clenched so hard it was amazing he didn't shatter his teeth.

"Walk away!" Gavin bellowed.

The crew jumped to his orders and grabbed the walkway and started to place it out across between the two ships. Travis's crew went to the rail as the board came across. They looked to Travis for instructions.

"Let him come." Travis chuckled.

Travis's crew backed away and formed a circle on the outer part of the lower deck. Once the board was secured Gavin hopped up on it. Two swords dangled from his hips. You could see the rage coming off of him in waves as he walked across. Jason and Thomas flanked his side. Behind them followed Jacob, Alan, and two men she recognized but was unsure of their names. She began to fidget. She didn't want Gavin coming over. The plan Travis had would crush him. She subconsciously began to shake her head no, her eyes begged for him to look at her. She had to tell him.

A cold steel blade pressed under her chin and against her throat. She frozed slightly. Morgan had wished she had more time trying to saw off the ropes. She began to slowly put tension on and off the rope holding her feet. By turning her heels out and then in. She could slowly feel them starting to become looser. She needed to get away. She needed to get to him.

Gavin's feet hit the lower deck followed by his crew. The silence was thick. Morgan attempted to lock eyes with Gavin but he was staring past her, his piercing gaze aimed at Travis. She tried to get his attention. She needed to warn him.

"Welcome to the Evening Star." Travis said as if he was introducing the title of a play.

"Evening star." Jason scoffed behind them.

"Travis. Give me Morgan." Gavin's voice echoed with authority.

Travis's crew seem to almost back away at the sound of Gavin's voice. It was terrifying.

"You have a thing for redheads now. I thought blondes were your thing. Want to see if her blood matches her hair color?" Travis said the smirk on his face growing.

Gavin began to close the distance between them. His hand clenching one of his swords.

"Stop right there or I'll slit her throat." Travis said as he dug the blade into Morgan's throat just enough so a small drop of blood ran down it.

Gavin tensed up. He wanted to go snatch her away from him but seeing the drop of blood he stopped.

"Enough. What do you want, Travis?" He growled.

"Seriously ...the map. Hand over the map and I'll hand over the girl. Map first." Travis said, rolling his eyes.

"Lower the blade from her throat." Gavin demanded.

"Oh fine." Travis said, lowering the blade.

Gavin reached into his back pocket and pulled out the rolled up map. He showed it to Travis. Travis all but did a happy dance behind Morgan. He acted like a spoiled child. Travis was distracted about how close he was to getting everything he wanted. He didn't feel Morgan shift. She had been holding the cold steel blade under her sleeve and seized the moment to use it. Morgan slowly let the blade slip down into her hands. She began to slowly move it against the rope. Travis was too occupied with seeing the map to notice the slight movement.

"Chris get it." Travis ordered.

"Gavin, don't give it to them! It's a trap! Christina, she's alive and behin-" Travis hand fell over Morgan's mouth.

Gavin stepped back. Did she just say Christina's alive? He glanced at Jason, his shocked face confirming.

"Travis-"

A loud bang was heard. Everyone seems to shift to the noise. All Gavin saw was platinum blonde hair running down the stairs towards him. His heart sank into his stomach. Travis's men moved out her way as she raced towards him with arms open. She crashed into his chest. Gavin's arms automatically enclosed around her.

"Gavin you're here." She sobbed into his chest.

"Christina." He whispered his hand going to the back of her head and ran down her hair.

"Gavin, you came for me." Christina whispered through her sobs.

He pulled back and caught her face in his hand. He studied her face as if not believing it.

"Christina." He said again with a hand on her tear stained cheek.

She placed her hand over his and brought her hand to his cheek touching him softly.

"It's me." She said to him,

"Gavin it's me. I know he made you think I- I was gone but I'm not. It's really me." Christina continued as her thumb ran up and down his cheek.

"Christina." Gavin said and pulled her into his chest and placed a kiss on the top of her head.

Morgan watched the scene unfold, her stomach sinking further and further. She knew what would happen next. The acid building up in her stomach as she watched. Christina was an amazing actress. The torn clothing, the sobbing even the loving touch she had; was all so real. She kept trying to get Gavin's attention with her eyes. He was too shocked. He was holding onto Christina like if he let go she would disappear.

"Are you ready?" Travis whispered into Morgan's ear.

Morgan began to panic. She shook her head fiercely no. Morgan watched in horror as Christina's hand slowly went to a hair pin in her hair. Morgan stiffened. It was just like the one she had in her own hands. She needed to stop this! This couldn't happen! Morgan watches the blade start slowly peeking through Christina's hair. Morgan inhaled through her nose trying to calm herself down. Travis's hand was still over her mouth. She moved her mouth slightly so his fingers would slip. She bit down hard. She could taste blood as her ears filled with his screams. He pulled away from her. She kicked her right foot hard away from her left and the rope holding her feet together snapped. She began to run towards Christina and Gavin. Travis's screams broke Gavin from his trance. He looked at Morgan confused as she came running at them. He shifted slightly trying to see what was happening.

Morgan pressed the blade hard into the ropes holding her hands together as she ran. She saw Gavin looking confused but it didn't stop Christina and he hadn't realized yet a blade was heading for him. His eyes fixated on Morgan trying to understand. As she reached them the rope holding her hands broke. With all her might she shoved herself in between Gavin and Chirstina. Her open palm hands slammed into his chest and pushed him out of the way. She turned slightly and as she did Christina's blade came down. The blade pierced Morgan's shoulder. She let out a painful scream as the white shirt she was wearing slowly turned red.

"Morgan!" Gavin yelled going to her as Christina ripped the blade out of Morgan's shoulder.

"It's a trap." Morgan said as he reached her.

Christina raised the blade again and was going to stab Morgan once more. Gavin caught her wrist.

"Christina!" He yelled at her.

She growled trying hard to get out of his grasps.

"Stop. What are you doing?" Gavin yelled as he tried to get her to stop fighting.

"Gavin... The blade was meant for you."Morgan said as blood leaked down her arm.

The realization hit him and he looked at Christina struggling in his grasp. Christina saw his reaction and started laughing.

"What's the matter Gavin? You think I loved you? How could I love you? You're pathetic. This whole thing was me. The fire; everything. I planned it all. I met Travis a month before I wandered up to you all helpless." Christina laughed harder explaining.

Her words stun him, his grip loosened as he tried to process. Gavin didn't understand. The words everything was her repeated in his mind as he took a step back confused, pain written on his face. He glanced at Travis whose smug look confirmed what she was saying. Jason walked over to Morgan worried about her arm but she shrugged him off and focused on Gavin. She was afraid for him. He looked broken. He had tortured himself for months about not being there when Christina had needed him. He let it consume him. He dropped the map on the ground and began walking back to Jason and Morgan. Christina followed him, her laughter haunting as she did. She raised the blade again. Gavin didn't even bother to notice as it came for the back of his neck. He was in a fog.

"No!" Morgan yelled as she ran forward.

Meeting Gavin, Morgan hip checked him out of the way. Her hand coming up and catching Christina's wrist and with her other hand she lunged her blade forward. Christina stopped. Pain rippled through her as she looked down at her chest. The red rose hair blade was plunged deep in her chest, right into her heart. She fell to her knees. Her mouth filled with blood as Christina glanced at Gavin before falling over.

"No!" Travis yelled from behind them as he raced forward.

Travis crashed on his knees in front of Morgan and rolled Christina onto her side. He shook her lightly. No response. She was dead before she hit the ground.

"You! You! You whore!" He screamed at Morgan as he drew his sword and stood.

Morgan stepped back getting space between them. The crew both Travis and Gavin, had been watching silently, not sure what to do. Travis went to slash Morgan with his blade. Morgan closed her eyes waiting for the blow but the blade never touched her. A loud clink noise echoed. Morgan opened her eyes to see Gavin standing in front of her; sword drawn and blocking Travis's. Travis' face was full of surprise as he looked at Gavin. Gavin had regained himself completely and now stood in front of him ready to end it all. Travis pushed against Gavin's sword trying to keep him back.

"Attack." Travis yelled to the crew members around them.

Jason, Jacob, Thomas and Alan drew their swords. Morgan stepped back from Gavin and Travis joining Jason and the men. Travis's crew drew their swords and started for the six men.

"Here Morgan I grabbed you the lightest one I could find." Thomas said with a small smile as he handed her a sword.

She smiled big at him as she took the sword. She cradled her injured arm and held the sword with the other. They were very outnumbered. Gavin glanced back at his men as Travis's crew enclosed them. Gavin shoved Travis hard with his sword breaking the stand off. They needed help and needed it now. Gavin looked to the Morning Star and whistled.

Within a second loud bangs were heard across the ship as grappling hooks were thrown across the way and Gavin's crew began to board The Evening Star. It quickly became an all out war zone. Men began fighting

everywhere. The sound of metal hitting metal echoed throughout the ship. Yells and groans were heard as men were wounded. Morgan scanned the ship as she tried to find a way to help. Her eyes landed on Thomas. He fought two men at once and the toll of it started to make him struggle.

Morgan rushed over to help with the sword in hand and ready to use it. She came up behind one, man he was too wrapped up in the fight he didn't see her coming. Morgan cranked back and hit him hard in the head with the end of her sword handle. He sank to the ground immediately without ever knowing what hit him.

Thomas locked blades with the remaining man. He nodded his thanks to Morgan and went on with his fight. She scanned the ship seeing where she could be of use. Her eyes looked for familiar faces and found Jason. She watched as Jason thrusted his sword through a man's stomach, blood sprayed out of the man as Jason pulled his sword from him. Seconds later another man was already attacking Jason. He was fine and handled everything coming at him. She shifted her gaze across the ship and found that Jacob was pinned in the corner of the ship against the stairs fighting three. He was doing amazingly well but there was no way he could keep going like that much longer.

Morgan began to make her way towards him to help. As she crossed the deck a strong hand grabbed a hold of her shoulder. The person's fingertips pressed deep into the wound on purpose. The pain seared through her in a hot burning wave. It went all the way down to her fingertips and without meaning too she dropped her sword. A clink was heard as the sword bounced to the ground. The sword was then swiftly kicked away from her.

"Come on, Doll, you're going to be my bargaining chip." Chris said, digging his thumb into the hole of her wound.

Morgans gritted her teeth against the pain. A small yelp slipped out as he dug into the puncture. Morgan scanned the deck as she tried to come up with a way to get away from Chris. Blood leaked out of the wound as he pressed harder into it. He was letting her know there was no way around this. He had her and that was it. She flinched under his grasp. Jason looked out across the way and saw what was happening. No one was around to help her. He needed to get to her and began to fight harder and quicker with the men around him trying to make his way to her.

The ship was a war zone, blood stained the deck and men were falling left and right. Gavin was locked in battle with Travis. Each giving their all into trying to end one another. They had made their way across the lower deck and now we're heading up the stairs. Gavin lunged at Travis, Travis countered their swords smash together as he took the taking the first step up the stairs. Gavin slashed at his legs and the blade caught him right above the knee. Travis growled in pain and brought his sword down towards Gavin's head. Gavin blocked and pushed upwards against Travis as he took a step up the stairs. Their swords clash against each other with each step. A small yell caught Gavin's ear. His stomach knotted up as he immediately recognized it. Something was wrong with Morgan. The next blow he made to Travis was hard and powerful. Travis stumbled backwards and took a step back. It gave Gavin enough time to search the ship with his eyes.

He spotted Morgan as she was dragged across the lower deck by Chris. His eyes scanned his crew; they were all in the middle of defending themself. Jason worked steadily to end his battle and he could tell he was making progress towards her but Morgan was getting farther away. Travis grinned as he saw Gavin distracted. He slashed at him and his sword sliced through Gavin's left arm. The wound stung as blood seeped out of the clean cut. Gavin looked down at his arm and back to Travis. His eyes filled with more hatred as the pain fueled him.

"Enough." He growled at Travis.

This needed to end now. He had to get to her. Gavin began sending attack after attack towards Travis. Each one is harder and faster than the last. Travis did his best to keep up as he countered each blow. His strength weakened with each strike Gavin sent. Travis backed himself up against the rail of the upper deck. Gavin delivered another blow but this time his sword slid down the handle of Travis's sword and struck Travis's hand. Travis let out a scream as his sword and thumb flopped to the floor. Blood squirted out from Travis's hand from where his thumb was now missing. The blood ran down his hand and onto the floor in a water fall fashion. Travis cradled his hand as he winced in pain. Gavin pressed the tip of his sword into Travis's throat.

"I should take you apart piece by piece." Gavin said, his voice deadly.

Travis swallowed hard. His other hand gripped the spot where his thumb used to be. He knew he was in trouble and fear quickly filled his eyes.

"Gavin. I. Brother don't." Travis started to say but Gavin pressed the tip into his throat more, blood dribbled down his throat from the blade in a slowly steady stream.

"Brother! Brother! I should cut your tongue out." Gavin said through clenched teeth.

Travis went pale white. Sweat beaded across his forehead as his mouth went dry. He was searching for something to get him out of this situation. His eyes looked past Gavin in desperation and then he saw it. He began to laugh.

"Oh poor Gavin you're not destined to win."
Travis laughed.

Gavin raised an eyebrow at him and without moving much he glanced over his shoulder. His stomach twisted and his chest tightened. He took a breath in as he locked eyes with Crhis. He had Morgan by her hair and on her knees in front of him. He yanked her head back with her hair and placed his blade to her throat as he matched Gavin's stare.

"Good job Christopher! This is wonderful!" Travis said as he went to move.

Gavin growled and pressed the blade further into Travis's throat as a reminder that he still had him.

"Chris leave her and go now. I promise if you walk away now, you'll live." Gavin threatened, his eyes still matched Chris, he couldn't look down at Morgan. He couldn't see how he was failing her again.

"No. I'll decapitate her before you even make it over here. You'll be left with a headless body to hold. I mean I might be doing you a favor. She talks way too much." Chris smirked.

"What do you want?" Gavin asked, the anger in his voice would scare a grown man.

"A ship. This ship. Your ship. Just a bloody ship." Chris said exasperated.

"Just a ship?" Gavin asked, his eyes went to look at Travis, amusement sparked in them.

"Aye a freaking ship!" Chris groaned.

Gavin nodded and before Travis could blink
Gavin pressed his sword into his throat and through it.
Travis's head went back detaching from his body and
into the sea. The headless body collapsed onto the
deck. Blood was everywhere, it covered the deck railing,
the floor and Gavin was covered in his blood. He turned
to Chris, a chilling sight. He bent down and wiped the
blood from his sword on Travis's dead body. Chris froze
as he watched him. He looked like a demon as he
straightened up and squared his shoulders. The rage in
his eyes burned into his. The rest of the ship went
soundless to Travis as he watched a blood drenched
Gavin walk to him.

"So you want to die a captain?" Gavin asked him
with a smile.

Chris was confused and as Gavin stepped
towards him he loosened his grip on Morgan. Morgan
smirked, it didn't matter that Chris's blade was still at her
throat; she knew what the outcome would be. She knew
she was going to be just fine. Gavin caught the smirk
and glanced at her. Morgan's smirk turned into a small
smile and she winked at him.Gavin paused his advance
just as Morgan threw her head back into Chris's groin.
Chris dropped his sword and his hands went to cup his
manhood. As he went down Morgan snatched his sword
that landed neatly on the ground next to him. She then
turned into him as she rammed the sword deep into his
belly. Chris slunk forward into the blade making

295

Morgan fell back onto the deck floor as he impaled himself further. Blood began to flow out of his mouth as he tried to talk. It happened so quickly, blood splattered across Morgan's face in speckles. Chris's eyes glossed over in front of Morgan as she looked up into them. She held her breath as she waited for him to move. A hand grabbed hers and slid her out from under Chris. She immediately went to fight. As she swung her fist towards the person's face. They caught her wrist.

"It's done love." His voice calmed her to her soul.

As she looked at his face, she felt everything melt away. She went crashing into his chest. Bloody or not she needed him near her now.

"Morgan I got you." He said as he wrapped his arms around her tightly.

The fighting stopped. The world seemed to freeze as the crews realized Travis was gone. All eyes looked to the upper deck and focused on a blood covered Gavin with his arms wrapped around Morgan. Gavin exhaled, having her safe in his arms at last. This whole time it was like someone had him by the throat. He couldn't breathe without her.

A cheer went up from the ship as Gavin's crew celebrated. Morgan went to pull back as she looked out over the men. She saw two completely different groups of men. One shocked and defeated the other proud and excited. Gavin tightened his grip around her telling her that she better not move away from him. She gave in and went back into his chest. He held his arm up and his crew fell silent.

"Your captain is dead. By the law of the sea. I am now captain. You are now loyal to me or dead. Make your choices." Gavins voice bellowed out over the crew.

"Who says-" one of Travis's men went to speak up.

Gavin snapped his fingers and a blade went through him. It was instant and the man was gone before he knew it.

"Anyone else?" Gavin asked, staring them down.

A "No Captain" was heard throughout the crew. Jason caught eyes with him and nodded. Gavin glanced down at Morgan nestled in his chest. A warmth spread over him. He had her. She was safe and she was his. He smirked and scooped her into his arms. He began carrying her down the stairs.

"I can-"

"Aye love. I know you can walk." He chuckled.

She gave into him as he walked to the lower deck and across it.

"Jason, I need to come up with plans. Leave the men here and meet me in my cabin." He said to Jason passing him.

"Captain." Jason nodded and began to give orders.

Gavin walked across the walkway to The Morning Star with Morgan in his arms.

Chapter Twenty Six
Begin Again

Gavin's feet touch the wooden floor of the Morning Star. His body instantly relaxed. He was back on his ship. He had planned to carry Morgan to the cabin but Claire rushed at them. He smiled and set Morgan down. As soon as Morgan was on her own two feet,Claire jumped into her arms. Morgan flinched from the pain in her shoulder but she ignored it. She squeezed Claire as tight as she could. There was a moment there when she was afraid she would never see her again. She held Claire even closer as the thought entered her mind once more.

"Morgan I'm so happy they got you back." Claire said as she squeezed her.

"I was so scared I wouldn't see you again." Claire whispered.

Morgan pulled back slightly to see Claire's face. She cupped her hands around her face.

"Claire bear, there isn't a force on this earth that could keep me from you. Ok?" Morgan said to her.

Claire buried her face into Morgan and hugged her again . Claire pulled back and studied Morgan with her big blue eyes. Something was wrong.

"You're hurt." Claire said shortly.

"It's ok. It's just a scratch. I am fine." Morgan said as she glanced at her shoulder.

"Gavin, go fix her." Claire said, sighing as she stepped away from Morgan.

Morgan looked completely shocked as she watched Claire step away from her. Gavin began to laugh from behind her as he walked to Morgan.

"Come on Love, you heard the lass." He said as he reached her, still chuckling.

"Really You two I'm fine." Morgan said firmly.

"Gavin!" Claire ordered a small smirk on her lips.

Within a second Gavin scooped Morgan off her feet. She was tossed up in his arms as Morgan let out a small shock yell. She spotted Claire as she held back her giggles. She narrowed her eyes on Claire.

"Traitor." She grumbled at Claire. Claire's giggles turned into her laughing like crazy; as Morgan was carried away.

"Gavin my feet are not injured-"

"Aye love I know you can walk." He laughed as he walked up the stairs to the upper deck.

"This will be the last time you hear me." She muttered as she rested against his firm chest.

His chuckle rumbled through his chest and made her smile, even though it was at her. She inhaled his warmth and closed her eyes slightly. His strong steady heartbeat made her realize how tired she was. She could doze off listening to it.

"Bring me water to my cabin." Gavin said to a crew member as he passed by him.

The man nodded and went to follow the order he was given. Gavin's feet reached the upper deck as he made his way to his cabin. He reached the door handle and turned the knob and used his foot to push it open. Morgan was still nestled into his chest as he made his way over to his desk. He sat her down gently on top of it. She groaned slightly, protesting as he stepped back away from him. He smirked and raised his eyebrow at her.

"I was comfortable." She muttered a frown appeared on her face.

He grinned, he liked the fact that she wanted to be against him still. That she didn't want to leave his arms. She was comfortable with him. He could get used to all of that. Her shoulder tore him from his thoughts as a look of concern came across his face. Morgan sighed as she saw the look and rolled her eyes at him.

"You're lucky you're wounded." Gavin said his voice low but playful.

"Hmm?" Morgan smiled innocently and blinked her eyes at him.

He shook his head as he removed a knife from his belt loop and went to the fabric of her shirt. She didn't even flinch seeing him with a knife near her. It made him smile. This woman who is constantly two steps ahead of everyone with a way out and a plan to fight; never shows an ounce of fear with him. The adoring smile stayed on his face and he cut the fabric away from the wound.

"Problems?" Morgan asked as she saw his smile, it was a little confusing to her.

"'Besides the hole in your shoulder, no." He said, as he shook his head.

"Then what's with your face?" She asked, chuckling.

"I was just thinking." He muttered as he looked at the wound.

The puncture would need to stay open. The knife had missed anything major. The bleeding had nearly stopped. Morgan sat on the desk admiring his face. He was a mess covered in blood and just had his whole world shattered for the second time. The last several months of his life was a lie but here he stood caring for her. She had never met anyone like him. She watched him mutter to himself something about the water that had not yet come. He glanced up at her and raised an eyebrow to her.

"Problems?" He asked her mimicking the same tone she had earlier.

"Besides you, no." Morgan answered her smile growing playfully.

"Me. I'm a problem? I believe this is like the third time or more that I am attending to your injuries. You're worse than any crew member I have ever had." He said a hint of frustration in his voice.

"You may have attended to my wounds but you owe me sir." Morgan said her eyes sparkled with mischief.

"And how is this?" He said a daring smile came across his face.

"I believe this is the second time I've saved your life." Morgan said, smiling proudly.

"Well I can't argue with that." His eyes grew darker and lust flashed across them.

"That's right." She tried to hold her own against his charm but the words came out as a whisper.

He stepped into her, closing the very small gap they had between them. Her breath caught in her throat as her stomach flipped excited. He leaned into her; his mouth inches from hers. She could feel her lips twitch with anticipation.

"And how can I pay off this debt of mine." He whispered his warm breath tickled her lips.

"I guess I'll have to think of something." She said her eyes stared into his.

She was having trouble thinking at all. Her whole body was needing his touch. Her skin felt like it was pulsing. She could hear her heart beating in his ears.. He smirked seeing the want in her eyes. His hand caught her chin and his thumb playfully pulled down at her lower lip. He watched it instantly quiver. His hand captured his face as his mouth came towards hers.

"Captain. I brought two things of water just in case." The crew members' voices echoed through the cabin.

Gavin sighed grumbling as he stepped back from Morgan. Morgan stopped herself from reaching forward and pulling Gavin back to her. Her eyes flickered over to the man who stood just in the doorway. The crew member didn't even realize what he was walking into. He came over to Morgan and set two large buckets of water down.

"Good to have you back Miss." He nodded to her, he caught a glimpse of Gavin's disapproving face and he quickly left.

Gavin grumbled more to himself as he watched the man leave. He sighed as he walked back over to Morgan. Her eyes searching his as she wondered if he was going to pick up where he left off. Instead he went to the desk draw and pulled some clean rags out of it. He came back around to her and dunked the rag in the water. Ringing it out he looked at her.

"This might sting a little." Gavin said with a half smile as he placed the wet cloth on her wound.

She gritted her teeth as he began to clean her shoulder. After several brutal minutes, her shoulder was clean. He smirked looking at her face. He drunk the cloth back into the water before washing the blood off her cheek and forehead.

"You're a little bit of a mess." He chuckled as he wiped her cheek clean.

"I am. You should see you. Most of the blood on me is probably from you." She said, shoving him lightly.

"Yeah." He said looking down at his blood soaked shirt.

As he looked down at all the blood that covered him intense emotions rushed through. He had not had any time to process what just happened. The last few months he had spent in misery, blaming himself for Christina's death and she was alive this whole time. She had planned everything. The woman he was supposed to spend the rest of his life with. She was nothing but a

giant lie. Travis, betrayal ran deeper than he could have imagined. He should have left him when they were boys. The image of Travis's head falling into the sea flashed into his mind. He didn't know if it made him happy or not. He felt empty.

"Hey what's going on? You ok?" Morgan's hand caught his cheek as she spoke to him.

Her touch instantly calmed him. There was something about her. He needed her. She drove him crazy but at the same time he never felt more at peace with her around.

"Just thinking." He said softly.

Morgan nodded. She studied him for a second before biting her lower lip nervously. He raised an eyebrow at her reaction. She slowly reached out and took his shirt in his hand. He didn't react but just watched her. She began to pull his shirt up over his head. Gavin leaned down and helped her take the shirt off. She dropped the bloody shirt to the floor. Her eyes wander over his bare chest. Her heart raced as she looked at him. That damn smirk of his was back on his face as he watched her.

"Now you're almost decent looking." She said to him, clearing her throat.

"Almost? I am more than decent looking all the time, Love." He smirked as he winked at her.

Morgan chuckled, taking her eyes off his more than decent looking chest. She tried to not let herself get caught up in the sight of him. She focused on how much blood he had on him. She took the cloth and motion for him to come to her. His smirk grew as he walked closer to the desk. She inhaled sharply, clearing her throat as she pressed the cloth to his chest. She felt the blood rushing to her cheeks as she ran the cloth over his chest and down his abs. She could feel her ears burning. She couldn't help but be embarrassed about how much she enjoyed touching him.

"So what do I owe you?" He whispered intently watching her.

"Owe me?" She whispered not trying to look at him right now.

"You said it yourself. You've saved my life twice now." He said not charging his tone.

"Well ... .you saved me from drowning so we will just say once." She smirked looking up at him.

"But you still owe." She added with a small chuckle.

"So what is it that you want Love?" He whispered hunger in his voice as he leaned into her, his hand resting on her thigh.

The small touch sent shocking chills through her. Her mind screamed you! In response to his question, she couldn't say it. She shut her eyes as she tried to calm herself.

"Another dangerous route with man eating sharks?" He smirked his hand, beginning to move up her thigh slowly.

"Actually, the dock that we just came from is fine." She said as she tried to control her breathing.

"The dock? You were off the ship maybe two hours tops and you've already started over?" Gavin asked his voice somewhere between shocked and hurt.

Morgan was in a little bit of daze at his touch that she didn't hear the hurt in his voice.

"Mhmm I got a job and a place to stay for me and Claire." She said quietly.

Gavin blinked, shocked at both her ability to get herself set up in such a small amount of time and hurt that she was able to move on from him so quickly. He tried to tell himself what did he expected her to do. He was going to leave her at the dock anyway. Morgan opened her eyes sensing something was wrong. She saw the hurt on his face before he quickly hid it.

"Gavin?" She asked him as her hand reached out and grabbed his hand.

"You want to go back to the dock?" He asked, changing his tone from hurt to just matter of fact.

She frowned, studying his face. She needed to give Claire a future and a home like she never had. She needed a childhood. How could she deny that? Especially when she was denied that her whole life.

"Aye. Claire, Gavin. I have to." She whispered her hand going to his face, her own voice sad.

He sighed, running his hand through his hair. She smiled softly, reaching up and grabbing his hand that was going through his hair. He was caught off guard by it.

"Gavin, I am not choosing between you and not you. I have to do what's best for Claire. You said it yourself. A ship is no place for a woman or a child." She said, squeezing his hand.

Gavin was about to protest when there was a knock on the door. Jason did not wait to be told to come in; he just entered. He cleared his throat awkwardly.

"Should I come back Captain….we are just kind of in limbo right now anyways." Jason said half way out the door.

"Jason, stay." He said his eyes were not leaving Morgan's.

"Captain?" Jason asked cautiously.

"Good. That's a start." He responded to Morgan.

"Jason. The Evening Star is yours." Gavin said, turning to face Jason.

"Captain I cant-" Jason started

"The Evening star and the map are yours. I left this life before and I wasn't really sure what returning to it would do for me. Jason, you are meant for this. You are meant to be a captain. You are my most trusted friend and deserve your own vessel." Gavin said, cutting him off.

"Captain." Jason went to interrupt again.

"No, I mean this. Ask the men who would like to continue to plunger and pirate. They can go with you to the Evening Star. Those interested in an honest life can start anew with me." Gavin said.

"What exactly do you mean Captain?" Jason asked.

"I'm going to go be a merchant or tradesman or whatever. I'm taking The Morning Star and being an honest man from now on. Go tell the boys Captain Jason." He said with a wink as Jason.

"Gavin?" Morgan asked, confused, her hand squeezed his in anticipation.

Gavin turned to her and stepped even closer to her. His hand went to the side of her face as he stepped to her. His eyes studying hers, want and need him as he looked at her.

"I'll be damned if I ever let you out of my sight again." Gavin said as his mouth claimed hers.

Epilogue

Morgan stood in front of the kitchen sink as she stared out the window. She watched the waves crash on the cliffs below. Gavin had built a house for them overlooking the sea. Morgan was in a bit of trance watching the waves break. A loud noise coming down the stairs drew her attention. Gavin dropped his baggage loudly on the wooden floor. The sound broke her from the trance. Morgan sighed slightly. Gavin smiled brightly at her and closed the distance between them. His hand wrapped around her waist as he pulled her back against him. She leaned into him, sighing happily. He leaned down into her neck placing small kisses in the crease of it.

"I have a few minutes."He mumbled into her skin.

She giggled slightly and turned in his arms. Her hand went to his cheek and he leaned into her touch.

"Aye but you need those minutes to get your butt down to the ship." She smiled.

"Do you have all the paperwork?" She asked him concerned.

"Aye, we've been to this trade port before it should be fine. I have all the official paperwork. I will be home before you know it.'" He smiled and grabbed the roll of papers from his back pocket then waved them in front of her.

She grabbed them from him and opened them. She glanced over them quickly checking the seals and everything. She frowned slightly, she hated staying behind.

"Love, you know if it was safe for you. I would be taking you." He said as he kissed her hand.

She glanced at the room. Their home was filled with trinkets from their many adventures. Elephant statue from India, she had sand from the northern islands in a small jar, along with sea shells from China's shores. This would be their great adventure. Morgan's hand went to her belly. Gavin smiled seeing her thoughts and dropped to his knees and placed his forehead against her belly.

"Daddy will be home before your mother even misses me." He said softly to her belly.

Morgan smiled down at Gavin, love filling her heart. She ran her hand softly through his black curls as he talked to the baby growing inside her stomach.

"Ariadne if she's a girl." She said to the top of Gavin's head.

He kissed her belly and stood up. A smile on his face. His hand went to her cheek as he pulled her forehead to his lips.

"Aye, I like it." He said, stepping back.

"Claire, if you don't hurry I am going to leave you here." He yelled towards the stairs.

There was a load of noise and a few crashes before a twelve year old Claire bounced down the stairs. She was wearing pants Morgan had fashioned for her, boots, and a loose shirt.

310

"Morgan, are you sure you don't want me to stay?" Claire asked, looking at her.

"Of course not. I know how you love the sea. You go and make sure Gavin does what he's supposed to. I will be fine if the babe isn't coming for at least another two months. Joyce is going to check on me if I need anything. You go have an adventure" Morgan said, walking over to Claire and kissing her forehead.

"We will be back in a month." Claire said and squeezed Morgan.

Claire grabbed her bag and nodded to Gavin before she headed out. Morgan felt proud as she watched her leave. They had gotten out in time. Morgan had made sure that she got the best out of the life she had to give her. It was thanks to a grumpy pirate captain. She smiled at her thought as Gavin raised an eyebrow at her. She shook her head softly. Gavin wrapped his arms around Morgan once more and began showering her in kisses. Morgan laughed, throwing her head back.

"Robbie will be up to do any lifting or labor things you need." He said as he stepped back from her but not letting go of her yet.

"I will be fine." Morgan said to him resting her forehead against his.

"Take care of yourself and the babe." He said to her,

"Aye and you take care of yourself and Claire." She said, pushing him towards the door.

"I love you." Morgan said to him.

"Always. I love you, always." Gavin said, stepping into her.

His hand went to her hair as he pulled her in for a kiss. No matter the number of times his lips had met hers; they still sent shivers through her. He kissed her like it was the first and last always. The want and need for her was always there. Morgan pulled back breathless.

"You can't keep them waiting. I will see you soon." She said putting her hand to his cheek.

"I'll see you soon." He said as He kissed her hand.

He stepped out the door and headed down the path that led to The Morning Star. Reaching the Star he looked to their house nestled in the cliff side. Morgan had already lit the candle. A light to guide them home. It was never goodbye, I'll see you soon.

S.E Dymek's Other works:

The Star Saga:
Book one The Morning Star
Book two The Evening Star
Book three The North Star

Book Two: The Evening Star

Claire is in training to take over her cousin's trade business. She is out to prove herself and nothing or no one is getting in her way. Her first voyage out to sea to complete her first assignment on her own and the unthinkable happens! Her ship is attacked by pirates. The tall dark sails of the ghostly pirate ship is vaguely familiar. Like something from a distant memory. She locks eyes with the Captain of the Pirates and her stomach flutters. There was something about his disheveled bronze hair and hazel eyes that called to her. Something told her that her whole world was about to change.

The Captain of the pirates is in debt and over his head in a bad situation. Not only does he owe a notorious pirate who is now calling himself the king of all pirates, he just became an enemy of the crown. His world was spinning fast and his problems were getting out of control quickly. Could this golden haired, feisty annoying woman be his

undercover angel? Will Claire help him right his wrongs and in return, him help her prove that she is worthy of running her cousin's business.

The Alpha's War Series:

Book one Between the Alpha's War
Book two Breaking the Alpha Council
Book three The Beta's Betrayal

Bleep from the back of Between the Alpha's War:
Jace shoved her up against the wall, his knuckles hitting it as he did. The wall cracking beneath his fist.

"I said you're going to listen to what I say!" He growled, tightening his grip slightly on her arms.

A smirk appeared on her perfect lips. The smirk that drives him insane.

"And I said I will do what I want." Nora said, her eyes daring him.

Nora comes home late one night to find darkness and blood. Nora's whole world was destroyed in one night. Downward spiraling into misery and struggling to be normal she bumps into Alpha Jace. The second Jace lays eyes on Nora he knows he must kill her. He knows her secret. Late one night in a dark alley Jace is about to end her life when his wolf howls Mate. A word he never thought he would hear. Nora on the

314

other hand instantly hates Jace. As she connects the dots. She realizes what ruined her life. She dives into this new world with revenge.

What will happen if others find out Nora's secret? Can Jace save her? Is Nora the key to saving them all?